Stealing Fates

Stealing Fates

K.A. Shady

Dedicated to eight-year-old me, who always knew what they wanted to be.

Acknowledgments

I could probably write a few pages for every person I'd like to mention here, but for the sake of time (and paper) I'll just hit the main ones.

I can't thank my parents enough for encouraging me to always pursue what I love, without their support I wouldn't be the person I am today.

I can't go a day without mentioning my wife, Kayla, who's loved me through so many ups and downs that I'm amazed she's still on this crazy ride.

My Besties and Beta-Readers Val and Tamra have done so much to keep me going on this journey. Without their encouragement, excitement, and energy I'm sure this project would've died a long time ago.

Last, but not least, Micah for being so awesome as to review my work without asking anything in return.

Contents

One

In Which a Thief Meets a Lord

Lilith

An early autumn breeze whips around me as I stand on the street corner, the air has just begun to chill with the oncoming winter and the scent of dying things has started to taint the air. The street is packed with tall houses, all stacked and pressed into their plots like there's only so much space for people. Carriages rattle past me, some are pulled by magic and scarcely make a sound, but most are pulled by horses, their hooves clopping against the cobblestones and their bodies steaming with sweat.

The sidewalk is packed with people trying to avoid the traffic on the streets. Most pay me no mind but the few who do wince when they take in my appearance. My clothes are thread-bare and hang awkwardly off my thin frame, all of them were discarded by other people, things they no longer care for that I took for myself. I push a dirty strand of hair out of my face as it comes loose from my sad attempt at a braid, the uneven strands refusing to remain plaited together.

I hold out a small cup to one of the passers-by. Desperately hoping someone would, for once, take pity on me despite how much I hate begging. Thunder rolls from the heavy clouds that hang overhead, the air becoming damp and bringing with it a chill. A sharp wind rips through me and I shudder, pulling my arms tight against my sides in a useless attempt to ward off the cold.

Down the street I see a lamp-lighter starting to make their rounds, signaling that it's getting too late for me to be on the streets. I sigh and look into my cup, resigning myself to the reality that I'm not going to get any charity tonight. That truth, while familiar, still stings. The sharp pangs of disappointment and rage burn through my veins, the dark magic in me writhing to meet it. But I can't let it out here, I've got an image to keep, and if I break it now I'll lose business in the future.

I take a few steadying breaths and look up as one of my frequent tormentors turns the corner. I inhale sharply as I tense and take a step back toward the building. I remember too well the last time I saw him, his breath ripe with alcohol as he shoved me against a wall. His presence makes me want to flee, to use the shadows to conceal myself. I bite my lip to keep from actually disappearing. I can tell by the way he's smiling that he's already spotted me, to trigger my magic now would make things worse.

"Well, well, well," the young noble says, crossing his arms over his chest and leering at me, "Still begging like a dog, Lilith?"

I turn my head away from him, not so much that I can't keep an eye on him but enough that he knows I'm trying to ignore him.

"You wouldn't have to do this if you'd just accept my offer," he says with a smirk as he steps closer, looking at me in a way that makes my skin crawl.

I bite the inside of my cheek so hard I can taste blood, but I don't reply to his jab and start to walk away.

He makes an annoyed sound and grabs my arm, spinning me into his chest, "Now you're ignoring me, you little tramp?" he snaps, giving me a shake that has my teeth knocking together.

"I already told you no," I say, tears springing to my eyes as he squeezes my arm and digs his nails into the flesh.

"Come on, I'll be good to you," his voice drops to a tone that he must think is sweet, but it'd be hard to miss the cruelty infusing the statement.

I struggle in his grasp and try to pry my arm free. I keep my lip clenched between my teeth, the pain giving me enough focus to keep my magic from reacting to my fear.

"No!" I cry, trying to yank my arm away and slamming my foot on his. His nails score my skin and the heavy boots he's wearing don't give under my weight, but my arm slips free so I try to make a break for it.

"Damn it," he snaps and grabs my wrist before I can get more than a step away from him, he yanks me back and shoves me toward the wall.

I cry out and try to get away again when I hear a quiet voice from my left, "Now, this can't be right."

I freeze and inhale sharply. Both Greg and I turn as one and see three men standing a few yards away from us. One is all muscle and dressed in dark clothes, his expression stern as he glares at us with his arms crossed. Across from him is a man that looks ghostly in comparison, with white-blond hair and icy blue eyes dancing with amusement as he surveys the scene. Behind the two of them is a third man, his features are obscured by the light behind him but he's wearing a nice suit and holding an intricately carved cane with both hands.

I don't see any weapons on them and, other than the dark one, they seem to only be observing the current situation. The well-dressed man seems to have some authority over the others by the way he holds himself and the value of his clothing in comparison to his companions.

"Am I truly seeing what I think I'm seeing?" The well-dressed man asks, his eyes scanning us and catching on where Greg is holding onto my wrist. I'm not sure who he's asking the question to or if he's asking anyone at all.

Greg is staring at the man in clear shock, his mouth opening and closing a few times as he tries to gather his wits, which I doubt he ever had. "L-Lord Graves! She tried to steal my wallet!" He pushes me away as he shouts.

I yelp as he shoves me into the wall. My head cracks against the stone and tears spring to my eyes but I manage to cry out, "I didn't!"

My vision goes blurry for a moment and in the few seconds it takes for my vision to clear, the man with white-blond hair has moved behind Greg and has his arms twisted up behind him. I sink to the ground as I stare at the scene in front of me.

The dark man moves in front of Greg with a dark look in his eyes and a dangerous grit to his voice, "You don't think we're going to believe that, do you?"

The blond does something that makes Greg whimper and try to stand up straighter. "When we turned the corner, we heard you trying to coerce this young woman into saying yes to a less-than-savory proposition."

"You know we don't take kindly to such things," The dark man steps forward until he's looming over Greg, then he looks over his shoulder at the third man, "What do you think, Boss?"

Lord Graves meets Greg's eyes, his voice gaining a flicker of emotion that I can only describe as contempt, "I'm just grateful that we happened upon the scene before any damage was done. Your application to join Aegis is denied and, given the circumstances, all subsequent requests will be rejected on principle. If I even hear rumors of you accosting people again, I'll see to it that matters are handled more thoroughly. Now go, before I change my mind."

Greg struggles against his captor's hold and yells, "She stole from me! I swear! She's a thieving little tramp!" He continues to struggle as the blond wraps an arm around his shoulders and leads him away, the motion looks friendly but I can see the tension in Greg's shoulders.

I press myself against the wall of the building to separate myself from the strangers. Confusion swirls through me as I wonder who the hell these men are. Why does their mere presence make an abusive bully nearly piss himself?

"Are you all right?" Lord Graves turns to me and holds out a hand.

I stare at his hand for a long minute then I nod and look at my knees, making myself even smaller to keep him feeling like the rescuer, "I'm all right, sir. Thank you for your help."

"You're not hurt?" he asks, still holding his hand out.

"Nothing that won't mend on its own," I say quietly, shifting my weight to stand.

"I'm not going to hurt you," he says, reaching a little closer, but not invading my space or moving very quickly.

I glance over and see that the two other men have Greg at the end of the street and are talking to him in hushed tones. Based on Greg's posture he's fucking terrified of them, but I still can't figure out why.

I look back at Lord Graves and hesitantly raise my hand, I note that it looks extremely dirty in comparison to his, but still accept the aid. I get a flash of a scene, for a brief moment, I'm staring down at a man whose eyes are glazing over with the pallor of death. Then, just as quickly, it's gone, and searing pain rips through my mind.

I scream and yank my hand away, scrambling to my feet and sprinting away. I just barely manage to keep my magic from lashing out as I round the corner and make it out of sight. I get a few strides before my magic flairs out and tries to coat the entire alley in darkness.

Philip

"Phil! She's a non-hostile psychic," Sam says and points toward a nearby alley, I turn in time to see the slim form of the beggar disappear around the corner. I can't keep the grin off my face as I jump over the building and land in the alley in front of her. I frown as I'm plunged into unusually deep darkness, then a slim form appears in the shadows. The beggar slams into me and I catch her by the shoulders. She looks up at me and stumbles back, her eyes wide and panicked as we take each other in.

She's wearing a dress that's little more than rags, with tears and smears of gods know what all across it. The loose fabric hangs from her near-skeletal frame in a worrisome way. Her hair is long and tangled, the strands covered in various mucks that make it hard to tell what color it naturally is. Her face is equally covered in mud and dirt, obscuring her features into something nondescript and forgettable. But her eyes are a brilliant emerald color that's unsettlingly familiar. In the darkness of the alley, they seem to glow ever so slightly but a closer look proves they're just normal eyes.

The panic in her expression makes me grin, which seems to further her concern. She turns her head to one side and looks me over before glancing over her shoulder, "How?"

"We all have our tricks," I say warmly, sliding my hands into my pockets and taking on a relaxed posture, "My boss didn't mean to startle you."

"He hurt me," she says, reaching for something at her waist.

I'm surprised she hasn't relaxed, I'm usually good at setting people at ease. I raise an eyebrow at her, "Well, he didn't mean to do that either. You can't be too careful in this city, never know when someone with ill intent is going to try and skim something off you."

Damien walks up behind her, cutting off her escape, but he's so silent she doesn't notice him. She pulls a small knife from a concealed spot at her hip and points it at me.

"That ain't gonna do much," Damien says dryly, "Besides, We're not here to hurt you."

She jumps and turns so her back is to the wall of the alley in a clear attempt to keep both of us in her sights as she starts to tremble, "Well if you don't mean any harm then why are you trapping me?"

Damien chuckles darkly and she turns toward him, the knife pointed at his chest. There's a brief moment where I swear her eyes begin to glow again, but it's gone in an instant.

"We want to give you this," I interject, holding up a visiting card with the Manor's information on it.

She looks at me and while her attention is diverted Damien slips through the stone and replaces her knife with a card. Her attention flips to Damien before he's completely returned to his spot.

She scrambles back and presses herself against the wall of the building. Her are eyes wide and startled as she looks between him and the slip of paper in her hand, "H-how?"

"This is a shitty spell," Damien says as he glares at her blade like the paltry thing has offended him somehow.

"I know the runes are kind of messy but I did them myself!" Her voice rises in pitch as she glares at him, the fear in her eyes giving way to indignation. She catches herself and presses her empty palm against the brick behind her, dropping her head to avoid looking at him.

"The runes are carved just fine," Damien says in his usual gruff tone, "even if they are a bit rough around the edges. The spell itself is shit; you should be more careful who you buy spells from. Read the card," he points at the card in question.

She scowls at the card and to my surprise an obvious flush spreads across her cheeks, despite the layer of dirt and grime on her skin, "I can't."

I sigh and Damien shoots me a concerned look, "Well, It's an address. Do you know where Empire and Fifty-Sixth are?"

"About,"

"Good, there's a big mansion there, takes up two blocks. If you go there our boss will see to it that you find a good job and can get off the streets," I smile brightly.

"And if I don't?" she says reproachfully.

I shrug and rock back on my heels, "Then you don't, the choice is yours."

"Why?"

"Really?" Damien snaps, glaring at me with enough venom to cow anyone else.

She glares over at him then looks back at me, "Why offer me this?"

I meet her gaze and I see something shining back to me in her eyes, it takes me a moment to place it, but then I realize it's hope staring back at me. I smile at her and plant my feet again, "Lord Graves employs people like us," I gesture between the two of us, "people with skills that aren't exactly typical or are a little more than most. You seem to have a bit of a flair that might be of use, and seeing as he hurt you it's the least he can do."

"He didn't have to hurt me," she says softly, but there's a strange glint in her eyes, a flicker of uncertainty that makes me feel protective.

"He didn't mean to hurt you with his shields, but the spell doesn't discriminate so there wasn't much he could do. Look, we're gonna leave you alone now, but you're welcome to stop by whenever." I wave a dismissive hand as if it's not a big deal then look at my brother, "Give her blade back."

He sighs and flips the blade in his hand, "It's not going to do her much good."

I roll my eyes, "Then give her yours and stop being a prick."

He shakes his head and flips the blade once more, catching the sharp end in his palm and holding it out to her, "Here, it'll cut through a good bit, but it's not much sharper than your average knife. If you come by the estate, I'm sure we can set you up with something better."

She turns her head to one side, regarding him for a moment before taking the blade back and sliding it into a small sheath on her belt that I didn't see before, "Thank you."

I smile brightly and stroll past her, I nudge Damien, "Come on, Brother, no need to torment her further."

Damien grunts but joins me. I hear her rush away, her bare feet scarcely making a sound even on the damp ground. We get to the end of the alley and I start whistling.

"Where is she?" Graves looks at us expectantly when we turn the corner, glancing around as if she's just going to pop out of the wall like Damien does.

"Didn't want to come with us. This one," Damien jerks a finger at me, "Let her go."

Graves looks at me with a raised brow, "Well?" he asks, accepting that I must have a good reason for such a decision.

"She'll come around," I say with a grin, unexpectedly giddy about this woman "She wants to see what kind of help we're offering, just needs a little time to warm up to the idea. That's all."

Damien sighs and scrubs a hand over his face, "She smelled like desperation and bad decisions and I'm pretty sure she's hiding things."

"I'd be more worried if she wasn't hiding things," I quip, "As I said, she'll come around. Gotta approach her like a shy animal, just wait and let her come to us."

Graves looks at the alley, his mouth set in a firm line. He's silent for a long while and the faraway look in his eyes tells me he's lost in thought. Finally he says, "I hope you're right, she's important somehow, but I can't figure out why."

Damien groans and stalks away, "Great, some desperate beggar is important, what next? We gonna adopt a shifter?" he throws his hands up and starts walking toward home.

I chuckle and stroll after him, "I'm sure all will make sense in time,"

Damien turns to point a finger at me, "Oh don't you go dropping that oracle-type bullshit. I don't like it from actual oracles, and I like it less from you, smart ass."

I laugh now as Lord Graves follows after Damien, subtly shaking his head. I just grin and continue to stroll after them, feeling more optimistic than I have in years.

Lilith

Once I'm out of sight of the men, I roll my shoulders back and stretch my arms over my head. I drop the card to the ground and pull out the two wallets I took. Greg's has a few notes in it, but nothing tremendous looks like he's a cheapskate as well as a monster. I shudder as I remember his roaming hands.

The other wallet, however, has about twenty notes in it, and I can't help but grin at the windfall. It'll easily set me up for a week or more if I'm careful. I go to pull the cash out but stop. The card's bright surface stares up at me from the dirt at my feet.

I stare at the ground, scrunching up my face as I contemplate the small paper and the dark ink on its surface. I wonder if it would be worth it to go see what kind of work they're suggesting and if finding a proper job would do me good.

I laugh at that. Of course it would be good for me to find a proper job, I just ain't cut out for proper. Besides they only offered to help me, not Gavin, and I can't leave him behind. I shake my head and close the wallet, not wanting to take the money just yet. I turn away from the card and take two steps before I stop as something dawns on me.

I wasn't afraid. Those three men didn't scare me at all. Instead, something about them felt familiar and safe. It was as though some deep part of me knew that I could trust them, that they truly didn't mean me any harm. Even when the two had me cornered, I didn't feel as if I was in any danger. Which is more than I can say for most people, even Gavin, who I've known for years.

I return to the card and pick it up, turning it over in my hands a few times and leaving grimy fingerprints behind. Confusion and concern coil through me, making me wonder what the fuck I should do. I close my eyes and look up to the sky, silently pleading with the universe for a sign. After a few minutes of pointless prayer, I shake my head and pocket the card, then set off into the city.

After weaving through a few alleys I find where I stashed my extra stuff; a thin coat and a small satchel, both worn to near rags but in better condition than my dress. I throw the bag's strap over my head and start moving again, heading out to find Gavin.

I get to the corner he usually begs on and he's not there, instead an older man I know is sitting on the edge looking desperate. The people around him ignore him, much as they do me. Those of us that beg in this city are often left to rot on our corners or in the alleys. The urge to scream and rage at these people hits me hard, they choose to ignore our plight so they don't have to feel bad. I clench my fists tightly and take steadying breaths.

I shake myself as I approach the older man, I smile and roll my shoulders forward to make myself seem timid as I approach, "Evenin' Carl."

The older man looks up at me with bleary eyes, "Lil?" he asks in a rough voice.

"Aye, seen Gavin today?"

"Nah, wasn't here when I got here. Haven't seen him in a few days," He says looking around him as if Gavin is just gonna show up. I spot a few well-dressed ladies, in their fluffy coats with perfectly coiffed hair, wrinkle their noses at the two of us. The day's frustration gets the better of me and I trip one of the ladies with a shoot of shadow as she passes by.

The woman stumbles but I reply to Carl, "He does that at times, likes to disappear. I'll find him."

"Any luck today?" Carl asks as I get a few paces away, his unsteady hand dropping the cup he's holding.

I pause and glance at my bag, worry for the old man makes me sigh. I pull out a couple of notes from Greg's wallet. "Got a bit, just don't go blabbing that I'm sharin' and try not to waste it on booze again," I say sharply as I drop the notes in his cup.

I stop at a few other shops and corners, no one has seen Gavin in about two days. I sigh and finally make my way to a shop that sometimes will give Gavin work. I walk up to the building and eye the gold lettering on the door, Gavin says it reads something like 'bastard brothers' oddities' but I don't believe him. For one Barry is the only brother that works here and neither he nor his brother are bastards.

I just shake my head and open the door, "Hello?" I call, keeping my voice small.

"In the back," Barry's voice calls from somewhere deeper in the shop.

The shop is filled to the brim with all sorts of random things. From books to couches, to jewelry, and even a big stuffed dog. It always smells a bit musty and strange, but the owners are always good to us and will let us do work for a few notes. I weave through the mess of assorted items and make my way to the back room, "Barry?"

Sitting at a large desk is an overweight man with a receding hairline and a set of big spectacles. "Aye," he says, not bothering to look up from the watch he's tinkering with, "What're you looking for today, Lilith?"

"Seen Gavin?"

"No, not in a week at least." He looks up now, a frown creasing his features as he takes me in, "Can't find him?"

I shrug and keep my expression relaxed so he doesn't know that I'm worried, "Only been looking for a couple of hours, it'll be alright." I toy with the card in my pocket and stare back at the older man who's still watching me with a furrowed brow.

After a few more moments of staring, he shrugs and goes back to the piece he's repairing. I stand there for a few more minutes. I know Barry won't mind me staying until he closes the shop, and he's the only person I know who might have answers.

"Say..." I begin, still toying with the card, "You ever heard of a summat called Aegis?"

Barry freezes and raises his head to look at me, "Where'd you hear about them?"

I nibble on my lip and shift my weight, the intensity of his gaze making my skin itch, "Don't matter, just heard someone talkin' about it. Wondered what it was."

He sets his tools down and gives me a long look, "Aegis is a group of nobles that keep dangerous magic out of the reach of dangerous people. Some people think they're just collecting the stuff to use against commoners if we ever tried to fight back. If you heard someone talking about it you should steer clear of them."

"Why? You said they're trying to protect people." I say with a frown, confused as to why he seems as frightened as Greg did earlier today.

"Aye, but you've got a touch of magic, right?"

I nod.

"Well not all of them are kind to people with magic. Some of the more radical ones would see you as a threat just for having magic. And if you're seen as a threat they would kill you outright, no questions asked."

"Some? Not all?" I ask, tilting my head and scowling at the big man.

"Aye," he nods his expression growing thoughtful, "The leader isn't the bad sort, nor are his most trusted agents, but some of the other members are a bit on the zealous side."

"Who's the leader?"

He gives me a hard look, "You're really curious about this, ya sure you just heard it in passing?"

I nod and offer a weak smile, "You know I like to learn stuff when I can, I'm just curious is all."

He frowns and then sighs, "A'right, can't do too much damage I s'pose. The leader of the Aegis is a man named Lord Graves, he organizes what the other members retrieve and handles particularly dangerous artifacts himself. He's a well-respected man and from what I understand has a good clip of magic too."

"Thanks," I offer him another smile.

He shakes his head, "Get on out of here, I've got work to finish."

I grin and duck out of the building and head out into the streets. I wander around for a while, my mind swirling with thoughts about what's happened today. I get onto one of the busier streets and cringe, I'm not in the mood to do any more thieving. So I shroud myself in shadows, allowing myself to become harder to notice.

I wander toward the little hut that Gavin and I have been camping out in. Wondering if he's there and I can talk to him about what we could do. They seemed like they wanted to help so maybe we can both get jobs. I'm so lost in thought that I don't entirely pay attention to where I'm going. A sharp wind breaks into my thoughts and I look around me.

I'm standing on the corner of Empire and Fifty-Sixth, my eyes widen and my mouth drops open. Looming before me is a mansion, the massive building is three stories tall and seems to dominate the entire block of the city. The dark stone has vines crawling up the walls and there are a few balconies and ledges on the roof. There are a few outbuildings and a stable on the left side of the house, as well as a garden and some open space on the right.

A large gate stands open at the edge of the property, the wrought iron dark from age. I step a little closer and see there are some vines coiled around the far sides of the gate where the hinges meet the wall. The whole place has an overwhelming feeling to it, but I find it more inviting than frightening.

I start to turn away but as I do a raindrop lands squarely on my nose, making me stop. I look up and more drops assault my face, I clench my fists and look back at the building. An aura of welcome permeates the air and I can't shake the feeling that I should go in. I grip the strap of my bag and squeeze, "Looks like you made your choice, Lilith." I mutter to myself then I drop my gaze and roll my shoulders forward, making my way up to the massive building and hoping I'm not making a terrible mistake.

Two

In Which a Prophecy is Spoken

Damien

The kitchen is in the midst of cooking dinner when we return to the manor. The whole place is chaos, with maids getting dishes moved and Cook barking orders, the big man's booming voice echoes through the kitchen. The fire in the hearth has a massive pot hanging over it, and the stove is giving off enough heat to make the room stuffy. Phil and Graves make their way around the bulk of the movement but I step into the midst of it.

I nab a piece of ham off one of the trays floating around the room and get a glare from Marie for my trouble, "If ya eat all the ham before it's served you won't have any appetite and the rest of us won't have any ham."

I shrug and grin, not bothering to reply as I shove the ham in my mouth. Before she can reprimand me further the outer door of the kitchen bursts open, startling the whole room to stillness.

Sarah, the local oracle and Marie's sister stands in the doorway. She's wearing her usual flowing dress, but her hair is wild around her face and her eyes are wide as she stands there, holding the door ajar and staring at me. I frown, surprised that she's looking at me of all the people in the room.

Based on the intensity of her stare, I'd say she's had a vision and has something important to say.

"Sarah?" Marie asks, eying her sister with concern.

Sarah shakes her head, "Graves, Philip, Damien, I need to speak with you. Now."

We all exchange a look. Samael nods and gestures at the door, "You know where my study is."

She hesitates then nods seriously and marches off toward the interior of the mansion. The three of us tail along behind her, all of us exchanging worried glances as she moves with uncharacteristic intensity.

Sarah barges into the office and marches right to the fireplace and begins pacing, her eyes fixated on the flames in the hearth.

"What's wrong?" Phil asks, feeding the fire as she paces around and seems to be thinking hard.

"Today you met a young woman. Yes?"

"Yes," Graves says, his voice matching his name, "Why?"

"She's important," Sarah says quickly, her voice becoming shrill, "very important! You have to go find her."

Sarah starts walking back toward us but I grab her arm, "You're gonna have to be more specific. What's so special about her? She smelled of desperation and fear."

She pries her arm from my grasp and starts pacing again, putting her hands to her head as she mutters, "Gotta tell you enough, but not too much, can't reveal too much cause it could go wrong."

Lord Graves crosses his arms, "I got the impression she was important too, but I didn't get any more information than that."

Sarah stops suddenly and turns to look at me again, *"She is the First. But she is also the last."*

Samael rushes to his desk and pulls out a pen and paper, quickly jotting down what Sarah is saying.

Her voice shifts, becoming airy and distant as her Oracle powers activate, *"The Seals are breaking -*

"and time runs short to heal the wounds of the past.

"The Scattered must be found, and their hearts restored.

"Lest when the Seals fail, all shall fall to Discord."

Phil frowns and looks at me, his concern seeping into the air like a miasma. I'm concerned too if she's talking about the seals to the hell gate... I almost don't want to think about the repercussions.

I stalk up to her and she looks up at me defiantly, "The seals are meant to be permanent. And how the fuck are we supposed to find Them? We've been looking for them for a thousand years and always failed. How are we supposed to do things right this time?"

Sarah shakes her head, "What those seals are meant to hold cannot be held back forever. Time is running out and without the Scattered to stem the tide Discord will prevail."

I groan and run a hand across my face before I growl, "You said she's first. Do you mean, the firstborn?"

Sarah doesn't reply which gives me my answer. Philip's face lights up, "That's good, right?" he looks at me with hope shining in his eyes.

"I don't know," I say, looking over at Graves where he's staring down at the paper he'd noted things down on.

He frowns, "Seals? The artifact we need to steal is sometimes called the First Seal. What do you know about it?"

I frown and glance at Sarah, who just shrugs at me as if that's helpful.

I sigh and look at Samael, but it's Phil that speaks, "About a thousand years ago there was a catastrophe that left the underworld unprotected and unregulated. No gods were willing or able to take up the role, so they created seals to keep it closed."

"How do you know it's these seals?" Graves asks with a scowl.

"Cause we were there when they were created," I say, "And Discord was responsible for the catastrophe."

Before he can ask more there's a knock at the door and it opens without a reply. Roland, the butler, sticks his head in, "Sir, there's a young woman here, she has a card."

"Told ya," Phil grins, looking far too pleased with himself.

Samael sighs and pinches the bridge of his nose before adding more to his note and turning to the door, "We'll discuss this more later, come on let's go see our guest."

We make our way down the stairs and to the receiving room where Roland always deposits guests. The room has a small fireplace, a few chairs, a bookshelf against one wall, and a large window on the other. The beggar stands awkwardly in the middle of the room, in her tattered dress and an equally tattered coat. Her hair is still dirty and messy but there are smears where it looks like she got pelted with rain. She looks comically out of place in the cleanliness of the room, especially as she looks around sheepishly.

There's no way this is her, there's no way she's the Queen. I think to myself as I take her in. Her aura is all wrong, it's saturated with fear, desperation, and malice. She's painfully human, her dark hair is dull, her skin is pale, her eyes sunken into her face, and even from here, I can see her collarbones.

This life hasn't been kind to her and, if she truly holds my Queen's soul, we may already be screwed.

We all stand there for a few minutes staring at each other. Finally, she clears her throat and wrings her hands, "So... ya said ya might have work for me?"

I scowl at her and glance at Sam, who's standing between Phil and me.

"Yes, I might," Graves says, folding his hands together and looking her over, "What skills do you have?"

She scuffs her toe on the floor and looks down as her shoulders slump further but looks up at him from under her lashes, "Well, I don't know much as far as books. I am fair at following directions and I can clean well enough. I ain't bad at learnin' either, just can't read."

The coy expression irritates me and I glare harder, taking a few steps forward and clenching my fists.

Samael doesn't react to her attempt at coyness and clears his throat, "While those are all good skills, I'm a little more concerned with your magical talents. You managed to glean some information from me before the wards took effect, which is no easy feat. Generally, those protections cannot be breached at all."

"I'm also curious," Phil interjects with a raised hand and a big grin, "on how you managed to nick my wallet after just briefly running into me in the alley."

I turn to frown at him, he didn't say anything about her stealing, but then she barks out a harsh laugh.

She's staring at us with disbelief in her eyes. The scent of her amusement hits the air a second before she bursts into a fit of giggles. Her voice echoes around the room infectiously and I find myself fighting back a smile by grinding my teeth together.

She doubles over for a moment, her arms wrapped around her waist as she gets a hold of herself. Eventually, she sits up and grins at us. The expression is a wicked thing that's dramatically contrary to her demeanor.

She rolls her shoulders and stretches her arms up over her head, popping her neck. Her entire presence shifts right before our eyes. The timid demeanor falls away as she straightens, replaced with a steady stance and eyes that I swear are glittering in the firelight. Finally, she tucks her hands into her coat pockets and rocks back on her heels.

"Now," she grins brightly, and I can't deny the hint of surprise I'm feeling, "if I'da known that you were looking for actual skills I wouldn't have put on the act. Though, I s'pose being able to act a part can be seen as a skill itself."

At this point all of us are staring at her, Roland's mouth is hanging open, my scowl has been replaced with shock, Phil is grinning like an idiot, and Samael is just watching her with his usual level of calm.

"There's no way," I say with a shake of my head. The easy switch in personality aside, her aura has shifted too. There's less fear and an undercurrent of magic that wasn't present before.

Her grin widens and she turns her head to one side giving me a satisfied smirk that's equal parts amused and condescending, "D'you honestly think anyone who's that soft would last a week on the streets? I mean, I understand that you rich folk might have a bit of a misunderstanding of how the world works; but I didn't think it'd be this bad."

My mouth drops open at the sassy response. I can't think of an appropriate reply.

Sam clears his throat, "So, you can put on an act to manipulate a situation in your favor, playing on the expectations of others. What other skills do you have? Also, how well can you use your magic?"

"Well, I got that weird thing when I touch people or things, sometimes I see odd stuff. Like with you, I saw..." she trails off as if she doesn't want to talk about what she saw, then shakes herself and continues, "Though it doesn't always happen. As for other things," she shifts her weight and then disappears and reappears in a shadow in the corner.

"And..." She reaches into the bag at her side and withdraws a wallet and holds it out, "I'm good a nicking stuff."

Philip walks over to her and takes the wallet from her, "Anything else?"

She frowns.

He raises an eyebrow at her, "If you give it back now, then there won't be any consequences."

She purses her lips and sighs, then pulls a pocket watch out of her pocket and drops it in his hands, "I woulda put it back when I knew if I was going to stay or not, wasn't sure."

"Are you sure now?" Sam asks.

"No, which is why you'll be needin' to present your case." She puts her hands on her hips and lifts her chin defiantly, "What do you want from me?"

Graves

I stare at the young woman, baffled by her audacity to challenge me like this. She's meeting my gaze steadily, a glint of mischief in her eyes as she awaits my reply. Most people can't meet my gaze, and if they do they quickly turn away. They find me too intense and are put off by it. But this woman is staring me down as if she's not the one at a disadvantage here.

"Are you sure this is wise, sir?" Roland is looking at her with concern as Phil returns his pocket watch to him.

"No," I reply, keeping my gaze on her, "Have you heard of Aegis?"

"Not 'til today; 'Was told ya collect stuff that's magic so common folk don't get it."

"That's not how it works," Damien scowls.

She shrugs and waves a dismissive hand at him, "I just told ya what I was told. It's not like you noble types go around tellin' beggars what you do all day."

I hold up a hand to keep Damien from going off on a rant, "We reclaim dangerous artifacts, and the organization is made up of both nobles and as you call them common folks. We recently found a very dangerous item. It is known to give the wearer god-like power; however, it also drives them mad."

She snorts, "And what does that have to do with me? Can't you just go buy it or something?"

Phil sighs and runs a hand across his face, "No, we can't."

"The current owner isn't willing to sell it," I chime in before he can go on a tangent, "we fear that they're already under the influence of the item, but they are not consistently wearing it. Since they are unwilling to part with it we've decided to take a different approach."

She shakes her head as a smile slowly spread across her face, "You want me to go steal it?"

I clench my jaw, her flippancy irritating me, "Yes, that is the plan."

"Tell me where and I'll go get it."

"You can't just waltz in there and get it," Damien snaps, "It's well guarded."

"Very," I echo his sentiment.

She rolls her eyes and puts a hand on her hip and gives us a look that's full of confidence, "I can jump through shadows, it's not hard for me to steal stuff."

Damien bares his teeth at her, "Aye, and I can walk through stone, if it were so easy as getting to the damn thing I'd have already gotten it." He has a point and the flicker of concern that touches my awareness tells me she sees it.

She looks hesitant for a moment then shrugs, and resumes her cocky attitude, "Alright, what sort of magic do I need to get it?"

"It'll take more planning than that." I say before Damien can start a tirade, "While I prepare plans I'd like you to stay here so I can evaluate your skills and determine the best way to go about retrieving the item."

She rolls her eyes and looks at me like I'm the dumbest person she's ever met, which rankles, "You think I'm gonna stay here? I'm not stupid."

Her defiance is starting to grate, but I can also see the need for her questions. I just wish I didn't feel like I'm the one at a disadvantage, I'm not comfortable letting her leave when Sarah made it clear that we need her help.

I take a steadying breath and say, "You will have room, board, and a new wardrobe. In addition to time to further explore your magic and learn self-defense, and anything else that I feel is necessary for the theft."

She shakes her head, "Not gonna happen,"

Phil rubs his face, "Come on, kid, it's not so bad." His voice is coercive, which usually makes people relax, but it seems to have the opposite effect on her.

Her eyes narrow and she crosses her arms over her chest, "And what reason do I have to trust you?"

"What reason do we have to trust you?" Damien snaps back, growling softly and taking a few steps toward her.

Phil takes a step towards his brother, the other man's hot-headed tendencies making all of us wary.

"None," She sneers as she stalks her way to the door, "This is exactly why my staying here is a bad idea. If you want me to steal for you that's all well and good, but I ain't gonna stay in a place that I can't trust anyone."

She comes to an abrupt halt as Sarah walks in.

"Lilith," Sarah says, "Give them a chance."

I look between the two women, frustrated that Sarah failed to mention she knew the newcomer. It would've been much easier to have this conversation with that knowledge, though perhaps the Oracle has a reason for that.

Lilith stares at Sarah for a long second, "Hey, Miss Sarah, you know these blokes?" she jerks a thumb at me.

"Yes and I think you should give them a chance," Sarah says gently, her voice coaxing, like talking to a frightened animal. Maybe Phil's earlier assessment of Lilith is accurate. The light read I have on her emotions says that she's cautious but curious.

"You think? Or one of your visions thinks?" Lilith asks with a wary look between me and the Oracle.

"Does it matter?" Sarah shrugs, "I give you my word that these men will not harm you. They may push your limits and put you in uncomfortable situations, but they will never bring you harm."

Lilith turns her head to one side and regards the Oracle with a calculating look, "And if they do hurt me?"

I have no idea what she expects the Oracle to do with that question. We certainly won't hurt her. Sarah would never hurt anyone and wouldn't be any match for us if for some reason she did. Though, I suppose that's not a good thing to mention.

Sarah raises her hand and covers her heart, "If they bring harm to you I will personally help you exact revenge."

"What the hells?" Damien snarls, moving toward Sarah with a dark look in his eyes.

I'm shocked as well; Sarah is a stalwart pacifist and if she's willing to get vengeance for this beggar, perhaps I underestimated her importance.

Lilith's eyes widen and she darts to Sarah's side. She reaches out and grabs Damien's hand which is raised slightly. "Leave her alone," Lilith snaps, putting her body firmly between the much larger man and the Oracle.

Damien stares down at her, his mouth hanging open as he looks at his wrist where she's holding his arm. Her hand is so small it doesn't even wrap around his wrist. Her slim frame looks so fragile it's as if he could break her in half with a thought. But she stands there defiantly holding his hand at bay as he stares her down. I'd be worried for her safety if I didn't know him better.

"What do you think you're doing?" Damien says each word slowly and deliberately as if talking to someone who has lost their mind.

Lilith glares up at him, baring her teeth in a snarl, "Don't fucking raise a hand to her. She said that to reassure me. I know Sarah's a pacifist and if she were willing to fight you then I can trust you. But I'm doubting that now since you just raised your hand to her."

"I'm not going to hurt her," Damien snaps, ripping his arm from her grasp and making her stumble, "I just wanna know why the hells she decided to reassure you and not us! We're the ones with things at stake here, given that you'll be living under our roof and you're a known thief."

"I don't care!" Lilith shouts back her entire body trembling, "Nobody hurts my friends when I can stop it."

"You can't take me," Damien snaps back, his fists clenched at his sides as he glares down at the small woman.

I'm too shocked by the defiance in her tone, so at odds with the waves of fear I feel washing off of her, to intervene in the scene.

Philip tries to step between the two but Damien is still shouting and Lilith looks ready to haul off and punch one or both of them.

The torrent of emotions swirling around the three of them is enough to make my head hurt. I feel my magic reacting to their anger and see the fire of the hearth climb higher as ice climbs up my palms.

"Enough!" Sarah shouts, quieting all three of them and drawing me from the cloud of emotion, she looks at Damien, "Enough. I already told you why you should give her a chance. And no matter your doubts about her, trust in me. Lil, my dear, I know you are hesitant to trust anyone, least of all men, but I give you my word."

Lilith runs a hand over her face and nods, "Aye, that you did. Fine, I'll stay and play nice, but one misstep from these assholes, and I'm gone." She swipes her hand out. That fear still lingers, but she's settled now that nobody appears to be in danger.

Sarah just smiles kindly, "Very well, in time you'll see this is where you are meant to be."

Lilith rolls her eyes and shakes her head, "Aye, Aye, next you'll tell me I'm something more than a thief."

Sarah's smile morphs into a grin and she pats Lilith on the shoulder, "Everyone is more than their profession, though you are an excellent thief."

Lilith turns to me and gives me an inquisitive look, "You're in charge here, right?"

"Yes," I shake my head to dispel the last of the emotions and magic then turn to Roland, "See that a room is made up for Miss Lilith. See to it that Miss Lilith gets a bath and some clean clothes, then a solid meal," I say to Marie who's standing at the door.

I turn back to Lilith, "Tomorrow morning I would like to discuss what will be required of you for your stay."

"Callam," She says, "My surname is Callam,"

I raise an eyebrow at her, "Very well, Miss Callam, would you be so kind as to meet with me after breakfast tomorrow?"

"Do I have a choice?"

"There is always a choice," I say seriously.

She just shrugs and follows after Marie.

Philip

I watch as Lilith follows Marie from the room, Sarah goes with them as well and just gives the rest of us a hard look. Samael sighs and looks at Damien, "Come on, we've gotta start getting this plan worked out, and you're going to tell me what you know about these seals."

We make our way up the stairs and to the office, Sam goes to the sideboard and pours a glass of something, and sighs.

Damien slams the door shut behind us and crosses the room in a few angry strides, "You can't seriously be considering trusting her, can you?"

"You're mistaking in whom I'm placing my trust," Sam says at length, not bothering to face my brother's rage, "I agree that there is no good reason to trust a stranger. However Sarah is an Oracle and, while I might not understand the purpose, I trust her judgment and her skill. Not to mention my trust in my own abilities which also suggest that Lilith will be useful."

Damien openly winces at the name and I wonder why he's so against Sarah's prophecy. This is a good thing, if this Lilith and the Seals are what we need to mend things, we'll be able to bring our friends back. We'll finally be able to fix how we failed all those years ago. I just hope that when they remember they'll be able to forgive our failures.

My brother scrubs a hand over his face and bares his teeth at me, "What're you grinning about? You can't honestly be fine with this?"

I smile brightly at him, "I trust Sarah, I trust Sam, and I'm certain that this is exactly where she needs and wants to be, even if she's not fully aware of it yet."

Damien groans and throws his hands up in the air, and storms from the room. I stare after him, noting that I need to talk to him about why he's so upset before he fucks us all over with his temper.

After a few moments of silence, Sam sighs, "Put together a training regimen for Miss Callam, she, like all who work for Aegis, will need to have a fundamental grasp of self-defense. Also, see what you and Damien can fetter out about her magic and its strength. I'll look into a tutor for other things."

"Okay," I nod and turn to leave.

"Wait," Grave says abruptly, "Damien said you were there, what can you tell me about the seals?"

I sigh and sit in the chair across from him. I lean forward and clasp my hands together, emotion choking me, "We were there. I... We worked for a king and a queen. Individually their power rivaled that of the gods, together they were practically unstoppable. They ruled the realm and guarded the gates of hell for a very long time. Then, something happened and they were taken from us."

I close my eyes and shake my head, "I can't talk about it much, the guilt gets to me when I say it all aloud. I'll write down what I remember and get anything Damien has too, as well as what we know about the seals."

Graves looks at me with a calm expression that I'm certain sees more than he'd ever admit. "That will help," he turns away from the sideboard and goes to his desk, not saying another word. I sigh with relief, taking the dismissal for what it is and hurrying from the room.

I weave my way back downstairs and pause when I hear raised voices, I follow the noise and find myself on the floor of one of the guest wings and peer down the hallway.

"No!" Lilith's voice is a sharp cry that echoes down the hall, "I can do this on my own!" she shouts louder.

I start down the hall when I hear Helga, the housekeeper talking.

"I doubt that," Helga says, her low voice more a rumble than anything but still it carries, "You're covered with enough dirt for another you!"

"I can still wash on my own," Lilith argues back, "Go, go find some clothes or something! You, you..." she trails off as if puzzled and then yelps suddenly.

I pick up my pace, wanting to make sure she's okay. As I turn the corner I find the washroom door open. A wide screen is in front of where I know the tub to be. Helga is standing by the tub with her arms crossed and a blustering Lilith is fully clothed and soaking in the tub.

"Now you let me help?" Helga asks, glaring down at Lilith who looks like a drowned rat.

Lilith glares back up at her and opens her mouth as if to oppose it then seems to notice something in the water and winces, then sighs heavily, "All right, you can help, but... I'm not a child."

"Course not, just a tiny lass," Helga grins now and crosses the room to grab a few things. I just shake my head and make my way to the kitchen.

Roland is giving out directions to a handful of maids and Barry is elbows deep in making what looks like porridge at the stove. Roland looks at me when I enter and approaches me, a wariness in his gait that has me on alert, "Damien is in a mood," he says, almost reproachfully.

"You say that as if it's my fault,"

"It usually is,"

I sigh and rub my neck, "Not this time, at least not entirely. He's not too happy with our new guest,"

Roland looks down at his hand where he's holding the pocket watch she nicked, "I can't say I'm ecstatic about it either, but if Sarah says that this is where she's to be..." he trails off and closes the watch, "It is not my place to question an Oracle or Lord Graves, I shall attend to my duties as always. But I shan't be so naive as to leave her unattended for too long."

I nod, "Fair enough, it's best to let him simmer for a bit, I'll get him feeling better in the morning."

Lilith

The behemoth of a housekeeper, Helga, ushers me downstairs. To my embarrassment, she had been right about how much dirt I'd been covered in, she ended up having to change the water twice. I'd thought I had been keeping myself clean enough, but it seems Helga's expectations are greater than mine. She leads me into the kitchen and I pull up short, there are a half dozen people in the room and all of them stop what they're doing to look at me.

My eyes trace the space to take note of the exits. There's a door across from the one we came through, and one along one of the other walls. The one across from me seems to lead outside, and there are a few windows that are just a tad too high for me to get to. There are multiple tables spanning the room, all of them covered in various plates and dishes. I try not to shrink back at the collective stares of the group, resisting the desire to flee.

"Sit," Helga says, pointing at a bench in front of me.

I swallow hard then roll my shoulders and lift my chin, marching over to the designated seat and trying to avoid the gazes of the others in the room.

One of the people present is the older gentleman whose watch I'd taken. I feel a brief wave of shame at my behavior, but I straighten my shoulders and ignore it. I don't owe these people any sort of loyalty, and I already returned the watch.

Once I'm seated Helga looks at the cook, "Barry, get her food. The rest of you, back to your tasks, she's a guest and will be treated as one."

One of the maids raises her hand, her eyes on me, "Isn't she a... thief?" she says the last word as if it's the greatest of sins, her voice coming out as a whisper.

Helga opens her mouth as if to speak but I beat her to it, "Just cause I ain't got the privilege of working in a noble house don't make me a bad person." I snap, my annoyance and nerves getting to me. My magic lashes out around my feet but I manage to keep it from doing anything too obvious, "And yeah, I'm good at stealin' but that's why I'm here and I ain't gonna be shamed for it. Especially not by some spoiled chick who ain't ever even had ta go hungry, let alone the mishap of living on the streets."

The maid visibly recoils from me and Helga crosses her arms over her chest, "That's quite enough, both of ya. Riley, leave Miss Callam alone. I said she's a guest, so treat her as such."

She turns to give me a side-eye look, "No need to snip at her, she didn't mean no harm."

"May not have meant it but still caused it." I snap back, keeping my fists clenched and trying to stare down the huge woman.

"Aye, that it can. Enough now," she takes a bowl of something from a man who I assume is Barry, "Eat."

I sigh and take the seat, eyeing the porridge in the bowl. I briefly wonder if the freaking cook poisoned it, given how most of the room is still giving me wary looks from the corners of their eyes. Helga puts a hand on my shoulder and squeezes it slightly, "It's not fancy. You should be able to stomach it, eat slowly."

I tentatively take a bite of the porridge and begin to eat slowly, as I do Helga strides away and starts giving more orders, most of which mean very little to me. Marie, the woman who'd helped get me settled, comes into the room with a basket that contains my old clothes. She walks right past me and to the trash.

"Hey," I ask, reaching for the basket, "Those are mine,"

She looks back at me then at the clothes, "We're getting you new ones; these are practically rags as it is and you'll need the protection as things get colder."

I frown contemplating her words as she waits silently for my reply, I run a hand through my hair and sit back down with a plop, "Okay, you make a fair point."

She smiles and pats my shoulder, "Don't worry, we'll get you proper clothes, and the type you want. It'll just be a few days before I can get the time to go out."

I nod absently and return to my porridge. After I've eaten my fill Helga leads me back into another part of the house. I keep track of the turns we take, making sure that I know how to get around in case I need to make a quick escape. She leads me up to a large door and smiles, "Here, your room."

I open the door and my eyes widen and I look up at the housekeeper, "There's no way," I say hurriedly, "I'm just... just..." I look around frantically.

"Ah," she holds up a hand, "This is your room, Lord Graves said to put you in this wing, and he gets the final say around here."

"Why though?" I ask helplessly, confused as hell.

Her smile softens, "Because while none of you know it yet, Sarah is right. You belong here."

"How can you be so sure?" I snap, glaring up at her.

Helga laughs and pats my shoulder, "I know because I've seen that look in your eyes before."

"What look?"

"That look like you've been fighting against the world. Like you've been alone for far too long. Like you're desperate for a place to belong and you're prepared to fight for it." Her expression is serious but there's a weight to her words.

"Where have you seen it before?" I ask though I suspect I already know the answer.

She grins, "Everyone here once had that look on their faces," she pauses, "Well, not everyone. Only those of us who're part of Aegis proper, and not just the household staff."

"So, you're saying that since I have that same look I belong here?"

She nods, "Aye, and that's not even taking into account that Sarah said so."

I go to argue again but just end up yawning. She smiles and turns me toward the bedroom again, "Go rest, you need it."

I hesitate then make my way into the room. I should explore the space and make sure it's safe, but sleep tugs at me, and the big bed on the far side is calling my name. I make my way over and crawl in, the comforter is warm and the bed is soft. I've scarcely laid down before I succumb to sleep.

Three

In Which Boundaries are Set

Lilith

A brisk knocking at the door startles me awake. I jump to my feet, tripping over the too-long dress and ending up smacking my face against the wood. "Shit!" I shout, causing the door to burst open.

Marie, Sarah's sister, rushes in, "Oh no!" she comes to my side and helps me to my feet, "I'm sorry, I didn't mean to startle you."

I shrug, "I'm always going to be on alert,"

She gives me a sympathetic look then nods, "Fair enough, let's get you downstairs to get some food in you. Then you can meet with Lord Graves to discuss your contract."

She leads me downstairs and into the kitchen, where once again I'm watched as if I'm an interloper. It takes everything in me not to snap at them or just leave so I don't have to face their judgment. Marie quietly hands me food and I keep my head down as I eat tiny bites.

As I'm finishing my food one of the young women who I think

is a maid returns and waves at Marie, who's still about in the kitchen. "Marie, Lord Graves asked me to see if the thief is ready to talk."

Marie gives her a scolding look then nods in my direction, "She's right there, ask her yourself."

The maid looks at me and frowns slightly, "Miss, Lord Graves wishes to speak with you."

I raise an eyebrow at her and nod, "Okay,"

We get to a large door that's slightly ajar, as I enter I take in the space, bookcases line three walls, rising almost to the ceiling, and the fourth wall has a large window on it. There are a few comfy-looking chairs situated around a large desk in the middle of the room. Sitting behind the desk, Lord Graves watches me with a steady expression.

I shift my weight and plant a hand on my hip, taking on a sassy expression, "You wanted to talk to me, sir," I add as much disrespect to the title as I can.

He raises one eyebrow at me. He sets something on the counter and it glows slightly green, "I've written up the terms of your contract. The twins mentioned that you're unable to read, so I've got here a truth charm. So you know that I am telling you the truth."

I inspect the charm and turn my head to one side, "How do I know you're not lying about the charm?"

"Test it yourself. If you pick it up it'll change color if you're telling a lie or not."

I pick it up and turn the small charm in my hand, "All right, the sky is green," I say flatly, the charm flares red and I frown and glance at Lord Graves, "That's an easy one, you could be controlling it."

"Then tell it something only you would know."

I hesitate and roll the charm through my fingers again, "My mother abandoned me."

It glows bright green and I swallow hard. I drop the charm back on the desk and step away, "All right, I believe it. Now read the contract."

"Would you like me to read it word for word, or will just the high points be enough?"

"Just the important parts,"

"Very well," he sets the papers down and picks up the charm, "I need you to help me steal a charm bracelet, which is currently being held by a noble in the city. The noble in question is holding a ball for the Solstice, and that is to be our point and time of entry. For you to effectively be present at the ball you'll have to take lessons and learn how to pass as a noble yourself. As well as self-defense and further exploration of your magic.

"While you are here learning the appropriate skills you will be housed, fed, and clothed. After the artifact has been retrieved, you will be paid a sum of 5,000 marks. If, at that time, I feel you would be an asset to Aegis I may offer you a permanent position within the organization." He looks up at me, his expression is almost blank.

The charm has remained green through his entire speech and I'm frowning slightly, "You'll give me all those things, just to steal a charm?"

"There is more about the charm than I'm willing to disclose at this time, but yes I will give you all that for simply taking the charm," he pauses, "And behaving yourself while you are here, I can't have valuables going missing or the like."

"I'm not so dumb as to steal from the hand that feeds me," I say dryly.

He raises an eyebrow at me, one of the only outward expressions he seems to have, "I'll believe it when I see it. Do you agree to the terms?"

I sigh and rub my hands on my skirt, "Yeah, I agree."

He nods and turns the pile of papers toward me, holding out a pen, "I need you to sign it, simply make a mark that you acknowledge as your own that way we are both in agreement."

I take the pen from him and stare at the page, the shapes on the page don't make any sense, but he points to a line at the bottom and I draw a small symbol that I've used before when working with Gavin.

Graves takes the papers and puts them in a folder, "Now, I believe the twins are in the training yard, they'll put you through some drills to test your fighting skills."

"I do have one question," I interject suddenly.

He gives me that flat look, "Yes?"

"I have a friend who might be looking for me." I wring my hands nervously, "If they find me can they stay too?"

"If they find you we can discuss it. Now go find the twins, the training yard is outside the kitchen and to the rear of the house."

Damien

The sound of fists hitting the leather bag helps release the anger boiling in me, my annoyance at the situation with the thief getting me more riled up than I care to admit. I can feel Philip behind me, watching my movements as I try to let off some steam. He's been standing there for some time and I'm not inclined to give him the attention he wants.

He sighs heavily, "Good news,"

I grunt.

"Graves wants us to teach Lilith how to fight, which means you get to put her through drills. From what I understand she'll be out here after breakfast and a brief meeting with Boss."

I spin to glare at him, "This is ridiculous, there's no freaking way that is her, she's barely a slip of a thing. If she..."

I stop and take a deep breath, trying to rein in my temper, "It's not possible."

"Damien, denying it isn't going to suddenly make it so. We've got to trust Sarah, she knows what she's talking about and has never led us astray in the past," he falls silent but I return to my assault on the leather bag, "I know you're worried about the consequences of this being our last chance, but we're not going to give up on them."

I spin on him again stalking toward him with a snarl, "If that girl is our Queen, then we're never going to get the chance to give up or not. It's going to fail. She's a frail, skinny, human. She may have a bit of magic, but she doesn't even smell right! She smells like desperation and sorrow! You can't seriously believe that she can do this!"

He stands his ground and stares at me with sadness in his eyes and far more sympathy than I want, "I know you're scared of watching them die again, but we have to believe in something."

I growl at him and start to swing, then I hear soft footsteps behind us and spin toward them, ready to fight whoever is trying to sneak up on us.

I stop short when I realize it's the thief. She's wearing an over-sized dress that hangs from her thing frame haphazardly. The fabric looks incredibly heavy and makes her shoulders slump. Her hair, while clean, is dark black and has a dullness to it that suggests poor nutrition.

Her eyes are shining green and she's watching us with a curious look on her face, "Do all siblings fight with their fists when they're annoyed with each other?" she asks with a knowing smirk, "I thought that was something you were supposed to grow out of by adulthood."

I scowl at her and Philip chuckles, "Most do, but Damien's havin' a bad day and can't be judged for his temper."

"Don't fucking encourage her," I snap glaring at him again.

He just smiles, "Well, looks like it's time to start with the self-defense training. Do you wanna do the drills or should I?"

I bare my teeth at him and turn back to Lilith, "That dress is going to get in the way, did Marie have anything else for you?"

She plucks at the dress, "I dunno, this is what Helga gave me after she scrubbed me raw."

I sigh and scrub a hand over my face, "Fine, come here. Phil, go find her some pants and a shirt that'll fit. And tell Marie that she needs proper exercise gear when she goes to get clothes for her."

Lilith carefully walks up to me, her eyes flicking behind me, "Should I be concerned?" the question is directed at my brother.

I snarl and get in her face, causing her to take a small step back, "Look, you little hellion, I'm in charge of making sure your tiny ass can keep yourself alive long enough for one of us to find you. So yeah, you should be concerned. Because I'm going to work you so hard your aches will have aches. And then, when you think you can't keep going, I'll push you further. When I'm done with you you'll be able to hold your own against just about anything."

She stares up at me with that same wariness as before, her eyes searching my face for something, and I'm not quite sure what she expects to find. Finally, she smirks, and her voice takes on a sarcastic tone, "Well, I guess you better get to work, 'cause right now I'm not even tired."

"Ah, Lil, I wouldn't..." Phil starts, but it's too late, my frustration spikes and I dart forward, picking her up by the waist and tossing her over my shoulder.

"Phil, clothes." I snap at my brother as I carry the now-flailing hellion toward the track.

"Put me down!" she shrieks, her fists banging into my back as she struggles.

"You want a workout, you'll get a fucking workout," I get to the edge of the track and plop her down, she scrambles back and starts to fall so I grab her arm and pull her to a standing position, "Your task will likely take you into situations where you'll have to run in a skirt. So for now, get running."

She looks down at her skirt in disbelief, the long fabric is already in her way, and if she starts running it'll just get worse, "You can't be serious."

I smile at her, more a baring of teeth than an actual smile, "Deadly."

She scowls and then grabs the end of the skirt and ties it up, "Fine, you fucking demon."

Her jab just makes my grin widen, though the amusement is quickly washed away, "Off you trot, hellion."

She returns my snarl and starts running, stumbling and cursing as she goes.

Philip

Marie looks up, startled at my approach, "What's wrong?" she asks, taking in my expression.

"Do you have some pants and a shirt for Lilith? Graves wanted her to get started on some training... then she went and provoked Damien."

She gasps and covers her mouth, "Is she going to be okay? Why did you leave her out there with him?"

I grab her arm and pull her back in front of me, "She'll be fine, he won't actually hurt her just run her ragged until she stops being a brat. Which, I'd be willing to bet, won't be anytime soon."

"I'll go find clothes if you promise to go back out there and make sure nothing happens to her." She pauses and glances at a few of the others who're giving us odd looks, then lowers her voice "There's something about her... and Sarah said she's important..."

"All right, I'll go keep an eye on things," I squeeze her shoulder, "Just hurry up with those clothes, Damien's got her running in that skirt you and Helga gave her."

Her eyes widen again and she dashes back toward the main part of the house. I sigh and head back to the yard, sure enough, Lilith is running around the track with the skirt tied up haphazardly, barefoot, and cursing violently in thieves' cant.

Damien is standing on the nearest side of the track yelling at her,

"Come on, Hellion, surely you're faster than that? A pickpocket like you ought to be able to outrun just about anyone."

She curses at him and tries to pick up the pace, only to stumble over her skirt.

"Do you think that's necessary?" I ask.

"If she wants to be a brat she can deal with it."

"This is going to end up biting you in the ass," I say flatly and crossing my arms, "She's going to resent you for being an asshole."

I watch as Lilith keeps running, then she slows down slightly and produces her knife from somewhere. Still moving, she uses the blade to make slashes in the skirt, freeing up her legs and giving her more mobility. I grin, impressed that she found a way to make running easier, but also not stop her motion. I turn to Damien to make a snarky comment, but he's watching her with a grim look in his eyes.

"I'd rather her resent me and be able to survive whatever this life throws at her; than be soft and watch her die," he says quietly, not taking his eyes off her.

I look back at Lilith who's picked up even more speed, she nears a section of track where the house overshadows it and she turns to face us. She's running hard and is clearly breathing heavily, but as soon as she's inside the shadows her expression becomes a huge grin and she disappears.

I take a step toward where she was, worried that she's decided to run away. Before I can get more than a step away Damien spins as Lilith reappears behind him snarling and swinging at him. "Bastard!" she yells, trying to attack him with the knife.

He dodges to one side, returning her shout with a feral smile, "Not fast enough, Hellion."

She snarls and shadow-steps around him again, trying to punch his ribs. He keeps dodging out of her way and she keeps trying to strike him, getting more and more agitated as she continues to miss every strike. Finally, she stops, panting hard with her hands on her knees, "Asshole."

"Aye," Damien agrees, "But I did get a good gauge on what you're capable of in a physical fight."

She glares at him, the expression falling flat since she's still panting and red-faced.

"Was that whole thing just to gauge her skill?" I ask.

He snorts, "Didn't start that way, sure, but it did end up that way. It didn't initially occur to me that she'd try to fight me. I am pleased to see you won't let people push you around."

She grunts and wipes her hair from her face, "Asshole,"

"That I am," he looks up as Marie approaches with a bundle of clothes, "Go with Marie and get changed, we'll do some strength-building exercises and you can do a few laps at your own pace."

She gives him a skeptical look and he just grins, "Go on," he nods at Marie.

Lilith sighs and flips him off as she walks away, "I'll kick your ass one day."

"I'm counting on it," he replies.

Once the women are out of sight I give Damien a dark look, "Why did you do that?"

He doesn't bother to respond, just turns back toward the punching bags and stalks away, "She doesn't smell right," he says, "If she's really what Sarah says then she should smell right, so I'm going to push her until she does."

I rub my neck and sigh, "I'm worried Damien, I don't want you fucking this up for us before we've even begun."

He grunts then nods, "Fine, I'll be careful."

Four

In Which the Tutor Arrives

Graves

I sift through the papers on my desk, twelve more reports from various agents about mysterious monsters all around the country. I rub my forehead as Philip comes in, looking annoyed, "You need to tell Damien not to be so hard on Lilith. He's out there making her do a hundred sit-ups and push-ups. She hasn't had a decent meal in gods know how long before she came here and he's out there pushing her like she's been a soldier her whole life."

"I gave her training over to you and Damien," I say without looking up, "given that Damien's one who does close combat more, it makes sense for him to be the guide on that. As such it's his call what he has her do."

"Damn it all," he growls, "She's only been here for two days, she's not up to this level of exertion. He's going to push her too hard too fast and it's going to hurt her or make her resent us!"

I set my papers down now and look up at him, "To be perfectly honest I don't care one way or another. She's here because she's important for saving the world, otherwise, I'm not concerned about whether or not she likes us."

Philip glares at me, "Really? That's it? That's all you've got? You said yourself she's important too."

"What exactly do you want me to say?" I ask looking back to the papers, "She's nothing peculiar, just a psychometric with a bit of shadow magic. I presume her psychometry is going to be of use in identifying where the other pieces of these seals are. Her shadow magic is the key to getting to the first seal without being caught. Besides that, I see no reason to be concerned with her opinion of us."

He runs a hand through his hair and paces away from me. I sit back in my chair and watch him; opening up my senses to get a read on his emotions I frown. He's agitated, frustrated, and scared. I don't pry deeply into his emotions, knowing better than to reach too far into an immortal mind. I wait as he paces back and forth for a moment then turns to me. He's glaring harshly and I continue to watch him steadily, knowing full well that he'll break and tell me what's going on.

With a soft curse, he turns away, "Look, I don't want us to push her away. There's... there's more to her than you know, there's more to her than Damien is willing to accept right now. If what Sarah said is right, she's not just going to figure out where the seals are. She's going to be instrumental in fixing the gates. Please," he says, his voice dropping low and desperate, "Tell him to be more careful."

I close my eyes and rub the bridge of my nose, "Very well, I will ask him to be conscious of the consequences and bring the training down to be more manageable, within reason of course."

Phil sags with relief and nods, "Thank you,"

"Her tutor ought to be arriving this evening, I suspect she'll want to speak with Lilith for a while. Ask Marie to have Lilith presentable to meet with Coral."

He winces and scowls at me, "Coral? She's a pretentious bitch."

"She's also the best of the best, if anyone can teach Lilith how to pass in high society it'll be Coral."

"Fine,"

"Thank you," I look down at the reports, having momentarily forgotten them in the course of our discussion.

"Oh, one other thing," I grab the top two, "There have been sightings of strange monsters throughout the region. I've got agents on most of the other cases but these two are in the city. They look like it might be the same creature in both, and I'd like you and Damien to look into them since we're here."

He takes the pages and flips through them briefly, "All right, once lunch hits I'll have Marie take charge of Lilith and we'll head out to work on these." He taps the papers against his hand and leaves the room.

I sit back again and close my eyes, doing something I probably shouldn't. I reach out my senses until they brush against Lilith's presence out in the yard.

First I notice her annoyance and frustration, the surface emotions burning brightly. I keep reaching and pushing to the deeper emotions, whispers of fear, determination, and confusion are circling through her. Strangely her emotions match my own of the last few days. I push a bit further and I feel magic push back, shoving me away from her mind and snapping my awareness back to myself.

I sit up and lock down my empathy, "Perhaps there is more to Lilith than I originally thought."

I make my way down to the main part of the house and find Helga and Roland arguing. "What's going on?" I ask, looking between my housekeeper and butler.

They exchange a loaded look as if they're privy to something I'm not. And their hesitation has me irritated, however, I don't press them, I simply wait. To my surprise, it's Roland who breaks first, "Some of the maids are frustrated with Miss Callam's presence."

"Frustrated?" Helga demands glaring at the small man, "They keep claiming she's taken things from them, or that she's said something rude."

"We cannot dismiss their concerns offhand," Roland snaps, their tones making it clear this argument has been hashed out more than once.

"Can't just believe everything they say either," Helga snaps, her eyes hardening, "You know many of them cannot be trusted."

"Neither can she!" Roland snaps.

"Is that what's wrong? You're arguing about what to do with Lilith?" I ask, drawing their attention back to me.

Roland sighs, "Yes, it seems she's created quite the divide in the house. I'm just trying to be cautious as we were advised." He gives Helga a challenging look.

The housekeeper just stares him down, "Caution, yes, but not ostracizing! She needs friends," she adds the last bit in a soft voice and looks at me with an accusation in her eyes. "She needs people to care about her well-being, not just what she can do for them."

I pinch the bridge of my nose, "This is ridiculous. Everyone in the freaking house is messed up over her. Phil and Damien are at odds more than usual, you two are upset." I sigh and take a steadying breath.

When I open my eyes they're still standing there looking worried. "Tell the others that complaints are to be handled as they usually are. If things need to be brought to my attention I'll deal with them. But the usual mediated conversation ought to be enough." I turn toward the sitting room where we take visitors, "Lilith's tutor will be here soon."

Lilith

I finish the push-ups and roll onto my back, panting. "Giving up?" Damien asks from a few yards away from where he'd been doing his exercises.

"Finished," I reply, trying to catch my breath. My lungs are burning from the strain and the cool air.

"All right, take a breather, then we'll do a run." He stops his set and sits up rolling his shoulders a bit.

I groan and turn to look at him, "We already did a run this morning." I put on my best pouty face, I don't expect it to have any effect, but it's worth a shot.

He's quiet for a moment then grunts and looks away from me, "Fair enough, we'll do some fighting forms then work on stretches. You're a slip of a thing so being nimble will work to your advantage."

"You weren't kidding about my aches having aches," I grumble as my muscles protest every little motion.

At that he chuckles and stands up as well, tossing me a water skin, "Drink, then we'll start with forms. It'll mostly be just getting stances right so not too much strain."

I take a few big gulps then wipe my mouth with the back of my hand and eye the big man suspiciously, "You're being nice today,"

"You too,"

"Too tired to sass,"

"Good," he waves at me to come closer, "Stand with your feet square to your shoulders."

I follow his directions until I'm standing in a way that satisfies him, he's got my feet braced and my shoulders set, he stands in front of me and holds up his hand, "Okay, punch."

"Your hand?" I ask with a frown.

He gives me a dry look, "Yes, my hand."

I shrug and do as I'm told, hitting the center of his palm.

He scowls, "That all you got?"

I shift my weight and try again, but he still seems unimpressed.

"One more,"

I growl a bit and try again, not sure what he's looking for or how to get it.

This time I hit his hand and he sighs, "All right, you're not using enough of your body. Your arms may be somewhat strong on their own, but you'll get a lot more energy if you start from your feet."

"What do you mean?"

He steps in front of me and leads me toward a large bag hanging from a post by the house, "Watch me."

He takes on that same stance and draws back one fist, his body shifting backward slightly as he winds up, then snapping forward as he slams his fist into the bag before bringing it back to him for protection. I turn my head to one side and approach the bag too.

Damien steps away from the bag and nods at it, "You try,"

"Okay," I frown slightly and take on the stance. I take a deep breath and recall how he moved, shifting my weight to the back foot before snapping forward with my fist, slamming into the bag as hard as I can. The bag is a lot heavier than I expected, causing my wrist to ache, but it swings slightly on its stand. I pull my hand back and shake it out a bit, "Ow,"

"Better," Damien says, then walks to a small trunk against the wall, "These will help prevent you from damaging your wrists." He brings back a few pieces of fabric, "Phil will have my head if you get hurt 'cause I didn't give you proper protection."

I stare at the fabric, confused, "Uhh,"

He sighs and grabs my wrist, pulling it toward him, "Wrap it like this." He holds my wrist as he wraps the cloth over my knuckles and wrist, the fabric adding support to the muscle and bone, "These are mostly for practice since you'll be attempting to push your body past your limits."

"What if I need them not in practice?" I ask as he secures the cloth.

"You shouldn't,"

"What if I do?"

He looks up at me with a harsh expression, "If you find yourself in a situation where you have to use your fists you've already lost."

"What?"

"You heard me."

"What the hell is that supposed to mean?"

"It means that you're tiny and weak which isn't going to magically change. So just don't go getting into any fucking fist fights and you'll be fine."

I scowl at him as I snatch the other cloth from him and wrap my hand the same way he had.

He rolls his eyes and gestures to the bag, "Do a few more shots, use the momentum to switch between hands."

I retake my stance and begin wailing on the bag, imagining it's his head.

Focusing on the task at hand I don't notice when Philip approaches, "Hey," he says from a few steps away, causing me to jump.

I turn to scowl at him and he just grins like I'm hilarious, "Don't glare so much Lil, I'm here to rescue you."

"What?" Damien growls.

"Peace," he holds up a hand to his brother, "we have assignments from the Boss, and Lilith needs to go inside and find Marie so she can get cleaned up to meet her tutor."

Damien grunts again and sighs, "Fine," he waves me off without another word. I sigh with relief and head inside, unwrapping the cloth from my hands as I go.

I find Marie at the kitchen door, she looks me over and winces, "Oh dear, come on, let's go get you cleaned up. I found a dress that ought to fit you better but it'll still be a bit loose. You're so tiny," she mutters the last bit to herself and ushers me toward the stairs.

At the top of the stairs, she pauses and turns to me, holding out a small piece of parchment, "Here you go, this is from Sarah. I helped too. The boys have their protections against magic, and you deserve some too."

I stare at the paper for a long minute then take it from her and open it up to find a necklace with a small pendant attached to it, "What is it?"

"It's a protection charm, it'll keep your magic under wraps as well as protect you from other magic too. Sarah said you ought to have it, but to remember that you're supposed to learn to trust."

I hesitate but shrug and slip the necklace over my head.

Graves

I stand in the library that Roland and the other servants have re-purposed into a sort of classroom. The bookshelves line the walls, but a large table has been moved in and it's covered in writing supplies and various etiquette books. There's not a ton of space for workouts and the like, but there's plenty of that outside and in the training room in the basement. I nod in satisfaction and turn to the door as there's a soft knock. "Come in."

"Coral has arrived and Lilith is getting dressed now," Marie watches me with a grim expression.

"I'll go greet Coral, bring Miss Callam to the sitting room when she's dressed." I leave the room without waiting for her to reply, but it doesn't spare me being hit by her concern for Lilith or her dislike of Coral. I don't give myself time to analyze why everyone seems so against Coral's presence, she's the best there is and they'll have to deal with it.

I enter the sitting room and find the tall elven woman standing in the room, inspecting it with a critical eye. Her long hair is twisted up into an elaborate style on her head and she's wearing an intricate dress that's a bit too formal for this. She turns to look at me as I enter and smiles, but I can easily spot the condescension in her eyes without having to tap my magic.

"Lord Graves, it's wonderful to see you," her expression turns smug and she soothes the fabric of her dress, "I wondered when you were going to admit that your skills could use work and seek out my talents. I'm sure I can be of great help to yourself and Aegis."

I keep my sigh to myself, while she is very good at her job, she doesn't work well with others and is a little too self-important, "You misunderstand. I am not to be your pupil, nor will you be joining Aegis. Your charge will be joining us shortly. They're a recruit with special talents that Aegis has use of. However, their social skills are currently lacking and they need some guidance. I trust you can manage?"

Her smugness fades to disappointment but is quickly replaced once again with confidence, "Of course I can manage. I can teach a dog to be well-mannered. Whatever their skill level my pupil will be a star before you know it."

"Very good,"

The door behind me opens and Riley, one of the maidservants walks in with a tray of tea, "Helga said to serve tea for three," she says softly, batting her lashes at me.

"Very good, thank you, Riley, you may return to your regular duties."

She nods and sets the tray down before leaving the room. Coral eyes Riley as she leaves then looks at me, "Is that to be my pupil?"

"No, your pupil is..." I fall silent for a moment, wondering how best to describe Miss Callam without making her out to be some sort of monster. After a moment I state, "Unique. I do not doubt her capability, though it should be said that she is likely to be stubborn."

Coral huffs, "She will learn or she will fail, the choice is hers."

I go to the door when I hear a knock. Marie is on the other side and looks wary, Miss Callam stands behind her with her head high but she's also seeping uncertainty. "Come in Miss Callam," I gesture for her to enter, "Thank you, Marie, that will be all."

"Are you-"

"Thank you," I repeat, and she sighs then leaves as Miss Callam walks in. The dress she has on fits her better than some of the others she's been given, but it is still too large for her and she's very clearly uncomfortable in it.

Coral looks her over and wrinkles her nose, "This is to be my charge?"

I raise an eyebrow at her, "Yes. Miss Callam, this is Dowager Coral, she's to be your tutor for etiquette, stealth, and impersonation."

"Impersonation?" Miss Callam looks over at me with a raised brow, "I thought I already proved I was good at that."

Coral snorts, and I find my lips quirking at Lilith's attitude, "While you showed that you can take on the persona of a beggar, you'll also be learning how to be a lady."

Now she wrinkles her nose, "Must I?"

"We went over this in your contract. You're to learn how to behave like a lady so you may pass at the ball, and any other events that may need you to behave like someone of higher society."

Miss Callam sighs dramatically, then turns back to Coral, "I see, in that case." She drops a very messy curtsy and bears her teeth in what could barely equate to a smile, "It's a pleasure to meet you, Ma'am."

Coral winces and shakes her head, "It looks like I have my work cut out for me. We'll begin with curtsies," she walks up to Lilith who watches her warily.

"I'll leave you two to it then."

"You're leaving?" Lilith asks, sounding frightened as her gaze flicks between me and Coral.

I raise an eyebrow at her, "Yes, I have responsibilities beyond your training."

"Oh, okay," she looks back at Coral with uncertainty.

I allow my magic to reach out to her emotions and wince, she's somehow gained defenses against the most basic of my abilities. I notice she's wearing a necklace with a familiar sigil and sigh, "You'll be fine. Coral is an excellent teacher. Someone will come to fetch you for dinner."

I find Marie in the kitchen working on part of dinner, she looks up when I approach, "Did you give Lilith a protection charm?"

She gives me an annoyed look, "You weren't going to, and she deserves to have some protection from the rest of you. Just as you have protection from her."

"Did you think that perhaps I had a reason for that?"

"You might have a reason, but whatever it is, it's a bad reason. Besides, Sarah is the one who insisted she has one and made it."

"All right, keep an eye on her."

"And you keep an eye on Coral," she counters.

I frown at the command, but simply shrug it off.

Five

In Which There is a Demon

Philip

I flip through the file that Sam gave me and read out the key points to Damien, "Looks like a low-level demon was seen prowling around the docks, based on the description."

"Demons shouldn't be able to get through," he growls and kicks a pile of rope rotting on the sidewalk, "The seals really are weakening, aren't they?"

"Did you seriously doubt Sarah?"

"More like wishful thinking. What kind of demon?"

"Not sure, description is rather vague. All they've got is a shadowy animal-like creature that had stalked and attacked a young woman..." I trail off, "Shit, this is near where we found Lilith,"

"Well, she's not there now so what's it matter? With any luck, we'll find the thing tonight and be done with it." He shakes his head, "An animal demon isn't going to be too much work regardless."

"Yeah, unless it's one of the Queen's pets," I snicker.

He winces at that, "Those aren't low-level animal demons,"

"Oh I know, I kind of hope it's one of those, we can bring it back for Lilith."

"No fucking way," He snarls, "The little Hellion will likely get up to enough trouble on her own. No need to get demons involved."

"Scared what kind of trouble she'd get in?"

He stops walking and looks at me, the haunted expression in his eyes that has me stopping too, "Yeah, I'm afraid of what might happen to her if she's not prepared for what's to come. And not just because the world might end," he then plucks the file from my hands and starts walking again.

"Well, we'll just have to make sure they're prepared, won't we?" I say as I jog to catch up with him. I'm trying to lighten his mood, but know it's a losing battle.

He grunts and turns his head toward an alley, "I smell something down this way,"

I scowl but follow him, keeping alert for anything out of the ordinary. We scour our way down the alley, Damien goes up to a pile of trash and sifts through it, inspecting the contents, "What've you got?" I ask, but gag when he pulls a piece of cloth away and reveals a gnawed-on corpse under everything.

"Fuck," I cover my mouth with my arm as he does the same but crouches closer to it.

"Couple days old, bite marks look like wild dogs, but it's been hidden so whatever it was is smart enough to make that decision," he says, "Means we're dealing with a flesh eater, based on what remains of the body. Probably not animal in origin, more likely humanoid with animal characteristics."

"Doesn't exactly narrow it down, there are a lot of things that fall into that category."

"Might not be a demon," he replies nudging the body around and looking at the wounds, "There are plenty of earth-based monsters that'll eat flesh."

"Fair," I concede, "getting any of the usual underworld scents?"

He uncovers his face for a moment and inhales deeply, before coughing and covering his face again with a scowl, "No, I'm gonna see if I can find any clear bite marks; you take a walk around and see if you hear any echoes."

"Aye aye," I salute him and walk away as he shakes his head. I walk the length of the alley and don't hear anything, but as I get to the entrance I hear a scream, I turn and there's nobody but Damien in the alley at the moment. I close my eyes and tune into the sounds I'm picking up on, another scream, a tearing sound, running feet, then another voice, a raspy voice that has the hair on my neck standing on end, "Such tasty morsels, just waiting to be caught," followed by another ear-splitting scream.

I jerk back to my senses and Damien is standing a few paces away looking concerned, "What did you hear?"

I rub my forehead trying to keep a hold of the sounds that are already fading from around me, "Screaming, and whatever ate our victim spoke, so definitely humanoid, however..." I trail off as I replay the sounds in my head once more, "Nothing to confirm that it was demonic in origin."

"I smelt some dark magic on the thing, but nothing strong enough to confirm it as a demon, though I'd be willing to put money on a human using black magic. Also, no clear bite marks, so that rules that out as a lead. We'll have to take it somewhere we can do a more thorough inspection."

I rub my neck, "I'll scout around a bit more, to see if I pick anything else up."

He nods, "I'll get a hold of Sam so we can get the body moved. I'll be sure to double-check for any symbols and the like."

I pause recalling the echo I heard, "It might be a Lich, it spoke of tasty morsels..."

"Got it," he walks off without further comment and I make my way around the corner. I stand on the sidewalk and look around, nothing sinister is nearby, but that doesn't mean much if we're dealing with an earth-side monster. I rub my neck again and stare down the street, something strange prickling across my skin. I spot movement near one of the other alleys and make my way toward it.

I near the end of the alley and stop short as an echo hits my ears. "All I have to do is say the chant, ten words and it'll let something through," The voice is masculine and the mention of a chant makes my stomach drop. If someone is summoning the demons then we're in a lot more trouble than we thought. I head further down the alley, trying to find another echo, hoping that the chant they used might be caught somewhere.

Halfway down the alley I hear a scream, the voice is still masculine, but there aren't any words this time. I curse under my breath and turn in a circle, it's a dead end. It leads me to believe that they pulled the demon across here, but I can't detect traces of portal magics. I stand there staring at the brickwork, hoping that I'll be able to find another echo as I stand here. Movement behind me has me turning abruptly and I curse as a large creature darts out from behind a pile of trash.

"Fuck," I snarl and leap after it.

I spin around the corner and it's already gone, I'm not sure where it went, but I've got a sneaking suspicion that it wasn't a normal animal. "Fuck," I mutter again and make my way back toward Damien.

He looks up when I approach, "Find anything?"

"Seems like someone summoned something across, not sure how though couldn't find the chant they used. Also may have seen a shifter sniffing around, but didn't manage to catch them cause I was distracted." I look around us and keep muttering about the stupidity of it.

He sighs and rubs his neck, "Great, just great. There's a team headed over to help move the body to the morgue." He jerks a thumb at the alley, "Come help me make sure we got as much of it as we can."

"Okay," I follow after him, glancing at the street for a moment before shaking my head.

Damien

I help the clean-up team move the body to the large table in the morgue. The poor men are horrified by what's been done to the body and two threw up just seeing it. I can't say that I'm not horrified, just that I've seen this type of shit before. It's not the first, nor will it be the last, body I've seen in such a state. Phil comes up behind me and sets down a few pieces that we'd found when we'd scoured the alley while waiting for the clean-up team.

"This is a fucking mess," He says staring at the remains with deep sorrow in his eyes.

"We can't do anything for him anymore," I say, "We'll just have to hope that the poor sap managed to hold onto something that'll help us figure out what the fuck did this."

He nods then looks at the agents who're assembled behind us, "Go back to your duties, no need for all of you to deal with this, it's a shit show as it is."

None of them argue, and most of them scramble past each other to get out of the space, which I'm sure has started to smell beyond what they're able to handle.

"I'll go get the doctor," he says, patting my shoulder and heading out after the humans.

I turn to the body and start going over it carefully. I grab a few of the magically floating lights and tap them on, giving me better lighting to inspect the wounds. Most of the injuries overlap, making it hard to get a distinct impression.

I roll the body over and wince, their entire back is shredded, likely where the killer managed to pin them. Phil returns with the doctor, both of them looking wary as they survey the body by my side. "This is quite a lot of wounds," the doctor says, scanning the body and looking a little ill.

I grunt in agreement, "Can you check internally and see if anything is missing?"

He looks at me then back at the body and nods, "Yes, I can look. But, with this sort of damage, I'd be surprised if there wasn't anything missing. Is there something specific you want me to check for?"

Phil and I exchange a look and Phil sighs, "If you notice any injuries that seem to be inflicted by something other than tooth and claw we need to know. Also keep an eye out for any sort of carving, marking, engraving, tattoo, or the like."

The doctor frowns, "What would that mean?"

"You don't want to know," I say sharply, "Just let us know if you find anything." I storm from the room with Phil on my heels.

"What is it?" Phil asks as he catches up to me.

"This is bad," I say roughly, "I'm pretty sure it's demonic, as much as I hate to admit it." I clench my fists, "If the line between worlds is blurring so someone with a simple chant can bring things across, we have even less time than I thought."

He puts a hand on my shoulder and squeezes, "I know, but we can't rush this," he says insistently, "If we push too hard it'll break them, just like the others."

I put my head in my hands, "Damn it, damn it,"

Phil squeezes my shoulder again as I take some steadying breaths, "We can do this; We'll get them through this. I know we can."

"But can they? If they can't handle it, if it's too much too fast, we're going to lose either way." I close my eyes and grip the back of my neck.

"You can't think like that, we have to keep up hope," he reassures.

"How?" I mutter, "How the fuck am I supposed to keep up hope when I'm not even sure that Lilith truly holds the Queen's soul?"

"Trust Sarah," he says, trying to sound helpful.

I snort, "You know how I feel about blindly trusting Oracles."

He sighs and squeezes me again, "I know, but we've got to find hope somewhere. Trust Sarah for now, and when Lil starts to get stronger we'll see it. We'll see for certain that Sarah is right."

I shake my head but don't argue with him again.

The doctor sticks his head out of the morgue, "Sirs?" he calls.

We make our way back into the large room and he's pointing at something on the base of the victim's neck, "Is this what you were looking for?" he asks.

We both lean in, it's a tattoo of some gang symbol, but it doesn't look magical in any way. I sigh and rub my face, "We should head back," I look at the doctor, "Send word to Hellgate Manor when you're finished, and if you find anything else."

The doctor nods, "Yes sir, I'll get on it right away."

Phil hooks an arm over my shoulders and pulls me out of the room, "Come on, let's head back and get some food or something."

Lilith

I stare at the book in front of me, it's covered in letters and Coral is walking me through each one. I scowl angrily at it, frustrated that I'm having to be taught like a child. "Is there any other way we can do this? I'm not a kid."

"That may be so," Coral says, her nose turned up at me, "But your skill in this matter is that of a child. So, we shall do this my way. If you show good progress over the next few weeks perhaps we can seek different methods, but as of now," she looks down at me, her eyes almost sinister, "You're to do as I say without any more argument."

I wince and look away, "Fine."

"It is yes Ma'am," she snaps, "Address your superiors with respect, that was the first thing I taught you this morning. If you cannot retain such simple information perhaps Lord Graves ought to find someone else to do the task."

I stand up abruptly, "You can't do that! I signed a contract."

Coral shakes her head, "That may be so, but as I understand it your contract is contingent upon you doing what is needed to be prepared. And if you cannot obey me, then you're not fulfilling your end of the agreement."

I freeze, wondering if that's true and if she could so easily get me kicked out of here. If a few words from her could keep me from continuing to be here like I'm realizing I want to be. I look down at my hands, which are trembling where they're pressed against the table. I take a deep breath and let it out, "Yes Ma'am," I say softly, taking my seat again and going through the letters once more with gritted teeth.

A few hours later Coral guides me downstairs and into the large dining room. I balk at the large space, "Aren't we eating in the kitchen?"

The Elf gives me a disgusted look and shakes her head, "No. You're to be acting like a lady and no lady of any good standing would eat in the kitchens with the servants. Besides you are in dire need of etiquette lessons. Assuming your manners over food are likely as bad as your curtsy, I've ordered the staff that you're to eat in here with my direction until I say otherwise."

I feel myself blanch, "Every meal?"

"Yes, every meal," she points at a chair that has a bunch of plates and other dinnerware set out, "Sit."

Swallowing hard I plop myself into the seat and stare at the tableware. Coral smacks me on my head with a fan she's been carrying all day, "No, no," she says, "Stand up again and sit gracefully. A lady does not flop into a chair like that."

I frown, but her words from earlier have me standing up and sitting back down carefully.

"Better," she says, "Now we're going to go over what each utensil is used for and in what order. Once we've gone over all of it then you'll be allowed to eat."

I swallow again, nerves flashing through me so fast I'm not able to keep up with them, "Yes Ma'am,"

She smiles at me with satisfaction and malice in her eyes, "Excellent, let us begin."

After we've gone over every item on the table, my head is spinning. I'm quietly muttering the items to myself as Coral steps through the door that connects to the kitchen, returning a few moments later with Marie at her heels. I look up at the witch with imploring eyes, silently begging her to rescue me. Marie's features soften and as she sets the food down she whispers to me, "Give me a moment, I'll fetch Lord Graves. If he's here she won't be too bad, just hold tight."

I nod, not sure how or why Graves would help me, but not able to question her either. I look at the plate before me and see that they're small pieces of bread with some toppings, each one looks like it'll easily fit in my mouth. Unsure what to do next I just wait for Coral's instructions. I look up at the elf and she's looking at me with open disdain, "I just told you what to do with a first course, can you truly not remember?"

I can't remember; there's been so much happening today that I'm scarcely sure what day of the week it is, let alone how the fuck I'm supposed to eat this. Hesitantly I reach up and pick up one with my fingers, silently begging that I'm right.

Before I've so much as get the piece off the plate Coral's fan lands on the back of my hand, causing me to drop the bite. I cry out in distress as the food falls onto the tablecloth. "What?" I say looking up at her.

"Do not simply pick it up!" She shouts, her voice shrill, "Yes they're individual bites, but use your appetizer fork,"

"Which is that?" I ask, looking at the short line of forks beside the plate.

She smacks my head with the fan again, "You really can't remember?"

I rub my head, then guess once again, grabbing a smallish fork and picking it up slowly. I stab one of the little stacks and raise it to my mouth.

Coral sighs dramatically then takes the fork from me to rotate it in my hand, "Hold it like that," she says, "You look like a savage the other way."

I frown and put the bite into my mouth, trying desperately not to let her open hostility get to me. I don't need her to like me, I just need to learn.

I'm finishing the first course when the door on the far side of the room opens. Lord Graves comes in with both of the Twins flanking him. Philip looks at me with concern and Damien is scowling but I'm not sure what about.

Graves looks across the table and frowns, "Why was I not informed we were having a formal meal?"

Coral steps away from me, her voice shifting from harsh and demanding to soft and simpering, "Why, Lord Graves! I was simply taking this opportunity to begin teaching Miss Callam proper etiquette. Her manners are," she glances at me with disgust, "Not up to noble standards."

"I see," Graves says, but his eyes flick to me and I find myself unable to meet his gaze head-on.

I look away and roll my shoulders forward. Less than a week ago I would've fought back against Coral's commands, but despite my reservations, I'm starting to like it here. If she says that I'm not good enough I could end up getting turned out. Again. So I keep my head down and bite my tongue to avoid saying something nasty.

"In the future, if there is to be a formal meal I must be informed. Miss Callam can learn the manners suited to a lady without all of this," he waves his hand at the table in front of me.

"But, My lord," Coral says, her voice becoming sickly sweet, "I thought you were leaving her training to me? I don't think a standard meal will be enough to teach her properly. She's quite the feral little thing."

Graves frowns but doesn't immediately reply. Philip comes my way and looks at the spread before me, letting out a low whistle, "Damn," he says, "This is probably the most complex place setting I've ever seen. If she ends up going to dinner this long she might explode from all the food." He looks down at me with a gentle smile on his face.

As if Philip's comment allowed him to come to a conclusion, Graves says, "It is highly unlikely for a ball that complex to occur anytime soon, and even if it did I doubt I'd go, let alone have cause to send Miss Callam. There's no need for this."

"But sir," Coral closes her mouth when Lord Graves looks at her and raises one eyebrow; I've noticed that he does that whenever someone tries to argue with him.

"Do not make me repeat myself, Coral. I do not make decisions lightly, as I'm sure you're aware. That being said," he turns to Marie who's standing at the door between us and the kitchen, "clear this mess away. We'll stick to our normal meal for the afternoon, and the five of us will be dining in here."

"If she's not going to be doing the full meal every day then she needs to eat in here for every meal," Coral practically shouts.

Philip snorts and glares at the elf before sitting next to me. But Lord Graves seems to be considering her words again. As servants return with place settings for everyone Graves nods, "Very well, until Miss Callam's manners have become more refined she'll have both lunch and dinner at the dining table. Breakfast can still be served in the kitchen."

Marie nods, "Yes sir,"

The rest of the meal is silent, however, there's a tension in the room that has me uneasy. In the end, I practically bolt from the room to escape all the pressure.

Six

In Which Toes are Stepped On

Graves

I walk into the house, folders in my hand as I look for notes on the creatures terrorizing the town. The twins are still out doing their research and there's certainly more to be done on the Seal we're supposed to find, but I'm still waiting for reports from some of my other agents. Not to mention dealing with the dissent from the various members of the household because of Lilith's presence.

It's barely been a week and somehow it's like everything is being turned on its head because of her. What's strangest to me is that it seems the younger staff are the ones having the most issues with her. I shake my musings from my head and hurry to my office.

I almost get there when Coral appears, dragging a bedraggled Miss Callam behind her. We both come up short when we spot each other, Coral's eyes light up with glee which has me concerned, "Lord Graves!"

Miss Callam pales when she sees me, and Coral drags her to stand between the two of us. "Lilith needs a dance partner," Coral says brightly.

"Can you not act as her partner?"

She shakes her head, "Of course not! That would be simply unacceptable. If she is to learn properly then she ought to learn with a man leading."

"Did you ask Roland? Or one of the other servants?" I press, not wanting to get roped into this. Though, if the expression on Lilith's face is anything to go by, she wants even less to do with it than I do.

"Roland is too busy, and none of the others know how to dance properly. I have already exhausted other options, my Lord. I am not incompetent."

I frown at Miss Callam whose eyes are begging me to save her from Coral's scheme. However, Coral is right, she must learn somehow, I sigh and nod at Coral, "Very well, I'll assist with today's lesson. However, we must make alternate arrangements for later lessons. I cannot always take time out of my day to assist."

Lilith looks defeated as she looks at the floor, and Coral's excitement ramps up. "Excellent!" the elf says, grabbing my arm and pulling me along as she pushes Miss Callam ahead of her.

We pass Roland in the hall and I'm able to hand the folders off and he stares after us as I'm dragged along. The ballroom looks a little sad as we're ushered inside. The curtains are only cracked open to let a minimal amount of light in, and the floors look dull from not being polished. I shake my head, realizing it doesn't matter.

Coral finally releases me and shoves Miss Callam out onto the dance floor as well, "We'll start with a waltz."

Lilith stumbles then straightens up and turns to look at me, she looks annoyed but also worried as we stare each other down.

"I didn't ask for this," she says softly, her eyes flicking down and her shoulders curling inward.

I hold my hand out, "I did, our best avenue to get you into the building that houses the seal is through the Solstice Ball. You will be expected to dance."

She sighs sadly and takes my hand, "Have you gone over the steps?" My question is directed at Coral but I'm looking at Lilith.

"Yes!" Coral trills, "She's been taught the steps, now it's about application!"

Lilith goes to protest but Coral turns the music on and starts counting and clapping. I start moving in response to the music and Lilith stumbles trying to remember the steps she was taught. She gets through the first few bars of the song and then steps squarely on my foot.

I wince and try to keep dancing, but Coral calls out, "NO!" She stops the music, "Lilith, I told you to pay attention when I showed you the steps. You must move carefully, gracefully,"

Lilith makes a distressed noise, "You showed them to me once! I'm not a fucking miracle worker!"

Coral ignores her completely and starts the song again, turning back she says, "Watch your language, Lilith, and shoulder's back!"

This time I don't move a muscle, Lilith is staring dejectedly at her toes. When we stand still through the first few bars she raises her head to look at me, weariness in her eyes. "Coral cut the music," I say flatly.

The elf begins to protest but I turn to look at her with a brow raised, "Do not make me repeat myself."

She grumbles softly but turns the music off. "Now, Lilith,"

"Miss Callam," she corrects softly.

"Miss Callam," I amend, "We're going to go through the steps slowly. You follow my lead and we'll speed up as you get accustomed to them, ready?"

She nods sedately and I begin to give her instructions on the steps. We move through the first two sets of motions and she starts to hum softly to herself, adding the music at a much slower pace that matches our movements. I keep our pace steady as she gets used to the steps, her humming is adorable and I find myself smiling down at her as she stares at our feet.

Lilith

I continue to hum softly as Graves leads me through the motions of the dance. I stumble over a step and step squarely on his toes, wincing I glance up and he has the tight look on his face. "Sorry," I mutter, feeling defeated for not being able to do this.

"Stop watching your feet."

"What?"

"You're focusing too hard on doing it right you're not letting me lead. The Twins have said that you're very adept and nimble in your combat training, this is not much different. Just relax and trust both me and yourself to get it right."

I hesitate, not sure how I feel about trust, but he is a Lord and I suppose this is something they're supposed to be good at. So I nod and take a deep breath to steady myself, "Okay,"

"I'm going to count out the steps in time, just keep your focus on me."

Before I can respond he starts counting out the beat and begins to dance. I make a noise of protest but he keeps moving, his hand on my hip almost pushing me as we move. I let out a hiss of air as I stumble over my feet, stepping on both my toes and his. I can't fathom why he's pushing me like this like he wants me to step on him. "Miss Callam," he says, "Ignore your feet,"

I glare up at him, "You're trying to make this difficult."

"Hardly, you're doing that just fine on your own. I told you to trust and stop watching your feet."

"I don't know the steps."

His jaw ticks, "Perhaps, but I do."

"And I'm supposed to just, let you be in control? Sorry, sir, but I'm not some simpering lady who's going to just do what you say without question."

His jaw ticks again and something heats in his eyes, it takes me a second, but I realize it's ire. I've irritated him. The next heartbeat has me wondering if I'm about to be dismissed as his eyes narrow on me, then his expression returns to neutral, "See?"

"Wh-" I stop my question when I realize we never stopped moving. As soon as I notice I look down and stumble over my feet again. I curse again and just close my eyes, which immediately helps the situation for some fucking reason. I squeeze my eyes shut as tightly as I can and try to relax.

"You're going to give yourself a headache, not to mention confuse anyone you dance with," Graves says, sounding more amused than upset now.

I shake my head, not wanting to screw it up again, "Let me do this 'til I'm more comfortable."

He sighs, and the exasperation in the sound is rather amusing coming from the normally level-headed man. "If you keep that up it's going to keep you from getting comfortable. Just..." he sighs again, "Just look at me."

"Cause your critical stare is going to be so helpful in this situation," I keep my eyes tightly shut as I continue to dance. I misstep again and land on his foot.

He grunts, "Would it help if I looked at Coral instead?"

"Why would that help?"

"Then my supposedly critical expression wouldn't be directed at you."

That causes me to open my eyes and look up at him. He's looking at me when I open my eyes but his gaze flicks to Coral as soon as he sees I've opened them. The considerate action might've made me feel more comfortable with him; if his jaw wasn't clenched like he was trying to crush his teeth.

Oddly the sight makes me giggle, "I dunno," I say, drawing out the word, "You may not be looking critically at me, but look like you're enjoying this less than I am, given how tight your jaw is."

His eyes flick to me again and his jaw tightens for a moment then relaxes slightly, "I was dragged from my work to be your partner for this."

"And I was dragged across the house for an hour and a half before we got to your office," I mutter, "She seems to hate me," I tack the last bit on with a soft sigh of defeat.

"She may be a bit harsh but she's the best of the best," he replies, but he looks back at her with a more scrutinizing gaze, "Though you're not the first in the house to express some concerns."

My eyes widen, I'm surprised that he's taking what I'm saying into consideration at all. I go to ask him something but movement at the edge of my vision causes me to turn. My eyes widen when I see a set of dark brown eyes staring at me from the bushes outside the window. I blink and they're gone, but I could've sworn it looked like Gavin when he's transformed.

Music kicks up from behind me and Graves speeds up the pace of our dance to match the music. My protests die on my lips as I realize I'm able to seamlessly transition into the faster pace with his guidance. I look at my feet and see that they're perfectly in sync with his and even looking down doesn't upset that balance. "See?" Graves says calmly, "You're naturally adept at this, all you had to do was relax."

"Perhaps, or maybe you've hypnotized me or something," I mutter under my breath.

He levels a cool gaze at me, "For all your bluster you often second guess yourself."

I wince, realizing I have been hard on myself this whole time. I look up at him and go to argue but the song ends and he releases me. "That's enough for today. I'll arrange for one of the twins or capable servants to act as your partner next time. Now it's time for you to get outside for training."

"But-" I start but as if on cue, the clock begins to chime. Signaling that it is, in fact, time for me to go outside.

I frown and shake my head slightly, "All right," I turn and leave, ignoring Coral as she stalks over to Graves with apparent irritation in her movements. I don't envy him for being on the receiving end of her ire.

Graves

Lilith, no, Miss Callam isn't even entirely out of the room before Coral is advancing on me like she's going to tear me a new one. I don't even blink as she gets up to me and snaps, "Why are you coddling her?"

I raise an eyebrow at her, "Coddling? I simply slowed the pace of instruction to meet what she needed. Instead of forcing her to be a master in a few heartbeats."

"She needs to learn how to adapt!" Coral yells as if I'm not standing mere feet away from her, "She can't expect to know how to do everything that comes her way."

"Yes," I reply dryly, "but to be ready to adapt she must have a foundation of knowledge strong enough to get her through it. You cannot expect her to know how to do everything immediately, and your purpose for being here is to prepare her for what she may encounter. If you cannot approach the situation with that in mind then perhaps I need to find another tutor."

Her face pinches in annoyance and her fists clench, anger radiates from her for a moment before she seems to regain control of herself. "No need, I will do what I can to teach her how to adapt. Though, it concerns me that both you and Philip seem to have taken a liking to the girl, despite her being an urchin and a thief."

"Her abilities as a thief are why she's here," I say, keeping my voice low, "and her family or lack thereof is not inhibiting her ability to do what she's been hired to do."

She raises her chin as if to find something else to argue about but I raise an eyebrow at her, which makes her hesitate. She looks away, crossing her arms over her chest and making a displeased noise, "I hope you know what you're doing. I doubt her trustworthiness and her ability, but I don't make the decisions here."

She turns and marches away before I can offer a rebuttal. I stand in the ballroom for far longer than is necessary, glancing out the window as the sun peers through. "Do I know what I'm doing?" I ask the air, "Or am I going on instinct, for once."

A soft laugh has me turning to find Marie standing in the doorway with an amused look on her face. I raise a brow and she laughs again, "Poor Lord Graves, doesn't know how to trust his instincts, always needs a plan."

I glare at her, "Are you here to do something, or simply to mock me?"

"Sarah says that this is one of those things you need to let happen on its own. There is no plan because this is not set in stone, things are constantly changing and the plans must adapt as well. Trust your gut, trust your advisers, and most importantly, trust fate."

I sigh and pinch my nose, "Fate? When has fate ever gone in my favor? This is going to be awful."

She laughs aloud again, "Perhaps, or perhaps all this chaos is exactly what's needed for everything to go properly. We'll find out one way or another."

I grunt but don't look up at her, "Have you forgotten I make most of the plans around here? What are any of us going to do if I can't plan?"

She puts a hand on my shoulder, causing me to finally look up, "We adapt," she walks away leaving me to ponder how in the world we're going to get through this without a plan, and whether I'll manage to survive it.

Seven

In Which a Stray is Found

Lilith

I rush into the yard, skirting around the house to the gardens that are outside the ballroom. I stand next to the hedge and frown at it, I don't see any prints or anything to suggest that something had been here. I stare into the pattern of leaves, trying to sort through the tangle of my thoughts. Before I can get too caught up in my mind I push through the bushes and search around for more signs that a wolf was out there. When I still find nothing, I exit the vegetation only to have someone lay a heavy hand on my shoulder and make me jump.

I turn and Phil is standing next to me laughing like an asshole.

I scowl at him and snap, "What the hell? You scared me!"

He grins, "That was the point."

I shake his hand off and smack it away, "Why the hell did you want to scare me?"

"Well, you're running late and I figured I'd save you a tongue-lashing from Damien by finding you first. I thought you'd gotten caught up with Coral, only to hear you stumbling through the bushes instead." He gives me a questioning look.

I turn away and brush the leaves off of me, "I was just..." I trail off, "I thought I saw something and wanted to get a closer look."

"What sort of something?" he asks as he waves toward the ring, "Also, we should head over to the training yard."

I huff out a breath and follow him, "It was an animal of some sort," I say, not adding that the animal looked like someone I knew.

"Not many wild animals this deep in the city. Most likely a squirrel or something."

"It looked bigger than that," I say as we get to the ring.

Damien is standing in the middle of the space looking annoyed. He zeros in on me and shifts into outright anger, "Where have you been?"

I plant my hands on my hips and glare at him, "Looking for something,"

"You're late," he snaps, "You're supposed to come right here after your lessons with Coral."

I roll my eyes, "Well, Coral made Lord Graves help me with dancing and he kept me longer than usual."

"Yeah? Then why the hell didn't you come straight here? I went to find Coral and she said you'd been gone for half an hour."

"I had to change, asshole." I snap, marching forward and ready to fight him.

He advances toward me and I can feel magic begin to stir around us, "So you wasted time coming out here then," he snaps, pointing a finger in my face.

I get my magic under control before it lashes out at him. However, I slap his hand away with one hand and try to punch him with the other. He catches my hand and shoves me backward, "I didn't waste time! I just went to look at something in the garden. It's not a fucking sin to take a gods-damned moment to myself."

Phil tries to step between us but I just slide to one side and jump from Phil's shadow to Damien's, bringing my fist around to try and punch the much larger man in the side. Damien easily catches me again, "You're supposed to be training. Your time isn't all your own."

"So I can't have a breather?" Magic swirls up my arms despite my desire to keep it under control.

"You shouldn't just take them, you need to ask at the very least," he snaps, readying up like we're going to spar.

I take a step back and glare at him, "Would you have said yes?"

"It doesn't matter anymore," he says tersely, his stance falling slightly.

"So no, you wouldn't have let me have a few minutes on my own to breathe. See why I just went off on my own?" I demand, crossing my arms now.

He scowls and stalks toward me, getting in my face, "You're supposed to be training."

"And you're supposed to be teaching," I counter, "Which you seem to be shit at since all you can do is be pissy with me. So how about you do us both a favor and fuck off?"

Phil makes an odd noise and manages to push between us, cutting off Damien's line of sight and holding his hands up, "Whoa, whoa, brother, calm down."

"That little-" Damien starts.

"You're taking out your anger about the demons on Lilith," Phil interjects, "I get it, you're pissed about it and need to vent some anger. But don't take it out on her, she didn't do anything wrong and you know damn well this whole thing is overwhelming. Cut her some fucking slack."

I stand there, confused as to why Phil is outright yelling at Damien. The two men stare each other down for a tense moment, until finally, Damien snaps, "Fine! Fine!" he shoves Phil away and walks toward the house, "Make sure she still gets some work in, don't go fucking soft on her."

Phil sighs as his brother storms off and turns to look at me, "Sorry Lil, Damien... he's..." he glances after his brother and shakes his head, "A lot is going on besides your training and it's starting to wear on him."

"But it's not wearing on you?" I ask, turning my head to one side and trying to see if he is different than he was earlier this week.

He smiles, "It is, but we don't handle that stress the same way." He looks after his brother again then back at me, "But that's an explanation for another day. Let's get some warm-ups done."

I frown but nod and follow his lead into some of the warm-up stretches they've taught me.

Damien

I stalk away from the training yard, leaving Phil to deal with Lilith and her attitude. I'm too agitated about the strange scents I've been catching lately and the bloody demons in town to focus on the girl's attitude.

I freeze a few yards away from the kitchen door and turn on a heel, scanning the gardens in front of me as I inhale deeply. That strange scent is around again, a mixture of desperation, manipulation, and dog. My lips curl into a snarl when I notice a flash of movement in one of the bushes, a flash of dull brown against the evergreen.

I launch myself at the bush and tackle the trespasser, knocking into the creature with a snarl. We roll through the plants as the animal that I now recognize as a wolf snarls and snaps at me. I growl right back and manage to grab him by the throat. I stand with the struggling wolf in my grasp as it thrashes and snarls. Now that I'm closer to it I can tell that he's a shifter, and more concerning than that is the similarities between his scent and the miasma that hangs around Lilith.

"Knock it off you stupid mutt," I snap, shaking him slightly.

Philip and Lilith are running in my direction, Phil looks frustrated as Lilith sprints toward me as fast as she can. "Don't hurt him!" she cries as she gets close.

I scowl at her, "Don't tell me what to do, Hellion, he's trespassing and will have to go see Lord Graves."

She looks flustered and glances between me and the wolf, "He's probably just looking for me,"

"You know him?" Phil asks with a deep frown.

"Yes," she nods, "This is Gavin, he's my friend."

Phil's brow furrows and he looks at me with an almost pleading expression.

Before I have a chance to say anything Graves appears with Roland at his side, "What's going on?" he asks eying the four of us.

"Found a trespasser," I say, shaking the wolf for good measure.

"He's the friend I spoke of," Lilith interjects, "You said you'd give him a chance."

Graves scowls, "I'm not fond of shifters," he says slowly, "And he was sneaking around, yes?" he looks at me.

I just nod.

"He was looking for me, I'm certain of it." She says quickly then looks at me with a glare, "If the asshole here would let him go so he can talk he could make a case for himself."

"Watch it," I snarl back, not making any move to drop the beast.

Graves sighs and covers his face with his hand, "Let him down so he can transform and speak. I did give my word that if he came around I would discuss the possibility of a job for him."

I sigh heavily and drop the shifter, who hits the ground with a thump. Lilith rushes to his side as he shifts back, he coughs slightly and looks up at her, "Lil," he says with a smile, "I'm so glad I found you."

She smiles at him, "Me too," she helps him stand then looks at

Graves, who's looking at the two of them with his normal neutral expression.

"So," Graves says, "Gavin, was it? Make your case as to why I should allow you to stay here."

Gavin looks at Lilith as if expecting her to answer for him, she smiles encouragingly and he looks at Graves now. "Well, I'm a hard worker, and I'm strong, and I'm Lilith's friend so surely she can vouch for me?"

Graves doesn't look impressed and turns, "I don't have a job open on the estate."

Lilith's eyes widen and she darts forward, grabbing Graves' arm, "Please! Let him stay, please, Lord Graves," She pauses and looks sad, "He's all I have,"

Phil visibly winces and even Sam's jaw clenches for a moment, and I find myself hurt a bit by the statement as well. Graves covers his face with his hand again, his way of hiding his emotions when he's losing control of them, "Very well, Roland, add the boy to the stable hands and give him to Barry as an assistant for carrying things."

"You can't be serious!" I step forward, clenching my fists.

Graves raises his head and looks right at me, "Do I often jest?" he asks dryly.

"I don't like it,"

"Didn't ask for your opinion," He looks at Lilith, "Your friend causes trouble and it'll fall back on you too, do you understand?"

Lilith nods, "Yes sir, I understand."

"Good," he turns away, "Go finish your training time with Phil, Damien help Roland get the boy settled."

"Are you sure that's wise?" Phil asks, "Damien can help Lil."

"I'm certain," he waves them off and I usher the boy forward as we make our way to the house.

We step into the kitchen and Sam says, "Damien, be sure that

Gavin understands the rules of the house. Roland, don't leave him alone for too long at any given time."

Gavin growls, "You're gonna give me a job but treat me like an interloper?"

"Yes," Graves says flatly, "Unfortunately for the rest of us, it seems that Miss Callam is quite fond of your presence and might leave if I turn you out. So for now you're allowed to stay. However, your presence here is extremely conditional, and should you violate those conditions you will be turned out." He steps closer to the boy and holds out his hand, "Welcome to Hellgate Manor."

Gavin glares at his hand for a moment, then grasps it and shakes it once, but releases Sam's hand as if it bit him and stares at his palm for a moment. In that brief moment, Sam walks away, "Damien, be sure to give him a rundown of the conditions of his stay, and ensure he knows the proper rules."

Graves

I walk into my office and place my palms on my desk. I close my eyes and take a deep breath; the shifter is bad news, but I can't turn him out yet either. When I touched his arm I saw a snake biting into his wrist, but on the other end was another head and it was aiming for mine. I'm pretty sure he's related to whatever force is out there working against us, or at least working to break these oh-so-important seals. But I don't know his exact role, or what his presence will cause, and it's infuriating me.

I take a few steadying breaths and look at the wooden surface, there's a layer of frost on the surface and it has my lip curling in disgust. My magic has been much more active lately and my emotions are getting riled up along with it, which just makes me more frustrated. What's more, is the fact that Lilith's defense of the boy made me angry as well. I take a few more deep breaths to calm my frustration until I can get the frost to fade away.

I straighten up from my desk just as the door opens and Damien walks in shouting at me, "What the hells are you thinking? That shifter is bad news! He smells like desperation, deceit, manipulation, and treachery. You can't fucking let him stay here."

I sigh and clench my fists tightly, frost forming on my fingertips again. Plucking a letter off my desk I hand it over to him, "I am well aware of the fact that the boy is bad news, however, I am under instructions from someone with more authority to let him stay for now." The letter is from Sarah saying that the shifter needs to be here, but not what or why, she also omitted that he's a threat.

Damien snatches the letter and reads over it, then drops it to his side and crumples it up, "So we're supposed to just let some shifter mutt hang around here with no solid information as to why and plenty of reasons to kick him out?"

"Apparently. I had a vision when I touched him, it looks as if he's been poisoned by something that is also reaching out to bite us. I hope that he'll lead us to whoever is pulling his strings and we can eliminate the threat."

Damien paces across the room and turns to glare at me, "This is going to backfire," he says sharply as if I don't already know that.

"I'm almost certain of that," I nod in agreement.

"Fuck,"

I sigh and flex my hands, still working some of the chills out of them, "I need you and Phil to keep an eye on him, and honestly keep a bit closer watch on Lilith too. I don't know how his presence will affect her behavior."

"Damn it all," he runs a hand through his hair then laughs dryly, "Well, there is one good thing in all this."

"Oh?" I ask, sitting at my desk and flipping through a few of the newer reports.

"Yeah, remember how I mentioned that Lilith had an odd stench that hung over her?" he looks at me expectantly.

I raise an eyebrow at him, he must be really worried if he keeps asking about it, "Yeah, what about it?"

"Well, the boy is the origin, not Lilith. In fact, in the last week, the scent has gone down a good bit, though with the mutt in the picture again that might change."

"Hmm, keep me posted on any changes. I get the feeling that it'll be a good indicator of how things are progressing, and whether they're going in our favor or not."

He sighs and rubs a hand over his face with another growl, "Damn it all, fine. I'll keep an eye on him, but one fuck up and I'm beating the shit out of him."

"No," I say flatly, "Violence will likely hurt our goals rather than help them. For now, Gavin is to be treated carefully, but be on guard."

He growls again and stalks from the room without another word. I sigh and cover my face with my hand before muttering, "This is going to be bad."

Eight

In Which There are Doubts

Philip

I lean against the side of the house, watching Gavin as Morris gives him the rundown on his duties. It's taking all my energy to keep myself from just finding somewhere to drag his sorry ass and hide his corpse. But Lilith would never forgive me, and Graves told me not to. I scrub a hand over my face, briefly wondering where the hell Damien's gotten off to.

As if the thought summoned the man he appears at my side, also glaring at Gavin, "Boss says we're to leave him alone, but keep an eye on him and Lilith,"

"Lilith isn't the problem here,"

He rolls his eyes, "Sorry brother, she cares for the mutt so we've got to keep an eye on her."

"You're just looking for any excuse not to trust her."

"I'd rather be skeptical and keep everyone safe than be too trusting and end up with the lives of the world on my head," as if it's that simple.

"What if..." I trail off as Gavin goes into the barn with Morris.

"What if what?" Damien asks, giving me a dark look.

I sigh and rub the back of my neck, "Nothing,"

"No, spit it out, what?"

I turn to look at him and meet his gaze, not allowing him to use any sort of intimidation on me, "What if your being so harsh ruins everything? What if keeping her at a distance like this just makes things worse? She's..." I look up to the windows above us, "It's her Damien, I know it."

"I'm glad you're so confident and all, but I'm not that certain of it and until I am I'm going to keep an eye on things,"

I groan and pinch the bridge of my nose, "Also..."

"What?"

"I think he may have been the voice I heard the other day."

He frowns, "The one near the body?" he looks over at Gavin now, his expression even more concerned.

"Yeah, I can't be sure, but it feels..." I trail off and shake my head, "I'm worried, I'm worried about what he means for all of this. I don't think I... I don't think I'll survive losing them again. I'm confident that Lilith is the Queen, but I don't trust him."

Damien stays quiet for a long while, his eyes resting on the boy. I'm not sure what he's thinking. But I hope he's considering my words.

"We still can't be sure," he says at last, "We can't be sure that Lilith has the Queen's soul, and we can't be sure that Gavin isn't a threat. And until we are certain, both of them have to be kept under surveillance."

He stalks away and I stare after him for a while, at the corner of the house he turns back and looks at me, something akin to pity in his eyes, "I know you probably don't believe me, but I want Sarah to be right too. I'm just not so naïve as to get my hopes up without solid proof."

He leaves me with that and I remain outside to watch Gavin, searching for some proof that'll let us get rid of him. Before he hurts her. Before he, like so many others, hurts my Queen.

Lilith

I race toward the servants' quarters as soon as my lessons are finished. I slide to a stop when Helga is in the hallway giving instructions to someone inside one of the rooms. The large woman looks over at me and smiles tightly, "Looking for the boy?" she asks.

I nod, "Gavin, yeah,"

She gestures down the hall, "Last door on the right," she says roughly.

"Thank you," I slip past her.

Helga grabs my arm as I pass and gives me a serious look, "I know you don't trust us, but he's bad news."

I hesitate and glance down the hall then back at her, uncertainty unfurling in my chest, "I..." I trail off, opening and closing my mouth a few times.

She frowns and glances down the hall as well, hooking an arm around my shoulders she leads me away from the hallway, "You doubt him,"

I swallow hard and look out the nearby window, "I am not a fool. Uneducated perhaps, but I... I know that not everyone can be trusted." I glance over my shoulder and down the hallway, "I also know that people change."

I look up at her and she's looking down at me with understanding eyes, "You fear change," she says simply.

"I fear what change implies. I fear what I may lose to change, but..." I trail off and look at my feet.

"But?" she prompts, still holding my shoulder and not letting me move away.

"I wonder what I'll miss if I don't change. And for some reason, I feel that what I will gain is far greater than what I have to lose." I finally look up at Helga, meeting her gaze, "Does that make me cruel or selfish? To be willing to give up something I care for because of the possibility of something better?"

The older woman squeezes my shoulder and gives me a kind smile, "No, you must do what is best for you, not the best for others. If change is coming and you go with it, then you'll grow. If those who are with you now will not change too, then you cannot let them hold you back."

I look at my feet again, "So, should I abandon them?"

She shakes her head, "No, that would be cruel. You reach out to them, offer a hand, offer help, but if they will not leap. If they will not go with you, then you must leave them there."

"What if I need help? I don't know if I can face this big change on my own."

She chuckles and squeezes me, "No need to fear, you are with Aegis now, you will always have help."

"I'm not officially a member of Aegis; Lord Graves says I'm just under a temporary contract."

She snorts and shakes her head, "Lord Graves may think you are temporary, but I think not. Besides, that man knows little of what's good for him, the staff does."

"A lot of the staff doesn't like me either!" I cry, suddenly feeling worse about the whole thing rather than better.

She chuckles and shakes her head, "Those who know best do, and they're the ones who matter."

"And who is that?"

"Me, Marie, Roland, Sarah, Philip," she lists off fingers then pauses for a moment and adds, "And Damien."

I make another distressed noise, unable to contain it, "Damien hates me! And Roland isn't too fond either after I stole from him!"

"Bah, Damien's just a grumpy bastard and Roland is already warming to you," she laughs and finally releases my shoulder, "Go meet with your friend and know that change is not bad."

I frown and shake my head. "You're as puzzling as Sarah, and I thought Marie was her sister!" I throw my hands in the air and walk away, the massive woman's laugh echoing down the hall after me.

I knock on the door that Helga directed me to and it opens a moment later. Gavin doesn't hesitate to wrap me in a hug and holds me tightly, "I'm so glad you're okay," he says in a rush, "I was so worried when I came back to the hideout, and you were gone."

He pushes me to arms' length and I shrug out from under his grasp, "Well, I tried to wait for you. But you weren't coming back and I couldn't find you. And I... I felt like this was a really good chance and didn't want to pass it up."

He frowns, "Do you really think you can trust these people? They're just going to use you until you're not useful anymore."

I frown back at him, "Isn't that how jobs work? You're paid for a skill or service and when you're done the job ends?"

He hesitates and frowns at me, "What are they paying you?"

"Well, room and board, and clothes," I pick at the dress I'm wearing, "And when I steal what they want me to, they're going to pay me five thousand marks."

"That's it? Surely a lord can pay better than that," he snaps, "You should ask for more."

I hesitate, "I don't know, that's a lot... and Lord Graves said that when I've finished this job he might have a more permanent thing for me."

He frowns, "What about me?" he almost whines.

"Graves gave you a job too," I remind him, "And he said you can stay as long as you do your job and everything."

"I don't think we can trust these people," he grabs my arm and starts pulling me through the door, "We should just go,"

"Wha- no!" I yank my arm out of his grasp, "I made a deal Gavin. I don't go back on my word, you know that."

He stops and drops his head, "Why do you have to be so stubborn?"

I cross my arms over my chest, "I've never gone back on my word and I'm not going to start now."

"Fine," he turns to look at me with harsh eyes, "When they abandon you when they run like everyone else, remember that I warned you."

I hesitate at the vehemence in his voice, then raise my chin, "I'm not depending on them. They're not my friends. They're my bosses. I'm doing a job. Whether or not I stay is up to whether they want to give me a job and if they choose not to that's not my fault."

He turns away and crosses his arms, "Fine, go get back to work then, Miss Callam," he says mocking Lord Graves's tone.

I clench my fists and turn away from him too, stomping off and heading back to my room.

Graves

I sit at my desk flipping through paperwork, I look up when an angry presence rushes past my door. I frown at the door, wondering who is that irritated and not quite recognizing the magical signature. Opening the door I stick my head out, whoever it was is now gone. I frown when the energy doubles back and appears at the end of the hall appears Lilith, her eyes flashing with irritation.

She stops when she sees me, her eyes widening, "Uh,"

"Everything all right, Lilith?"

She hesitates, "I, uh..." she trails off looking frustrated, "It's fine,"

I'm not sure what prompts the question, but I say, "It doesn't seem like it's fine,"

Lilith gives me a sharp look, "What's it matter, Lord Graves?" she asks, her voice as sharp as her expression.

"I find it rather annoying when someone is running around my house throwing their emotions around. So it matters for my comfort."

She recoils, "Well, you can't expect everyone to keep all their emotions in check all the time! And call me Miss Callam!"

I step from the room and cross my arms over my chest, "I don't expect people to keep things in check at all times, I have magical protections for that. However, when someone's emotions are so strong that I can feel them halfway across the house even with my protections there is a problem, Miss Callam." It takes all my willpower to keep the anger out of my tone.

She stands there defiantly, her eyes flashing with emotion and I can feel her magic coiling through the hallway. I'm not entirely sure how long we stand there, glaring at each other down the hall. But it's long enough that I feel uneasy, and my magic begins to react to hers; forming frost on the ground and causing the windows to fog over.

Finally, she looks away, her shoulders dropping and disappointment replacing her ire, "It's nothing important, I overreacted."

"Somehow I doubt that," I say dryly, though I'm not sure why I'd doubt her testament, or why I trust that she would not be one to overreact, "However, I won't press you further. I suggest you get to bed and get your emotions under control. It's unladylike to behave like this, Miss Callam."

She gives me another angry look then nods, "Of course, sir," the way she says the honorific sounds more insulting than respectful.

I watch her walk away, her emotions now locked down so far I can scarcely detect them. As she disappears around the corner I frown, there's a glimmer of something on the floor of the hallway.

As I approach I realize it's not truly there, it's a part of a vision. I crouch next to it and see it's a snake, similar to the one that I saw earlier with Gavin. I scowl, looking up to where Lilith went and worrying about the implications of the beast's presence. I look back down, it's just the head of the snake, and it looks as if it's been torn asunder. I reach out to touch it and it dissolves.

I sit back down at my desk and rub a hand across my face, "Was it on her? Or did she take it off him? Or did she take it off herself?" I wonder aloud. I stare at the door for a long while, using my magic to keep track of Lilith's emotions. When I find myself circling my thoughts, wondering about things I can't possibly fix tonight, I get up and go to bed.

Nine

In Which Things Begin to Change

Damien

The house is quiet as I make my rounds, I can barely contain my agitation over the arrival of the mutt the other day. I don't want him here and I'm on edge because of the threat he poses to everything. That's not evening taking into account the shit that's happening in the city lately. I scrub a hand over my face and try to calm down by continuing my surveillance of the manor.

I keep my footfalls light while I prowl around, I get a whiff of deception and uncertainty from the guest hall. Looking down the hall I see Lilith peeking her head out of her door. I step back and keep an eye on her, watching closely as she looks both ways and steps out of her room.

She goes further down the hall, toward the windows and I stalk after her, keeping to the darkness and small recesses of the hall. She winds her way through the house, slipping through a few offices and out another door in the same room. Her route is ridiculous and I can't figure out what the hells she's up to, but I know she's up to something.

She loops back around to the servants' quarters and slips down a set of back stairs towards the kitchen. I frown as she goes inside, briefly wondering if, during her roundabout route, I missed someone else wandering around. I stand in the doorway just out of sight as she makes her way to the pantry.

Lilith looks around her again as she opens the pantry door and slips inside, I'm about to follow after her when she returns with a small box. I frown as she hums to herself and pulls out a cookie crunching into it happily. I stare at her from the doorway for a long minute, not quite able to process what I'm seeing.

Once I get a grip on myself I walk away and find a place to lean my back against a wall. I scrub a hand over my face and laugh to myself, "Cookies, She sneaked around and did that loopy ass path for cookies."

I laugh a bit more and shake my head, "Adorable little hellion."

I return to my rounds, making sure to keep clear of Lilith's winding path between her room and the kitchen.

The next morning I seek out Marie, she's cleaning one of the less-used guest rooms. "What do you want?" she asks as soon as I open the door.

"Why do you assume I want something?"

She shoots me a dry look over her shoulder, "You rarely seek me out unless you want something, usually a request for a specific food or some random weapon or tool."

I snort and shrug, "Fair enough."

"Well, what do you want then?"

"Ah, there's a box of cookies in the pantry, it's pink with flowers on the outside?"

"What about it?"

"Can you make sure there's a good stock of them?"

She stops and turns to look at me now, her brows furrowed as she looks me over, "What? Sarah had me buy them over a fortnight ago, certain that one of you would absolutely love them. Then when I got them you all ignored them. I even offered them to you directly, and you turned up your nose and wanted nothing to do with them. Why the sudden desire to keep a stock of them?"

We stare at each other for a moment, but I'm the one who caves and looks away, "Well, ah…" I trail off.

Marie crosses her arms over her chest and gives me a severe look, "Answer the question or I'm not doing it,"

I sigh and look at the ceiling, "Lilith was sneaking around last night to get some and I just want to make sure there's plenty there for her."

Her eyes widen, "You, want me to make sure there are plenty of cookies… for Lilith?"

"Is that so outlandish?" I ask, scowling at her now.

"Ha! Yes, it is. Since the moment she arrived, you've been all but hostile to her and now you want me to make sure she has sweets?" she shakes her head, "If I hadn't heard it with my own ears I'd scarcely believe it. But here you are," she waves her hand at me.

I cross my arms over my chest and glare down at her, "Are you going to do it or not?"

"Of course, I'm going to do it, she may be mischievous but she's still a sweetheart. I'm just still shocked that you, of all people, are the one asking me to do it. Philip, I would have expected, hell even Roland has taken a liking to her this week. But you, as I said, have been antagonizing her since day one."

I grunt, "She's still a pain in the ass. But I will admit she's growing on me a bit,"

She eyes me seriously and then smiles slightly, "If you say so. I'll make sure there are cookies for her, I'll even start putting them out for her lunches so she can have a few then. Is that sufficient for you?"

"Yes, thank you,"

She chuckles and turns back to her cleaning, "I also promise not to tell anyone you're soft on her,"

"I'm not."

"Uh-huh," she says, but I can tell that she doubts me.

I grumble under my breath and storm from the room.

Philip

I trot my way down the stairs and stop on one of the landings. Lilith is standing in the hallway with a bucket, which is sloshing in her hands as she tries to lift it to the top of the door. I smirk and make my way to her side, keeping my steps light so I can startle her. "Lemme help," I say, taking the bucket from her and balancing it above the door on the molding.

She yelps and turns to look at me, her eyes wide, "You're... helping me?"

I grin, "Of course, though, if this little trap is for Lord Graves I will have to stop you."

She wrinkles her nose at me, "I'm not an idiot. I'm pretty sure I can get away with pranking almost anyone in the house, except him. So yeah, I'm not that stupid."

I chuckle, "Fair enough, who's this for?"

"Coral," she says, her tone flickering with animosity, "The Bitch has been treating me like shit; quite frankly I'm tired of it. But if I complain I'm just seen as being whiny or not wanting to do my job. So here I am, making her life miserable the only way I know how." She hands me a length of rope.

"Tell me how you really feel," I reply dryly, but I take the rope and secure it to the bucket properly.

She snorts, "Sarcastic much?"

"Back at ya," I grin over at her, "I'm surprised you decided to do a prank like this, given that you can't reach the doorway."

"Gavin was going to help me," she says, visibly pouting, "But he got roped into some task in the barn."

I roll my eyes, "Be careful around him.".

She rolls her eyes at me now, "I know him better than I know you, so forgive me if I ignore your advice."

I sigh and look at her, "You may know him, but that doesn't mean he can be trusted."

She raises an eyebrow at me, "Are you going to lecture me on my choice of friends, or are we going to finish setting this up?"

I shake my head and return to the bucket, getting it situated properly, "There," I point at a doorway a few paces away, "When do you expect her to come out?"

She glances out the window, "Within the next five minutes, hopefully. Sometimes she takes forever to get ready, it's kind of ridiculous if you ask me."

"That's lady folk for you,"

She wrinkles her nose, "If I ever take two hours to get ready for anything then just shoot me and put me out of my misery."

I snort at that and cover my face with my hand, "Sassy little thing, aren't ya?"

She grins up at me, batting her eyelashes innocently, "You just noticed?"

I shake my head and point at the corner, "We can hide just there, and I can hear her getting close to the door so we won't miss the good stuff."

Lilith giggles now and darts for the corner, the sweet sound making me grin. She settles into place and I realize I never asked what was in the bucket, "What's in that?" I ask, looking down at her.

She looks up at me, her grin widening to something almost sinister, "Nothing too bad,"

"Lilith," I take a step toward the door.

Lilith grips my arm and pulls me back with a pleading look in her eyes, "It's just water with some twigs and leaves in it, nothing permanently damaging, I promise."

I frown at her, but the sincerity in her eyes has me stepping back to stand beside her, "If you're lying to me I'm going to make you do drills for an extra hour this afternoon."

She nods and her grin returns.

I stand at her back as we watch the hallway, peering down at the door to Coral's bathroom. I hear Coral muttering to herself as she nears the door, putting a hand on Lilith's shoulder I whisper, "Here she comes,"

Lilith bounces slightly in anticipation and I grin. The door opens, the bucket falls, the water splashes and Coral screams. The elven woman is drenched in water and there are sticks, dirt, and leaves caught in her hair and on her dress.

The pounding of multiple sets of feet alerts me to other people coming, "How badly do you wanna see this fallout?" I whisper hurriedly.

She looks up at me with concern, "What?"

I look down at her and her emerald eyes are boring into me, "If we stay we're going to get caught, are you okay with that?"

She frowns, "Ah... will I get in trouble?"

"Maybe," I admit, "I can try to take the blame but that doesn't mean you won't get caught in the crossfire."

"I don't want to get in trouble if I can avoid it," She says, looking sadly at Coral and her drenched gown.

"In that case," I hook an arm around Lilith's waist and step through the wall, moving us through the house and clear to the other side and out into the garden.

Lilith yelps when we appear outside, her hands gripping my arm like a vice, "What just happened?"

"Stone walked," I explain my arm still looped around her, "Just took us outside into the garden so we're not likely to get caught."

"Won't they know it was us though?" she looks up at me.

I look down, noticing for the first time how small she is standing next to me. I grin, "Ehh, they'll think it was one or both of us, but they'll be hard-pressed to prove it. Given that we are outside."

She grins, her eyes lighting up, "That's amazing, but... I do need to head toward the classroom."

"Yeah, I'll walk you back," I let her go and hold my arm out for her.

She loops her arm with mine and we make our way back toward the house. "So, I've seen you essentially teleport when you've entered shadows, can you do that from any shadow to another?"

She shakes her head, "No, they have to be within a certain distance of each other, but if it's a big shadow like the one cast by the house I can get pretty far without having to move."

"Ah, which is how you jumped from one end of the house to Damien's shadow that first day."

"You both looked shocked when I did that."

"It's not a common skill. Shadow magic in itself is hard to come by and moving through them like that is impressive too."

Lilith beams up at me, "I'm aware. Most people don't appreciate a thief that can disappear on them. You two still managed to catch me though."

I chuckle, "We're used to tracking the more unique magic types,"

"I'd say I'm offended, but alas, I am one of a kind," She fluffs her hair over her shoulder dramatically.

I laugh at that and shake my head. We turn the corner to the front of the house and Damien is standing there glaring, "Where the hell have you two been?"

"In the garden," I reply with a grin.

He scowls further, "Doing what?"

"Talking about some of my skills," Lilith chimes with all the innocence of a cat with a mouse in its mouth.

Damien's eyes narrow, he probably suspects there's more to it, but Lilith's statement isn't a lie so he can't be sure.

My grin widens, "Something wrong?"

He sighs, "Someone rigged up a bucket to dump water all over Coral as she was leaving her room." He eyes us critically, "And I caught you two's scents near her door."

"My room is in the same hall," Lilith says with a roll of her eyes, "Of course, you'd smell me near it."

"And I met Lilith in the hall this morning," I add, also not lying.

Damien shakes his head, "You two are going to get into way too much trouble," he mutters to himself, then looks up at us with another glare, "I won't tell anyone, Coral probably deserved it, but don't make a habit of it."

My eyes widen, surprised at his admission. Beside me, Lilith's eyes light up, but she keeps her mouth shut and doesn't spill that we were responsible.

Damien waves at the house, "Go be ready for your lessons, Coral will be in a mood all day but if you're already there when she finishes changing she can't be mad at you."

Lilith nods and then skips off, looking happy as a clam.

Once she's out of sight Damien says, "You shouldn't encourage her,"

"Like you have room to talk, seeing as you're enabling her to sneak around for cookies."

He spins to face me and scowls, "Don't you dare tell her that,"

I laugh and pat his back, "Don't worry brother, your secret is safe with me."

Graves

Coral stands in front of me, her hair still damp as she points a finger at me. "I'm certain it was that little brat! She misbehaves and causes all sorts of problems around here."

I stare at the woman and shake my head, "There's no proof of what you're saying. Yes, Miss Callam may be a bit troublesome at times, but that doesn't mean she did this." I wave at her to highlight the fact that she's still dripping wet.

I suspect that Lilith did indeed pull this little prank, but I'm also certain that there's no way to prove that. I'm not sure if I'd call it protecting her, but there was no harm done and I can't find it in myself to be angry with the result. Coral seems to need a bit of a dressing down.

Coral clenches her fists and glares at me, "So you're going to protect her too?"

I raise an eyebrow at her, causing her to take a hesitant step away from me. "If you can provide proof that Miss Callam had anything to do with this then I'll see to it she's properly chastised. However, without any proof or indication of who might have done it, I'm not going to dish out any sort of punishment."

"So that's it? There are to be no consequences?" she snaps, "Nobody is going to be held responsible?"

"For what?" I ask, not understanding why she's so hell-bent on someone being blamed for it, "You're unharmed, your clothing is unharmed, and the floors can easily be cleaned. It's a harmless prank, Coral, there's no need for anyone to get into any trouble."

She scowls at me, just as Lilith turns the corner with a bright smile on her face. She hesitates when she sees the two of us standing just outside the library door, "Is something wrong?" she asks innocently, but her eyes scan Coral and I catch a flicker of satisfaction.

"Yes," Coral snaps, "Someone dumped water on me." The elf

stalks toward Lilith, keeping the younger woman pinned with a stare, "You wouldn't happen to know anything about it?"

Lilith blinks at her, keeping her expression serious, "Can't say that I do." Her eyes flick to me and I catch the mischief in them that looks a lot like Phil's, "I got up early and was walking in the gardens with Philip."

I can't keep myself from snorting, the statements aren't outright lies, but it's clear to me that she's omitting parts of the story.

She looks at me, "Do you not believe me, sir?"

"I believe you," I concede, but I don't bother to add that I also know she's not telling us everything, "I've already told Madam Coral that since there's no trace of the culprit or culprits, there's not much else to do. And seeing as no harm was done, I see no need to pursue the matter further," I raise a brow at her, "That seems the wisest course, no?"

Miss Callam nods enthusiastically, "If nobody is hurt what's it matter? Pranks are pranks," she shrugs, "And a bucket of water is probably the most harmless thing I can think of."

"Please don't think of anything harmful," I say quickly which earns me puzzled looks from both women. I shake my head, "I've already got one prank-happy person in the household, I don't need another."

"Who's also prank-happy?" Lilith asks, turning her head to one side, but there's a knowing glint in her eyes that tells me she already knows the answer.

"If you can't figure it out on your own then perhaps you're not as perceptive as I've given you credit for," I say dryly, not entirely sure why I'm bantering with her, but enjoying the challenge in her eyes.

She plants her hands on her hips, "Oh?"

"Yes. Now, the two of you have something you ought to be doing," I turn to Coral, "If I find anything that incriminates anyone I'll be sure to hold them accountable. But, as I've said, with no harm done I can't find a good reason to seek further action."

I'm halfway down the hall when I pause and look back, they're both in the Library at this point, but I call out, "Miss Callam?"

Lilith looks back at me with concern, "Yes?"

"Don't forget to give Phil his wallet back when you see him again."

Her mouth drops open and Coral glares at both of us, then Lilith throws her head back and laughs, "I never keep anything I take from people I live with." Her expression spreads into a huge grin, "It's a good way to get on people's bad sides."

"I'm sure," I agree, then return to my office.

Ten

In Which There is Not Enough Food

Damien

I rub a hand over my face as I make my way to the training yard. I need to stretch before Lilith's training, otherwise, she'll notice I'm stiff and never let me hear the end of it. She's been getting stronger by leaps and bounds, it's been just over a month and she's already becoming a force to contend with.

I'm walking past the library when I catch a scent, I stop short and turn to look at the door of the room. It's cracked slightly and I can see Lilith on the other side with books balanced on her head. She's reciting something to Coral but I'm more focused on the scents coming from the room.

I walk up to the door, inhaling deeply as I try to sort through the natural and supernatural scents. I close my eyes and inhale again, finally catching what I was looking for. I'm able to dismiss Coral's sickly sweet scent off hand. There's another fragrance seeping from the room that I hadn't allowed myself to hope I'd find again. It's a subtle, lightly floral scent with an undercurrent of apples and hints of sage. It wraps around me like a comforting blanket.

I hurry to the kitchens, needing to get some space from Lilith and that scent. I lean against the wall near one of the side doors, my preferred hiding spot for when I need a bit of space. I close my eyes and keep my breathing steady.

"She's a bitch," someone behind me says, "Acting like she's better than us 'cause she's got a contract with Aegis. Damien and Lord Graves barely even like her! And as soon as she's done what they've asked I'm sure they'll turn her out."

"I don't know," that voice I recognize as Riley, one of the serving girls who's a shameless flirt, "Philip is really taken with her, and so are Marie and Helga. They might convince Lord Graves to let her stay. And I've noticed that Damien has been nicer to her lately."

"Then we'll have to find ways to stop it," the first person says brightly, "Maybe we can sabotage her some..."

I keep my head down and remain still, I need to hear as much of this as I can.

"That would be unwise," Marie's voice cuts into the room.

The two girls gasp and I sigh, "W-we weren't going to do any-thing!" the first girl says, "Well, not anything harmful. Just some pranks, you know, like Lilith and Philip."

Marie makes a skeptical noise in her throat then says, "Get back to your chores and leave Miss Callam alone. She's working very hard to do her job and that's more than I can say for you two lately." They scurry out of the room and I hear Marie leave too.

I head to the training room and find Phil in the space already doing drills. He looks up as I approach and frowns, "What's wrong?"

"Depends on which thing you're referring to," I mutter.

"Okay, what's got you looking ready to kill someone?"

I grunt, "Apparently some of the maids aren't too pleased with Lilith's presence. I heard a couple of them talking about how much they dislike her. We'll have to keep an eye on them, we can't have them hurting her."

His mouth drops open, "Okay, okay, I'll keep an eye out. However, I'm going to need you to back up and explain why you're suddenly a stalwart defender of our dear Lilith."

I look away from his probing stare and cover my face with my hand, "Fuck. Phil..." he doesn't press further, just waits for me to say something.

I sigh and rub a hand over my face before admitting, "The miasma cleared."

He frowns, then his eyes widen and his face lights up, "You can smell her scent now." It's not a question.

I nod.

"And?"

"And if those brats hurt my queen they're going to wish they'd never even thought ill of her, let alone dared to do something to her." I snarl, baring my teeth at him, "And if you think I'm suddenly going to start going easy on her you're gonna be disappointed. I'm going to push her harder now. I'll be damned if something happens to her because I didn't prepare her well enough."

He lets out a whoop of excitement and claps me on the shoulder, "I won't tell her anything, I'm just glad you've finally come around."

I grunt and shake him off, "Asshole."

"Are you going to tell Graves about the change? He said to keep an eye on it, right?"

"I will, but not just yet," I see Lilith approaching from behind him, "For now it's time to do some exercises with Hellion."

He turns and grins at her, "Lil! Right on time."

Lilith

Phil looks overly pleased to see me today, and Damien looks grumpy as ever. But when he looks at me there's a softness in his eyes that I swear wasn't there even earlier today. I don't have time to ponder it before he says, "You're late."

I scowl at him, "Coral kept me a bit long, apparently not knowing all the noble house crests after two days isn't good enough."

Phil sighs, "She's a hard ass, but she is the best."

"She hates me," I say with a shake of my head, "but I'm done dealing with Coral for today. Now I want to beat the shit out of something."

Damien laughs, "Bring it on, Hellion." He waves his hands at me, a sinister smile spreading across his face.

I find myself smirking back then throw myself at him with as much force as I can muster.

As we're working through the drills I feel myself getting dizzy, even though I've been eating regularly it's apparently not enough. I keep moving as fast as I can but things start to sway.

I lose focus and stumble, Damien grabs my arm and frowns, "Hellion?"

Shaking my arm away I look up at him and scowl, "What?"

"You almost fell over," he says looking me over, "Are you all right?"

"I'm fine, just a little worn out."

He raises a brow at me but shrugs and steps back, "Start that drill from the top."

I brace myself to begin again.

"Wait," Phil interrupts from the sidelines, "Lilith, come here," he points to the ground in front of him, I hesitate and make my way to his side.

He takes my arm and pushes my sleeve up, he stares at my wrist; the joint is skinny, the bones almost visible through the thin skin. Philip traces the veins and looks up at me, "How long have you been here?"

I frown, not sure what that has to do with anything. Damien walks up behind me and stands at my shoulder, also looking down at my wrist.

"About six weeks? Why?" I look at my wrist as well as if I can tell what they're looking for.

Damien grunts, "You should be putting on weight and muscle by this point."

"Yeah," Phil agrees, "Have you been getting sick with the food still?"

I look away, pulling my wrist from Phil's grasp, "No, the food is great."

"Then why do you still look like skin and bones?" Phil prompts gently, his eyes filled with concern.

"Coral says I eat like a heathen and that ladies only eat a little at a time. So she limits me to eating only a few bites of one or two things at meals."

"What?" Damien growls.

"I didn't stutter," I snap back, turning to glare up at him.

"Fuck," Phil says, rubbing a hand over his face.

Damien growls again then picks me up, throwing me over his shoulder and marching toward the house.

"What are you doing?" I screech, "Put me down, you big oaf!"

"Not a chance in hell," he growls, "We're going inside and you are eating a decent fucking meal."

I'm stunned by the sharpness in his tone and look over at Phil who's following after us looking equally annoyed. Damien kicks the kitchen door open and plops me down at the table, then looks at Marie and Barry, "Get her food, as much as she wants, and whatever she wants."

"But Coral is putting lunch out now," Barry says.

Damien bares his teeth at the man, "Who the fuck has more authority here? Me or that elven bitch?"

Barry recoils from his words and Marie's eyes widen, "Y-you," Barry stammers.

"Damn straight, do as I fucking say," he turns back to me, a fierce look in his eyes, "Sit here, eat, and at every meal eat however much you want. Got it?"

I nod, still not sure what the fuck is going on. Before I have the chance to ask, Damien walks out of the room and storms off. I can hear him slamming doors and making a fuss. Phil gives me a look that makes me think he's pitying me, but he smiles, "He's not mad at you,"

"I'm so confused..."

His smile widens and he ruffles my hair, "Damien's not as much of an ass as he likes to pretend he is."

I just frown further, "Where are you two going?"

His smile fades, "Seems we've got to have words with Coral," he also walks off before I can respond.

I look back at Marie who is standing there looking sad, "She's been keeping you from eating?" the older woman asks.

"She said I ate like a pig..." I look down at my hands.

A grunt from behind me has me looking up, Helga is there with a scowl on her face, and I half expect her to call me a pig too. Instead, she grabs a plate of food from the counter behind her and plops it on the table in front of me, "Eat,"

"But-" I try to argue, but she scowls at me.

"You heard Damien," Marie says, "He wants to make sure you're eating enough to be able to keep yourself safe. He may be a bastard, but he does care."

I nod numbly and pick up a spoon to dig into the food in front of me.

Graves

I stare at the spread on the table, Coral is prattling on about something but I feel uneasy. There's strange energy floating around the house and it seems to be coming from multiple sources. I turn toward the dining room door just as it opens inward, slamming against the wall with enough force that I hear plaster crack. I wince as Damien storms in and marches up to Coral.

"You," he grabs her by the collar and pulls her in close enough that she's forced to look him in the eyes.

Her eyes widen and she tries to push him away from her, "What in the world?"

He bares his teeth at her, and they lengthen into fangs and his skin begins to take on a grayish cast, "Listen here, Bitch,"

"Damien," I snap, "What is going on?"

He looks at me, his eyes black with his magic, "This bitch," he shakes Coral, "Has been monitoring Lilith's food intake."

"Of course I have!" Coral snaps managing to shove him away in his distraction, "She eats like a pig if I don't."

Phil walks in just as Coral finishes her sentence, and Damien grabs the elf again.

"Damien," Phil says, "Get your temper in check for a second,"

Damien growls at his brother but releases Coral, shoving her into a chair at the table, "Stay right fucking there."

Coral's eyes are wide as Phil sighs, "Graves, as I'm sure Damien has mentioned, Coral is monitoring how much food Lilith is eating. It seems Coral has been limiting her to very little food at any given meal. Which is taking its toll on Lilith's already under-fed body. She almost passed out today while she was sparring with Damien."

I frown and look at Coral, "Is this true?"

Coral crosses her arms, "Of course, it is! She eats like a pig otherwise."

Damien growls and steps toward her again, "What does it matter how much she eats?"

"She's perfectly thin already and doesn't need to put on any weight. If she gets fat no-" Coral doesn't get to finish before ice spreads from my hands across the table and all the flames in the room leap to ridiculous heights.

"You've been starving her to meet your ridiculous expectations?" I demand, unable to keep my ire in check. How dare this woman try to control Lilith like this, how dare she put her health at risk?

Damien and Phil are staring at me now too, eyes wide.

Coral looks horrified, but stammers, "She's still put on weight."

"Not enough!" Damien shouts, over his momentary shock at my outburst, "She's working her ass off to train and she was already starving before she came here. And you dare to say that putting on healthy weight is a bad thing?"

Coral remains speechless as the three of us stare her down. After a long while, she says, "I didn't think any of you cared that much."

Damien growls and bares his teeth at her, "I may be a hard ass, but even I wouldn't starve someone just to keep up fucking appearances. Besides the fact that both heavy magic and intense physical training require more food than normal." He steps closer so he's looming over her, "And remember this, I care about Lilith a whole hell of a lot more than I care about you. You pull something like this shit again and I'll personally kick your self-righteous ass out on your face, consequences be damned."

Coral looks at me as if expecting me to help her in some way.

"There wouldn't be any consequences to him from me. Lilith's presence has far more weight than yours. I can find another tutor, but I cannot replace Lilith," I know that Sarah's prophecy incorporates Lilith and I can't afford for her to leave, but I'd be a fool not to acknowledge that my concern goes past her usefulness. And a fool not to recognize that I've also been trying to control Lilith, I'll have to correct that as soon as I can.

Coral blanches and shakes herself before standing, "Very well, I'll stop monitoring her food intake. But she still must eat with my supervision or else her manners will deteriorate."

"One of us will be joining you for meals then," Phil interjects, "Can't trust you not to fall into old habits."

Coral huffs and looks away, "Fine,"

I pinch the bridge of my nose, "Which one of you wants to be in charge of that?"

"I will," Phil says, "Lilith and Damien together usually results in either violence or yelling," he grins at his brother.

"Like you two don't get into any trouble, we've all seen the pranks you two get up to," Damien snaps.

I roll my eyes, "Thank you, Phil. Damien, there's a file on my desk that needs to be looked into, I think your tracking abilities would be best suited to it," He walks off without replying, so I look at Coral, "Lilith will eat in the kitchen today, she'll rejoin you tomorrow, with Phil's company."

Coral scowls at me, but nods again, "Very well,"

Eleven

In Which a Secret Slips

Damien

Lilith stands with her feet planted and her eyes focused on me. I smirk as she scowls, "You wanna run that by me again?"

"Stop holding back! I can fight you without you coddling me." She demands, shifting her weight slightly and creating an opening.

"Oh? You think you're all that? Think you can face me if I don't hold back?"

"That's what I fucking said!"

"Fine," I snap, "Let's do this," I launch forward not giving her any warning. She shadow jumps behind me, aiming a kick for my side. She changes direction at the last second, avoiding my side to land a blow to the back of my knee. The joint buckles and I stagger, her strength has come a long way, especially since she's been able to properly eat over the last couple of weeks.

She goes to land a punch on my head and I catch it, shoving her backward and regaining my footing. She hisses slightly, her eyes glowing in the afternoon light. I can smell her magic getting stronger in the air around us and feel the hairs on my neck stand on end. I square my shoulders and bare my teeth at her, she returns the gesture and then darts toward me.

I dance back and she shadow jumps again, getting behind me once more. I spin quickly and catch her leg in mid-air. Her eyes widen as I shove her foot backward, sending her sprawling to the ground. I grin wickedly, taking it as a victory; I reach my hand out to her, "Nice try, Hellion,"

She takes my hand and yanks, hard. The magic in the air shifts abruptly, and the scent of apples and sage becomes suffocating, making my eyes widen. My shock makes it easier for her to shift me off balance and as I start to fall Lilith scrambles up. Her shadows latch around my wrist and shove at my ankle pushing me further over. I topple face-first into the dirt as she dances away.

She looks down at me with a smirk on her face, she's looking down her nose with her chin raised and there are still shadows dancing around her feet and hands. "First rule," she pants, "Never assume your opponent is defeated unless they are unable to move of their own accord, or they openly concede their defeat."

I stare at her, the scent of her magic fills the air around us, and I realize she has access to far more magic than she's let on up to now. She's two or three times more powerful than we'd thought and, based on how she just used it, is more skilled than she's been letting on too.

"Well?" she asks, raising an eyebrow at me as she keeps her guard up.

I shake myself and hold up a hand, "I concede."

She grins and takes my hand, helping me to my feet, "I told you I could take you."

I look down at her, and the magic dissipates as she locks it down again. "What did-" I stop short when I notice a stable hand walking by, whistling a bright tune. I grunt and grab Lilith's arm, "Come with me," I drag her to one of the offices, needing answers.

Lilith

Damien drags me through the house and toward one of the offices, his grip on my arm is tight but not painful. He's growling a bit and muttering to himself, he pulls me into the office and turns to glare at me. "What the hell?" I demand, yanking my arm out of his grasp.

He barks out a harsh laugh, "I should be asking you that. I don't know how you've been doing it, but your little shield faltered. I caught scent of how much magic you have," he taps the side of his nose, reminding me of his secondary abilities.

I freeze and step away from him, "W-what are you talking about?" I manage to stammer, but I know he'll be able to tell that I'm freaking out.

He raises an eyebrow at me and turns his head to one side, "What am I talking about? You know exactly what I'm talking about. You slipped up and your strength was exposed. What I can't fathom is why the hells you've hidden it this whole time. Do you know how much that power would help with your training? Do you know how much stronger you could be right now?"

I look away and cross my arms over my chest, "I don't know what you're on about."

He frowns and walks closer, I take a few more steps back, trying to keep him at a distance, but I bump into the desk behind me.

"Hellion," he says in a low voice, his tone sounding ominous.

I look at my feet and try to make myself smaller, memories swarming me of the other times people knew about my full power. Mother's silhouette walking away as shadows dance around me. Lisa yelling for me to leave and chasing me from the hovel she'd been raising me in. I grab one of my arms with the other and squeeze, feeling my throat get tight as the nails dig into my skin. I prepare for the rejection that I'm certain is going to come; for the inevitable loss of yet another place I've started to see as home.

Damien steps close enough that I can see his boots, "Lilith," his voice has dropped in volume, becoming gentle and coaxing, he reaches up and covers my hand, gently pulling my nails from my arm, "What happened?"

"I-" I shake my head and try to pull my hand from his.

"Please," He says, looking at the marks on my arm and running a hand across them, "I want to help," he pauses and purses his lips as if he's thinking. "I know I can be an ass, but I'm trying to make sure you're capable of protecting yourself no matter what comes your way. I can't do that if you're not honest and showing me everything you can do."

I squeeze my eyes shut and try to grab my arm again, Damien grabs my hand before I can dig my nails in. He squeezes my hand and then hooks a finger under my chin and lifts my head, "Lilith," he says, using his thumb to rub my cheek, "Look at me."

I shake my head and he sighs, "Hellion, I can't change the past, but if I don't know what happened I can't stop it from happening again."

I slowly open my eyes and look up at him, "I can't," I whisper as tears fill my eyes, "I can't show it, please, don't make me."

He frowns, one hand rubbing my arm gently, "Why not?"

I try to look away but he grabs my chin to keep me from moving and gives me a probing look, "People always leave," I whisper, "When I've shown what I can do they leave."

I try to look away again and he lets me, "I... I like it here, and I don't want to be sent away. So please, don't..." I trail off, not entirely sure what I'm asking for, but knowing that I need to ask.

He gently squeezes my arm and pulls me toward him, surprising me by wrapping me in a hug and holding me to his chest, "All right, I won't say anything. But I promise you this, no matter what you can do, you won't scare me. You won't scare Phil. You won't scare Graves."

I'm too startled to reply for a moment, then I relax into the hug and press my face against his chest and grip his shirt, "You can't speak for them," I mutter.

He chuckles, "I've known them for a long time, I think I can make a good guess."

"You don't know all I can do either, I didn't even use all of it. How can you be so sure that you won't turn me away when you do see it?"

He puts me at arm's length and searches my face, "I'll show you, but you have to promise me something."

I frown and eye him warily, tears still tracking down my face, "What?"

"Promise me you'll tell them when you feel it's safe to,"

"Like... tell Graves and Phil what I can do?"

"Exactly, not right away. But when you feel like you can trust them not to leave or send you away, then I want you to tell them." His expression is stern, but I can see a glitter of warmth in his eyes.

"All right, but you have to show me why you're so sure they'll be fine."

He steps away from me, "Promise not to scream,"

I snort and roll my eyes, "Get on with it, Demon," I stick my tongue out at him.

His smirk spreads into a grin and he takes a deep breath and lets it out. He glances down at himself then shrugs and pulls his shirt over his head, my eyes widen in surprise. Before I can say anything I sense the magical pressure in the air relax as Damien transforms from a tall man to a towering creature.

His skin has shifted to look like a dark gray stone, he's gained some height and small horns protrude from his hairline. I stand there staring, not quite sure what to say, then he bares his teeth, and a set of dark, wings spread from his back making him seem even larger.

My eyes rake over his body, taking in details that are unique but feel familiar to me. Scars crisscross over his chest like a lattice of pain and strength. I find myself slowly walking closer, my eyes catching on to two symbols that are tattooed under his collarbones. The patterns aren't something I would say I recognize, but they feel familiar too. I raise my hand to trace the one on his left, the ink is slightly raised and some scars cross over it as well, breaking up the lines.

I raise my eyes to his and he's looking at me with a soft expression. I know I should pull my hand away but the feeling of his skin is reassuring, despite its stony texture. "What does this stand for?" I ask quietly, my fingers still tracing the shapes.

"A Queen," he says gently, "A long time ago I pledged myself to a royal couple, it was the tradition at the time to ink their symbols on your skin to show your fealty. I stayed by their side for a long time and would have stayed longer had circumstances allowed; but alas, things went wrong and they were taken from me."

As he speaks I get flashes of images, of battles won, laughter shared, and joy lived. I start to pull my hand away but he grabs it and pins it to his chest, "How did you do that?" he asks a look of awe on his face now.

"What?"

"I just..." he trails off then shakes his head, "Did you see some of my memories? Cause I just saw some things I thought I'd forgotten."

"I didn't mean to," I say hurriedly, "I just, you talked about them so fondly. I guess I lost control a little bit. I'm sorry,"

He shakes his head, "No need, it was nice to remember some of the good times," he releases my hand and steps back.

I look away now and fidget slightly, "Um, you're really not gonna tell anyone?"

"Nope," the magical pressure returns and he pulls his shirt on, "Come on, you used a lot of magic and should eat a little something before going to study."

I frown up at him, "You're kinda weird sometimes,"

He grins, "Comes from being older than you think I am,"

I snort and shake my head, "Whatever,"

Philip

I stare in shock as Lilith and Damien come into the kitchen. Lilith looks disgruntled but unharmed, and Damien looks pleased with himself. Marie touches my arm and I jump slightly, "I swear he looked angry with her when he dragged her through here."

"I believe you, seems whatever they talked about has calmed him down. I'll see what I can find out," I walk up to Damien as he points at a seat and Lilith takes it without either of them speaking a word.

Damien sees me approach and raises an eyebrow at me, "I thought you were doing research."

"I was until Marie came running into the library looking for me. You stormed through here like a bat out of hell dragging a startled Lilith behind you," I cross my arms over my chest and give him a severe look.

He winces slightly and rubs the back of his neck, "Ah, it's nothing."

I scowl then glance at Lilith who's watching us with a curious but worried expression, "Was it nothing?" I direct the question at her.

"Honestly, I think he was just mad I kicked his ass,"

My eyebrows raise at that, "You kicked his ass?"

"Barely," Damien growls.

"You conceded, that's not barely," Lilith snaps, taking a bite of the food Barry delivered.

"You conceded?" I turn back to Damien who's glaring at the back of Lilith's head.

He shakes his head finally and shrugs at me, "Yeah, I did. She managed to knock me down and I figured that was enough of a win."

"I tricked you," Lilith chimes, not turning away from her food, "You assumed I conceded when I didn't."

"Rule one," I start.

"Yeah I know," Damien snaps, "You finish eating, Hellion, I need to talk to Phil alone for a bit."

Lilith shrugs, "I don't care," she waves a dismissive hand at me and I can't help being reminded of a queen dismissing a servant.

Damien grunts again, "Hellion,"

She shoots him a look over her shoulder, "You were leaving, Demon,"

I frown at the exchange, ready to question it, but Damien grabs my arm and leads me away. "What was that about?" I ask, pointing a thumb at Lilith.

He rolls his eyes, "She's got a big head cause she beat me, once."

"But she did beat you, you conceded," I point out.

"So you all keep reminding me," he mutters, "Look, I..." he trails off and scrubs a hand over his face, a move I know is associated with nerves.

"Are you, worried about something?" I ask, frowning at him as he glares at me over his hand.

He sighs and drops his hand, "Yes, I'm worried," He glances over my shoulder where he can still see through the kitchen door, "I'm worried about her, she's afraid of her power."

"She's never shown any sort of fear of her magic, she's always willing to do whatever sort of practice is suggested."

He shakes his head, "I promised not to go into specifics. Just keep an eye on her and don't hide so much of your magic."

"What the hells are you on about?"

He glares at me now, "I said I wouldn't go into specifics. Suffice it to say that Lilith is a bit afraid of what she can do and we need to stop hiding our magic as much. The same goes for Sam and Marie. She needs to see that there is a lot of magic in this house already and that she has nothing to fear. I'm going to go talk to them after this,"

I just stare at him for a while, very confused at this abrupt shift in his concern for her. He's been a hard ass on her this whole time and has barely let me know that he cares, and now he's practically yelling at me. I take a deep breath then nod, "All right, stop hiding magic so much, got it."

He sighs with relief, "Thanks,"

"Sure, you'll just have to explain to me why the fuck you're being so protective all the sudden,"

"Eventually," he says, then stalks away to go gods know where.

I stroll through the house, unable to keep myself busy this morning after Damien's vague instructions about magic. I tuck my hands in my pockets, puzzling over what could've happened to make him suddenly so protective. As if conjured by my thoughts a current of magic laces through the air around me and I turn to see I'm standing in front of one of the offices. I turn my head to the side and approach the door, an echo of a voice whispering through the crack in the door. "I like it here, and I don't want to be sent away. So please, don't..." my heart clenches as I realize that the voice is Lilith's and it sounds like she's sobbing.

I turn toward where I'm pretty sure Damien is, ready to tear him a new asshole, but stop short as another echo reaches me, this one in Damien's voice, "...I promise you this, no matter what you can do, you won't scare me. You won't scare Phil. You won't scare Graves."

I stand there for a long time, wondering what in the worlds Damien found out that scared Lilith so much, and what's more, changed to make him sound so tender as he comforted her. I resume my search for my brother marching through the halls in a hurry as a few of the servants cry out at my pace.

I open the door to the upstairs balcony and, sure enough, Damien is perched there on the ledge staring out over the yard. "What did you find out?" I demand, "You saw something or smelt something, or felt something, I don't know. But She was crying and you were being nice!"

He looks at me and sighs, "I can't tell you,"

"Why the hells not!" I shout, marching to his side and ready to shake him senseless or shove him off the ledge, I'm not sure which yet.

He gives me a wry look, "I promised I wouldn't,"

He's silent for a long while then sighs, "She proved to me she's the Queen again. I promised not to speak of it; but aside from that what I found out, she tricked me, she felled me, and..." he pauses, "And I showed her my true form and she wasn't even phased. Honestly, I'd say she was impressed."

I raise my eyebrows at him now, "You showed her that you're a gargoyle?"

He chuckles, "Yeah, she's scared of her abilities, I thought seeing what I am would help her. And it did, I just didn't expect her to be quite so relaxed about it."

I stare at him then sit back on my hands and stare out into the yard too, "Now what?"

"Now we do everything we can to keep her alive," he says blandly, but I can hear the undercurrent of fear in his voice.

"Right," I sigh and we fall silent, staring out over the yard and the city. I wonder what all we'll have to protect them from now.

Later...

I flip through a few pages of the case files and rub my face, "This is getting worse," I mutter, we need to find a better lead cause putting down the animal we found a couple of weeks ago didn't stop the attacks. I look out the window and see that it's getting very late, I wouldn't be surprised if the entire house was asleep at this point. I sigh and stand up, may as well get some sleep and see what I can dig up in the morning.

I open my office door just as Marie walks up, her hand raised to knock. I frown down at her, "Something wrong?"

"I found Lilith asleep in the library and needed someone to carry her to bed."

"Couldn't you just wake her?" I question, frowning at her.

"I tried..." she trails off, "She's been working very hard, and it looks like she fell asleep while studying. I thought..." she trails off.

"It would be better if she stayed asleep," I finish.

The witch nods at me and smiles sweetly, "Will you?"

"Yeah," I nod and shut my door, "I'll help you get her moved."

I step into the Library and stare at what has become a disaster zone. Books are laying open on almost every table, papers are strewn across the floor and the fire is still lit but has died down to embers. I look across the books and see that it's a variety of things. From noble crests to types of magical creatures to different countries. And the papers on the floor are numbered and placed in a series of dance steps, each page has at least one footprint on it.

I look to see Lilith curled up in one of the chairs, a blanket and a book on her lap. She's got her face propped up on one hand and she's leaning awkwardly against the side of the chair. I chuckle and glance at Marie, "Let's get her settled then clean this up. Coral will have her head if she finds the library like this."

"She's been working so hard," Marie states, looking down at Lilith with motherly affection.

"I know," I agree, "She deserves a break."

"Too bad we can't give her one," Marie says humorlessly.

"Don't be so sure of that." I set Lilith's book aside and easily pick her up out of the chair.

She's put on some weight since she's been able to eat properly but is still much lighter than she should be. She sighs and leans against my shoulder as I carry her to her room.

"What're you going to do?" Marie asks as she tails after me.

"Oh, a lie here, a well-timed question here, and a little bit of charm."

She pulls back the covers on Lilith's bed and I set her down. "Should I be worried?" she asks.

I ponder the question for a moment, "Perhaps, but it largely depends on how much lying I have to do."

She shakes her head and we go back to clean up the library.

Twelve

In Which the Fair is in Town

Philip

I open Sam's office door without preamble, "Boss," I say brightly.

"What do you want?" he says without looking up from his papers, "And since when can people enter my office without asking?"

I just keep grinning, "Knocking is for people who you don't respect and as a courtesy from those you do."

"And what makes you think you land in that category?" he asks dryly, sounding annoyed.

"The fact that I'm still standing here," I reply cheerfully, "But debating whether you respect me or not isn't what I came to talk about. I was wondering if Lilith could have the day off?"

"Why?" he says still not looking up.

"She's been working her ass off and I think she deserves to have a break. I'm not necessarily thinking we let her loose in the city unsupervised, just maybe a chance to get out of the manor and do something other than study and exercise."

He sets his papers down now and looks up at me, his eyes narrowed as he looks me over, "You want to just... walk around town?"

I stick my hands in my pockets and rock back on my heels, "Well, the fair is in town and I thought it might be fun for her."

He stares at me for a long while, but I know better than to keep talking, he'll answer when he's ready. Finally, he sighs, "Take Damien too, if I let just you and Lilith off into the city alone who knows what sort of chaos will pop up."

I frown, "And sending Damien is going to curb that? You do realize they fight almost all the time, right?"

He sighs and gives me a dark look, "You all seem to think I'm not aware of what goes on in this house. I may not always be present but I do keep up to date on how things are. Yes, Damien and Lilith are often at each other's throats; but I also know that Damien pushes her because he's worried he won't be able to protect her or teach her well enough to survive what may end up being the end of the world. And Lilith pushes back because she's afraid of what trusting him, and us would do."

"Why doesn't she push us then?" I ask, crossing my arms and glaring at him.

"She pushes you by seeing with what and how far you'll help her with her pranks, when you encourage and help her she gets frustrated because she sees what she's doing as a way to be difficult. As for me, she pushes me by testing my control and my patience. She doesn't fit into any parameters or expectations I have and she knows it, so she's constantly pushing further and further to see when I'll get fed up."

I stare at him for a long while, both of us silent as he glares at me. I relax a bit, "So is that a yes?"

He groans and looks away, "Yes, take Damien, and don't let them fight." He waves me off and returns to his paperwork.

I salute him even though he's not looking and walk off to find Lilith and my brother.

I find Damien with Marie in the kitchen, he's awkwardly holding a tray that she's stacking food on. "What's this?" I ask looking between the two of them.

Marie looks at me and says, "I told Coral that Lilith is sick, we're taking her food."

I chuckle, "No need for feigned sickness, I told you I had a plan."

Marie frowns, "Oh? What's the plan entail?"

"She's not sick?" Damien asks with a scowl at Marie.

"I talked our esteemed leader into letting Lilith have the day off." I declare brightly, "And what's more is I've been permitted to take her to the fair in town, assuming of course my dear brother accompanies us. Apparently, letting Lilith and I roam the streets without escort would result in issues Graves doesn't want to deal with." I say the last sentence as if I'm confused by the idea.

Marie snorts, "Aye, that sounds right. Though," she side-eyes Damien, "You sure Graves has thought through sending Damien?"

Damien grunts and we both look at him, I can't tell what he's upset about. Whether it's the expectation that he and Lilith don't get along, or that everyone seems to be questioning it. Before any of us can move past the odd silence a thin form zips through the door.

Damien

I'm not entirely sure what prompts me to do it, but I sense movement behind me and my arm snaps out to catch the form sprinting past me. I have half a moment to figure out that I've just snatched Lilith off the ground with an arm around her waist before she beings to flail, "Put me down! I'm late!" Her elbow swings toward my jaw and I lean back before it makes contact, but that doesn't deter her from trying to squirm away.

"No you aren't," Phil says with far too much enthusiasm, "I got you the day off. And, if you stop trying to rearrange Damien's face, I even have a surprise for you."

She stills in my grasp and stares at my brother who's in front of us, I can't see her face but it's fairly easy to imagine the skeptical expression she's now got. "A surprise? Why do I feel like getting a surprise from you is a bad idea?"

"Cause it is," I say flatly. I should let her go, but she doesn't seem intent on getting away at the moment, and for once not having her annoyance directed at me is rather nice.

Phil grins, "Aw, come on Lil, it's a nice present, I promise." He covers his heart with one hand and raises the other as if swearing an oath.

She snorts and relaxes slightly, almost leaning toward me, "Yeah? And on what do you promise? Cause I know for a fact you're trickier than me."

"Damien's coming too," Phil points at me.

Lilith looks back and up at me, seeming to only just realize that I've got a hold of her still. She raises an eyebrow at me and I do the same to her. Then we both turn back to Phil, "Doesn't help," we reply in sync.

Phil's grin widens and he sighs dramatically and looks at Marie, "Now they're ganging up on me."

I snort and Lilith giggles, the sound almost innocent, "Ganging up on you would imply that we've done something to you," she says sweetly, "But I don't think our doubting your lack of trickiness is necessarily our fault."

He frowns at her then sighs, "Fine, fine." He waves his hand dismissively, "I have acquired permission for one Lilith Callam to have a lovely day out of the manor. Assuming of course she is in the company of both Philip and Damien Jones. What exactly the plans are, I would like to keep a surprise. Does that satisfy you both?" his eyes flick between the two of us, but he's got a pleased glint in his eyes.

Lilith frowns at him, her eyes narrowed in suspicion, then she looks up at me, a question on her face, "You agreed to this?"

I can't contain my surprise at her even bothering to ask me, but I nod without much thought, "We felt you needed a break," I say, even though Phil and I hadn't actually discussed it.

Her eyes narrow again then she nods as if coming to a decision, "Very well," she says stepping out of my hold and smoothing down her dress, "I just need to fetch something before we go, okay?"

"Sure," Phil says with a grin, "Be quick don't want to miss all the fun." His grin widens and I shake my head at him as Lilith trots off.

Once she's out of sight Phil grins at me, "Thanks for going along, you could've said no."

I just shrug, "And deal with your bitching? I'd rather just go to the fucking fair." I mutter but I just plop myself down at the kitchen table and stare at the polished surface.

My brother stands there for a while, silently watching me, then he says, "You know, you're allowed to care."

I wince but ignore him.

It's not long before Lilith comes trotting back down the stairs with a coat and gloves on. "What did you need to get?" Phil asks, giving her a warm smile.

She just grins and tucks her hands in her pockets, "Just something for a friend."

Phil and I both frown at her but he shrugs it off, "All right, let's go," he offers her his arm.

She hooks her arm through his and I get up to follow them out.

We wander toward the park, where the fair is set up and I'm on high alert, the threat of the demons making me fidgety. We get near the park and Lilith scans the street corners. I'm not sure what she's looking for but she abruptly releases Phil and veers off toward one of the corners.

"Hey!" I cry, darting after her as Phil also turns and follows.

When we catch up to her she's standing next to an older man with graying hair and sad eyes, he's peering up at her looking confused, "By the gods," he says in a raspy voice, "Is that you, Lilith?"

"Hey Carl," Lilith says with a sweet smile, "I'm glad to see you still up and kicking."

The old man barks a harsh laugh, "Up at the very least," he looks her over holding a hand out to her, "Where the hells have you been?"

She takes his hand and crouches down next to him, "I got a job," she explains, "it's a good one, I'm working in a big house and they pay me really well."

He eyes Phil and me, giving me the impression we're being judged rather harshly at the moment, "Who're these blokes?"

She glances over her shoulder at us, her eyes scanning our faces for a moment as well, then she breaks into a grin, "Friends,"

He raises a brow at her, "Aye? That so?"

"Yup, they're assholes, of course, but it takes assholes to deal with my crazy ass. Yeah?"

He chuckles, "True enough," he frowns at us then at her, "If you've got such a great job, why're you here?"

Her expression shifts slightly and she reaches into her pocket, pulling out a roll of something, "Well..." she says slowly, "I know you can't do normal type work, and I know that people 'round here ain't that nice."

She turns his hand over and presses the roll of what I can now see are five notes, "So I brought you something to help through the winter. It... it's ain't as much as I wish I coulda brought... but..." she trails off as the old man stares at the money in his hands.

His eyes fill with tears, "No, no, lass," he says the last word in a choked voice, "You don't need to give me your earnings, you don't." He shakes his head and tries to hand her the money back.

She presses the bills into his hand and closes his fingers around them, "I saved these just for you. I've got all I need, food, clothes, a place to sleep. I know you don't have that and I always did what I could to help you, just like you always helped me when you could." She looks into the old man's eyes with deep conviction, "Please, Carl, take it."

He hesitates and looks at the money, then at Lilith, and nods, "All right lass, all right," he shakes his head as he pulls the money back to him, "Can't say no to that face."

Phil chuckles, "I'm not sure anyone can say no to her."

Carl laughs outright, "Aye, aye." He squeezes her hand, "You run along to do what you'd intended, aye?"

Lilith nods, "All right," she straightens up and looks at Phil, "To the park?" she asks.

He holds his arm out, "Yep, come along."

They walk off and I stand by the man for a moment, then he says, "You lot are taking good care of her, right?"

"Best we can," I say, looking down at him. I pull a card from my coat and hand it to him, "Here, I'm not sure what they can do, but see if the folks at this address can help you find work."

He grunts and pats his right leg, "Can't do much anymore, leg's gone bad." He pauses for a moment then narrows his eyes at me, "Why are you doing this anyway?" he waves the card at me.

I shrug and can't stop myself from looking at Lilith, "It takes a lot to get on Lilith's good side. I'm not always sure I can trust her judgment, I feel like I can this time."

He huffs out a breath then looks stricken, "Wait, the boy, the shifter. Do you know where he is?"

"Gavin?"

"Yes, him." The old man nods quickly, "He- he's bad news. She met me after she met him so she wouldn't hear a word of him being trouble. But I know that the boy is bad news, keep him away from her if you can."

"I've been trying," I admit, "But it's hard not to give in to what she wants."

He nods understanding but still wary, "Just, be there. Be there when he finally shows his true colors so she doesn't have to face that betrayal alone."

"I will."

Lilith

I trot along next to Phil as we make our way to the park, I notice that Damien doesn't immediately follow us, but I keep quiet until we're almost to the park. "Where'd Damien go?"

Phil glances over his shoulder and frowns, "Not entirely sure, he probably saw something he wanted to deal with."

"He won't bother Carl, will he?" I hedge, worried about the old beggar.

Phil gives me a dark look, "Do you honestly think he'd hurt the poor man?"

"No, I just worry. Carl has always been nice to me. He was in the war and got hurt, then abandoned by the military when he wasn't useful anymore."

Phil wraps an arm around my shoulders and squeezes me to his side, "Don't fret Lil, I'd be willing to bet Damien is giving him as much help as he can."

I smile up at him, relieved at the idea, "Good,"

We turn the corner and I gasp, spread out before us is the faire. The entire park is swallowed in tents and people. I can't help the giddy excitement that fills me as I look at everything. The doors on the colorful tents flip open, revealing actors and peddlers and everything in between. The sweet smell of spun sugar and fried foods fills the air and I find myself bouncing on my toes. I look up at Phil, "I'm going to explore!"

He laughs, "Sure, just stay close, if you go get into trouble without me Graves will have my head."

I grin, "I wouldn't jeopardize my taste of independence by getting in trouble." I pause and frown, "I didn't think to bring money for me."

He shakes his head and gives me an amused look, "Always looking out for your friends, eh?"

I nod, "I'm not going to change my mind, Carl needs the money far more than I do."

He smiles, "Well, luckily for you I brought you some spending money." He hands me a few twenty marks and I stare at them.

"I can't take this," I mutter, not able to grasp why he's giving me anything at all.

He shakes his head and puts the money in my palm, "This would be a terrible surprise if I didn't at least ensure you got to do a few fun things."

I look up at him "Are you sure?"

"Certain as the grave," he says with an unusual amount of seriousness.

I grin brightly at him then, impulsively stand on my toes and kiss his cheek, "Thank you, Phil, this is wonderful." I dart off before he can react to my action and duck into a nearby tent where I saw a few pretty pieces of jewelry.

I look through the shining jewelry and I'm vaguely aware of Phil following me into the space. The peddler approaches me with an overly bright smile, "Hello miss, is there anything I can help you find?"

I look up at him and smile in return, "No, I'm just looking for now."

He frowns and glances at Phil, "Surely your date would like to get you something?"

I chuckle and shake my head, "That's his decision, and," I glance over my shoulder and Phil raises a brow at me, "Not exactly a date."

Phil chuckles and winks at me, "Not exactly."

I shake my head and return to the jewelry, my hands pass over a few rings, their silver sheen bright in the light of the room. I avoid the rings and pause at the earrings, a shining pair of moons blink at me and I stare at them with a frown. "Something wrong?" Phil asks, "Did the earrings offend you?"

I shake my head, "No, I like them but," I raise a hand to my ear, "My ears aren't pierced."

"I can pierce them!" the salesman says brightly.

Phil scowls at him, "No,"

"But-"

"No," I agree, "If I'm going to get them pierced I'm going to go through someone I trust. Though," I look at the earrings, "I will take them."

His face lights up, "Wonderful!" he collects them and the money changes hands.

We resume wandering but don't get far before a gruff voice says, "There you are."

I look over and Damien is approaching us, a giant ball of spun sugar in his hand. I stare at the mass of fluffy sweetness, "You don't like sweets," I blurt.

He rolls his eyes, "Good thing this is for you then, huh?"

My eyes widen, "Really? You got it for me?"

His mouth twitches in a slight smile and he holds it out to me, "Aye, I'm not a total asshole."

I squeal, delighted, and snatch the sugar from him, pulling a section off and putting it in my mouth. I moan softly and grin up at him, "This is amazing! Thank you."

He smiles for real now, "No problem, Hellion, just don't go getting crazy on us."

I giggle, "Yeah, yeah, don't get into trouble and all that. I'm not entirely reckless."

He snorts, "I beg to differ."

I laugh and hook my arms through both of theirs, "Come on, let's go explore!" and with that, I drag them through the fair, and both of them seem to enjoy themselves too.

Thirteen

In Which There is an Invitation

Graves

I'm on my way to my office and turn a corner, pulling up short at the sight before me. Lilith is walking down the hall with her nose in a book. Her raven hair is in a long braid which she's draped over her shoulder, and she's wearing a simple green dress that practically floats around her slim frame. I find myself standing in the hall, staring at her as she approaches, mesmerized by the change a couple of months have made in her. She moves more like a lady now, though there's still that undercurrent of mischief in the lift of her lips and the glitter in her eyes.

"Are you all right, sir?"

Lilith's voice breaks into my thoughts, causing me to practically shake myself and focus on her. I blink at her a few times, desperately trying to catch my bearings and not quite sure what to say.

After a few beats of silence, Lilith smiles slightly and gestures behind me, "I seem to have caught you on an off day, if you'll just step aside I'll get out of your way and to my lessons."

I turn and see that I am between her and the door to the library. I step out of her way and gesture for her to move in front of me. That soft smile remains as she glides forward, we make eye contact and I finally find my words.

"You look lovely," I say, almost stumbling over the sentence as it leaves my mouth.

Her smile grows, the mischievous expression shifting to pleased, "Thank you, sir."

Once the door is closed I wander the rest of the way to my office and open the door, the twins are both situated in the room already, discussing what looks to be a folder of reports. Damien turns and raises an eyebrow at me, "What's up with you?"

I wave him away and take the file from him, "What do the reports say?"

Phil gives his brother a look then shrugs, "There are two dozen more sightings of demons and the like in the city. So far nobody has found any gates or portals that could be letting them in; however, there is some debate as to whether such things are needed for these creatures to be crossing between realms."

"Is there a pattern to where they're showing up?"

"Not that anyone can find," Damien growls and runs a hand over his hair, "This is getting worse,"

"No shit," Phil snaps.

I flip through the files a bit more as they banter out their frustrations. I pause on one page, a map of the city with all the sightings marked out. The spots seem random, but something about their placement seems familiar as well. Grabbing a thin piece of paper I trace out the lines between the points, seeing if I can find their shape. I repeat the process a few times, starting with different points and trying new paths, and I'm so engrossed in the process that I don't notice when the Twins go quiet.

"Sam?" Phil's voice draws me away from the page, "What're you doing?"

I look down at the desk, "These points, they seem familiar for some reason. I'm trying to draw them together to see if there's a symbol we can search for."

They both come to my side and peer down at the page too, Damien looks frustrated and shakes his head, "I swear we've already done this."

Phil grunts, "We can't discard the possibility, Damien,"

Damien continues to argue while I pause for a second then turn my head to one side, I could swear I've seen something like this before but I can't recall where. Damien snatches the map from me and stalks across the room, his anger puffing off of him in waves, "This is absurd," he snarls.

I sigh as Phil follows his brother, keeping myself silent I open my eyes as the door is pushed open.

"Sir?" Roland says from the doorway, "There is... There's a letter, regarding one of the city's aristocracy hosting a ball."

The twins stop their bickering and look up. I hold my hand out for the letter, "When is the event?" I ask, knowing full well that the Butler already has the information, despite wishing to read it myself.

"In a fortnight, sir, at..." he trails off giving me a wary look, "It's at the Hurst estate, sir."

Damien bares his teeth and sets his shoulders, I can see the fight coming for me as he inhales, "No fucking way,"

"That's not your decision," I counter, "If these sightings keep increasing at the rate they are we're going to need to get that seal faster than we thought. Lilith needs to practice and this is the only ball on the books. We will be going."

"No! You're not going there! That, that... BITCH is just going to try and manipulate you, or hurt you, or, or..." he seems at a loss for words for a moment, his eyes casting about the room, then he seems to settle on something and snaps, "Or Lilith!"

Phil turns to glare at him.

"What reason would she possibly have to disturb Lilith?" I ask, unable to hold back the ice in my tone, feeling protective of Lilith as much as I'm angry with him.

Damien doesn't back down and meets my gaze, "You think Clarissa is just going to let someone else have any of your attention? She barely let us be around you when you were courting her. Besides, she'll just get jealous of Lilith hanging around you."

"For one, Clarissa is a married woman, I see no reason for her to care who I'm seen with. Also, there'll be no 'hanging around' as I'll be Miss Callam's escort for the evening."

Damien snorts, "As if that will matter to Clarissa,"

"I truly doubt Clarissa cares enough to antagonize me, let alone Lilith," I say flatly, trying to close the matter without further argument.

"Then I'm going with you," Damien snaps, "I'm not letting the two of you go into that without making damn sure nobody bothers you."

I pinch the bridge of my nose, "You're overreacting, and no, you can't come with. I doubt Clarissa would even let you in at this point. However, as a compromise, I will take Philip with me. Is that fair?"

Damien sighs dramatically, "Fine, but only cause Phil is going. And when shit hits the fan I get to say I told you so."

"You may say whatever you wish, as long as you remain here for the night."

"Ah, Sir?" Roland says from the door, sounding a bit concerned as well.

"Yes?" I ask, looking at the older man.

"There are also two notices from the local authorities, apparently whatever has been attacking people down by the docks got two more victims last night."

Damien curses and slaps the arm of his chair, "What the fuck? I thought we got that one!" he looks over at Philip.

Phil rubs his face, "I don't know either," he stands up and takes the papers from Roland, "We'll look into it," he looks over at me, "You should go let Lilith know about the ball, I'll let Marie know to make sure she's got a dress."

Damien launches himself to his feet and snatches the papers from Philip, "Let's go,"

I roll my eyes and take the invitation off my desk.

Lilith

Coral tuts at me repeatedly, giving out corrections left and right as I try and fail to create an illusion on the table. I bite my tongue, using the pain to focus harder on the image I'm trying to create. Coral gives another command, then flings the curtains open, flooding the room with even more light. I wince as the sun hits my face and the vague shadow shape flickers and then disappears. "FUCK!" I shout, unable to keep my temper in check after two hours of this shit.

Coral spins on me, her eyes livid, "Watch your tongue!"

I look up at her, my magic rising like a tide, "Watch what you're doing! I'm trying to work with SHADOWS here. Opening the gods' damned curtains while I'm working is just diminishing the shadows I have to work with. Are you intentionally sabotaging me?" I demand the last with a wave at the curtain.

She scowls at me and stalks closer, "How dare you?! You petty, ungrateful cur. I am trying to teach you how to be a lady and a good magic user. If you cannot make do with changing situations you are not worthy of your position."

I take a step back and look away, not willing to get into a fight with her. "Fine, it seems I'm struggling with this too much, is there something else we can work on?"

She sighs dramatically and shakes her head, "I suppose. Your language needs work." She gives me a stink eye, "Though, come to think of it, have you ever spent time in the company of a gentleman?"

"Uhhh, Lord Graves generally joins us for dinner, and he's been helping me with dancing."

She shakes her head, "Not what I meant," she smiles slightly, a bit of maliciousness in her eyes, "In that case, I think we should seek out someone to do a little trial run."

"Meaning?"

Her smile widens and she turns to the door, "I think we should seek out Lord Graves and the three of us shall go on a stroll."

My eyes widen, "I don't know if that's-"

"It's a fine idea," Lord Graves says from the door.

I jump and spin, he's looking at me curiously and Coral is grinning cruelly, "What?"

Lord Graves raises one eyebrow at me, "I think it would be a good idea if you were to get some experience out in the real world so to speak. I already have some errands to run in town."

"Excellent!" Coral says, grabbing my arm roughly and I tense, "Give us a little while to get ready and we'll meet you in the foyer."

I look at Graves pleadingly, the treaty on my lips to beg for him to change his mind. Coral drags me toward the door and Lord Graves grabs her arm, halting our motion altogether.

"Actually," he says slowly, meeting my eyes, "I think it would be best for Miss Callam's learning if she and I were to run the errands ourselves. Without your company," he looks at Coral on the last statement.

"But that's complete-" she cuts off as Graves raises his hand, putting it in her face.

"I didn't ask you for your opinion, nor do I care to hear it," her eyes widen in shock as Graves offers me his arm, "Come along, Miss Callam, let's go fetch your coat."

Coral still has her nails dug into my arm, and I'm staring at Graves, baffled by the sudden, unsolicited shift in plans. Graves sees that I'm not moving, his eyes flicking down to where Coral has a hold of me, then back to me.

"Do you not wish to come?" he asks slowly, a question in his gaze that almost seems more than what he's openly saying.

I blink at him, my thoughts wheeling as I realize he's giving me the out.

I shake Coral's hand off and she scoffs at me, "You can't be serious Lord Graves," she says hurriedly as she grasps for me again, "She's not prepared for such an excursion on her own!"

"Strange," I say before she or Graves can reply, "Merely a moment ago you said I was perfectly ready for such a thing. And now you wish to change your mind? It's starting to sound as if this little adventure was not for my benefit as much as you would have Lord Graves believe." Her mouth falls open as I step away from her and casually link my arm with Graves'.

Coral gapes at us for a long moment then shakes herself and smooths her dress, "So be it," she says sharply, "If that is what you wish, do not come complaining to me when things go awry."

"Noted," Graves says dryly before turning us to the stairs. Coral doesn't say anything more but follows behind us, her presence like a looming evil at my back.

We enter the foyer where Marie and the Twins are having a hushed discussion. Marie looks up and smiles.

Damien frowns, "What's going on?" he asks, eyes flicking across all three of our faces.

"Coral suggested that I take Miss Callam into town," Graves says, "to help her learn what is expected of her in public as much as at home. I think it's an excellent idea since I have errands in town regardless." He turns toward Marie, "Could you please fetch Miss Callam's coat?"

"Yes sir, gloves are probably necessary as well," Marie nods to herself and walks away in a hurry.

"Are you sure that's wise?" Damien asks, concern on his face.

"Yeah," Phil adds, "We've got that case you sent us on, we can't go with for protection."

"There's no need for guards, we're only going to a couple of places and we'll be back before sundown," Graves says.

"This is outrageous!" Coral shouts, pointing a hand at the Twins, "You two should be more offended by this! It's inappropriate! It's unacceptable! Being seen alone with this reckless little tramp will ruin his reputation!"

Damien frowns and rolls his eyes, but Phil looks furious and stalks toward her.

I take a step back, fear spiking in my veins despite a bone-deep knowledge that he won't hurt me. I bump into Graves as Phil marches past us and towers over Coral glowering as if he's going to tear her apart.

The blond man glares down at her and bares his teeth slightly, and I'm swamped with a hit of dark magic as he says, "Watch your tongue. The only one whose reputation is at stake right now is yours. If I ever hear you speak of Lilith like that again I'll make sure your reputation isn't the only thing in shreds when I'm done."

Coral visibly cowers back, her eyes wide and staring. I briefly see the air shimmer around Philip, revealing an even paler version of himself with bloody red lips, white eyes, and fangs bared at Coral. But before I can fully process what I'm seeing the image fades and Philip steps away from Coral, who has gone pale as a sheet. "Am I clear?" Philip asks.

Coral doesn't say a word but turns and sprints off in the direction of her room. I stand there for a long minute, staring after her and very confused.

Philip

I turn to Graves and Lilith, Graves has an eyebrow raised and is giving me a serious look. I ignore that and look at Lilith, she's got a puzzled expression on her face as she glances between Coral's retreating form and me. She finally settles her gaze on me and raises an eyebrow as well, the expression so like Graves' that I almost laugh.

I tuck my hands in my pockets and smile as if threatening bodily harm is the most normal thing in the world, "Don't you two have somewhere to be?"

"I don't think that level of threat was truly necessary," Graves says dryly.

I shrug and grin a bit wider, but there's nothing friendly in it, "You can think what you like, boss, but you'll have to forgive me if I choose to act differently."

Graves sighs and rubs his forehead as Marie returns with Lilith's coat and gloves. He looks at Damien, "Don't let him go getting into a fight,"

Lilith snorts as Marie helps her into her coat, "There's a twist," she says, a smirk on her face.

"Oh?" Damien asks, raising an eyebrow at her.

"Yeah," She says, giving him the sassiest look I think I've ever seen, "You're the one most likely to get into a fight, what with you being such a grumpy ass."

Graves sighs again, "Miss Callam, please don't antagonize Damien right now. They're supposed to be going on a case."

Lilith turns and goes to say something sassy to Graves, but he gives her that raised brow and she sighs, "All right, I do suppose it is unladylike."

"Very," he replies, holding his arm out to her, "We should go,"

She nods and takes his arm and they leave the house.

Once they're gone Marie says, "Um, do you think that's a good thing?"

I smile, "I think it's an excellent thing. However, I do wonder what they think."

Damien grunts, "She didn't sass him when he gave her his signature look."

"Which means?" Marie asks.

I grin and rock back on my heels, "It means she respects him enough to do as he asks, even when he doesn't actually ask."

Marie smiles at me, but she seems uncertain as she does, "So good?"

"Yes," I nod, "I think it's good," I start toward the door, waving at Damien, "Come on, Brother, let's go find what's causing problems."

He sighs and shakes his head, "Yeah, let's go."

As we walk away I whistle to myself, unable to keep my excitement in check.

Fourteen

In Which Perceptions Change

Graves

We walk out of the estate and down to the street in silence. After a block or so Lilith says, "Thanks,"

"For?" I ask, not quite willing to acknowledge my behavior on my own.

"For taking me out, for not letting Coral come with, for..." she pauses and I feel her shrug, "Everything I guess."

"It's-" I begin.

"If you say it's nothing I'm going to elbow you in the gut." She snaps, then pauses and sighs softly, "Sorry,"

"You're right, I was going to say it's nothing." I admit, "Truly, I've noticed that Coral seems to be actively oppressing your true character. And if I'm honest, it doesn't sit right with me in the slightest; When I asked that you learn how to be a lady I didn't realize it would be at the expense of your nature and I apologize."

She stops mid-stride and turns to look at me, her eyes wide.

She's silent for so long that I get uncomfortable and snap, "What?"

She smiles, a wide genuine thing that I want to see more, "You do like me."

"Certainly if that weren't the case I wouldn't allow you in my house."

"You just apologized to me!" she says with a grin and leaning against my side, "You don't apologize to anyone."

I almost smile and just shake my head, "Don't be absurd," I start walking forward again, and she keeps stride with me, "I apologize whenever I'm wrong," I pause for a beat, "but I'm rarely wrong."

She laughs, "Somehow I doubt that," she bumps into my side again, "If you're right all the time, I bet it stings to be wrong."

I give her a side-long glance, "Bumping into me is not appropriate behavior, Miss Callam." I advise, "However, being wrong isn't something I'm ashamed of or in any way upset by. It's simply something that happens, people are wrong all the time. I just have a very good knack for being right."

"I suppose when you put it that way…" she trails off, and her emotions shift to somber, "I wish I could say I was almost always right."

I look over at her and she's visibly deflated, "What makes you think you aren't?" I ask, unable to leave her like this.

She shrugs then looks up at the sidewalk and keeps her gaze averted, "So many times in my life I've done what I thought was right and it blew up in my face. I'm wrong more often than I'm right, and it makes for a lack of confidence in my decisions. Even this," she waves at herself with one hand, "I wonder if it's the right choice. I wonder if living somewhere I'm expected to be one way, where someone actively dislikes me, is a good idea."

I don't immediately have an answer for her, so we walk in silence while I collect my thoughts. I know that Damien doesn't dislike her, seeing as he's rather doting on her when she's not around. I also have a solution for the issues with Coral, I hope.

So, when we round the corner that has Sarah's shop on it I say, "For starters," she startles a little, which I ignore, "I'm going to talk to Coral about your instruction, I want you to know how to behave like a lady, but I don't want you to become a doll. Your personality shouldn't be sacrificed for the sake of appeasing Coral's need to be controlling. As to whether or not being here is the right choice," I hesitate then look over at her and she's regarding me with her head tilted to one side, her curiosity brushing against my psyche, "Despite my original misgivings, I think you being here is an excellent idea, so take that as you will."

A small smile tugs at her lips, "Yeah? Guess it can't be too bad, seeing as you're always right."

I snort and she grins, "Come on," I tug her toward the shop, "I do have other things to do today."

Her laugh dances around me as she shakes her head and follows along, "Bossy."

I push the door open and wait giving her my usual raised eyebrow, her grin widens as she steps inside saying, "Thank you," and I can't help but wonder if she's talking about the door or not.

I follow her into the building and she's stopped just inside, her eyes light up as she takes in the space. There are bundles of herbs hanging from the rafters, jars of questionable liquids on the shelves, but most importantly is the sparkle of magic all over the place. "Miss Callam," I say quietly, "I take it you've been here before?"

She shakes herself and looks back at me with a smile, "Yeah, Not a lot mind you since it's a bit outside where I used to live, but I've been in Sarah's shop before."

I smile back and her face lights up, "Well if you see anything you'd like we can grab it, but we do have to get some specific things," I pull Marie's list from my coat.

Lilith nods and smiles as she comes to stand beside me, "Lead on," she says warmly.

I offer her my arm again and she takes it with a grin. We step up to the counter when Sarah bursts out of the back in a cloud of perfume, "There you are!" she cries, and I can't tell if she's happy or distressed.

Before I can think on it further she rounds the counter and envelops Lilith in a hug, "I'm so glad things are going so well," she gushes.

Lilith laughs, "Miss Sarah, I've asked you dozens of times to ask questions before you congratulate me on how things are."

"Sarah doesn't know how to ask first," I hold out the list to Sarah.

Sarah doesn't even look at the list as she reaches and grabs a bag off the counter, "Here, there are the things you need. However," she takes Lilith's hand, "I need Lilith to pick something out real quick."

"Don't you already know what I'm going to pick?" Lilith asks dryly, but she lets herself be pulled away regardless.

"I have a good idea, but not everything is set in stone," Sarah says brightly, glancing at me she says, "Wait here,"

I sigh, "We do have other places to be,"

"Yes, yes, you'll get everything done." Sarah waves me off as they disappear into the depths of the store.

Lilith

Sarah leads me away from Lord Graves, her arm wrapped around my shoulders. We move around a few shelves and she leans close, "So how do you feel things are going? I know what I've seen, but tell me the truth."

I look up at her with a frown, "Don't you know the truth?"

She shakes her head, "I know what I see, and I've seen that things are on a path that seems good. But if you are unhappy with the path then it can be changed."

We come to a display case and she pauses, looking at me expectantly.

I sigh and put my hands in my coat pockets, and sigh, "Well, I think things are going well, but I'm worried."

She nods, "That's good, worries are normal. Things are changing, and they will continue to, just be ready for it."

I nod, but quickly change the subject "What do you need me to pick out?"

She grins now, "Here," she turns to the case, "I'm making you a present, and I need you to pick a charm for it."

I look into the case and look it over. There are a dozen charms arranged on a velvet cloth tucked behind a glass pane. My eyes skim over the charms, skipping across most of them but catching on two. One is a silver circle with elaborate swirls through it; The other is a blackened charm of a crescent moon with a cross coming off the bottom of it. Without asking I open the case and grab the moon, I trace my hands across it and then grab the circle as well. Using my hands to trace the patterns, they feel familiar for some reason and I can't recall why.

Sarah stands silently behind me as I look both of them over. I look at her, one charm in each hand. She looks at me expectantly. I hold both hands out, "I want these," I say.

"You only need one," she says, holding her hands out for both charms regardless.

I nod, "I understand, but these..." I trail off as I open my hands, showing her both charms, "These are mine,"

As I say it she smiles and takes them from me, "Very well, then I'll use them both."

"You knew I'd pick them both, didn't you?" I ask giving her a probing look.

She grins wider, "I can't tell you that, as I'm sure you're aware."

I throw my head back and roll my eyes, heaving a heavy sigh as she shakes her head.

She takes my hand in hers and says, "There is something I need to tell you though, and it's important that it remain between us, do you understand?"

I hesitate, the seriousness of her tone instantly putting me on edge, "Sure."

She nods, "This has to be cryptic mind you, oracle things and all."

I frown at her but nod regardless.

"Each seal holds the final shard, of that which they have searched for so hard. And when that piece finds its place to rest, from its bearer it shall not be wrest."

I stare at her, "Am I supposed to understand that all?"

She chuckles, "It'll make sense in time. Come on, let's return you to Graves before he gets himself worked up."

I snort at that and shake my head "Graves has two moods, annoyed and thoughtful. I don't think he knows how to get worked up."

She smiles, her eyes twinkling, "He certainly can, but he makes a concentrated effort not to."

"I will admit that I'm pretty good at upsetting him," I sigh softly.

Sarah makes a tutting noise and shakes her head, "I think you'd be surprised by the true core of his concerns." She wraps her arms around me and leads me back to the main part of the store.

Lord Graves is, to my surprise, pacing back and forth in front of the sales counter. He gives Sarah an odd look, his expression more intense than usual, "I did say we have other places to be,"

"And I said that you'd get to everything," she says with a roll of her eyes, "Lilith and I needed a moment to chat," she squeezes me, "You've got everything you need and I have what I needed from Lilith. Now off you go," she waves me toward him and he sighs and holds his arm out for me. I shake my head and hook my arm over his before he leads me away.

Graves

I lead the way toward the tailor I usually use, now that I've gotten what we need from Sarah I want to get Lilith fitted for the balls she's to attend. It suddenly occurs to me that I don't recall telling her she's going, "Oh," I stop short, she jumps and looks up at me with wide eyes, "We received an invitation to a ball for the week after next, we're actually on our way to a tailor to get you an appropriate dress."

"Oh? Really?"

"Yes, we'll likely get a pre-made dress for the first ball, however, we'll need to get a custom dress for the Solstice ball. I presume you don't want to try and steal something in a full gown," I raise an eyebrow at her.

She giggles and nods, "Yeah, that would not go so well. Will your tailor be able to make a dress that'll work?"

"Yes, this is the tailor we use for all the Aegis business, as well as personal. They'll be able to modify the dress however you'd like to make it workable for your needs."

She nods and falls silent, her eyes growing distant as we resume our walk.

I wonder what she's thinking, after a few blocks she says, "I think a fuller skirt will be good, if we can make it so the majority of the skirt can come off that'd be best. I'll need to wear breeches of some sort underneath, and a place to put tools and such."

My lips twitch, not quite a smile, but I'm pleased with her quick conclusions, "I'm glad you have a plan, Miss Callam. I wasn't sure what you'd need."

"You can call me Lilith," she says, my eyes widen and I stop to look at her. She looks up at me and a blush floods her cheeks, "What?"

"Thank you," I say, keeping my voice soft, "I appreciate that you feel comfortable enough with me to allow that. I know you were quite adamant about me calling you Miss Callam before." I can't help feeling like she's given me a grand gift, even though nearly everyone calls her by her name.

She looks away, "I was only adamant about it because you were so concerned about being called Lord Graves. I thought you were looking down on me. But I've realized that's just how you approach everyone, so there's no need to worry," She smiles up at me.

"The main reason for that is I prefer to keep a bit of distance. Though..." I glance at her, "When we are alone then you may, if you wish, call me by my name."

"I would, but I'm not sure I've ever actually heard your given name."

"Truly? Nobody else has let it slip?"

She shakes her head, "Nope, I'm pretty sure a large portion of the staff don't know, and the ones that do know won't say. Even the twins rarely call you anything but Graves or Boss."

"Huh, I hadn't thought about that. Well, my name is Samael, and as I said if you wish you may call me that when we are alone."

Lilith gives me a contemplative look then nods as if she's come to some conclusion, "It's a strange name, but Samael certainly suits you."

I stumble and I spin to look at her, she's giving me a puzzled look. I'm not sure which I'm more shocked by, the fact that she heard my true name or the lurch my heart gave when she spoke it. "Are you all right?" she asks, putting a hand on my shoulder and tipping her head to one side.

"I'm fine, I was just surprised,"

"Why? You just told me I could call you by your name."

A small part of me wonders if I should tell her the truth, but the thought is short-lived as I realize how dumb the concern is, "I have a fairly intricate spell in place which makes it so only certain people can hear my name, others only hear Samuel."

"Who can hear the right name?" she asks her brow creasing further.

I can't help but smile at her, which makes her face light up, "Only those I can trust can hear my real name. There are precious few people who have heard my true name since the spell was put into place. I'm pleasantly surprised that you fall into that category,"

Her expression turns mischievous, "How do I know I can fully trust you?" she asks with a raised brow, which echoes my usual mannerisms.

I return the expression, "It's safe to assume the trust can go both ways, but if you are genuinely concerned, then we can talk to Sarah and Marie about it."

She sighs with a roll of her eyes, "What, no lengthy explanation of how trustworthy you are?"

"Would it have changed anything? I'm certain you have already decided if you can trust me; but as I said, we may bring it up with Sarah and Marie if you are concerned."

She purses her lips as if thinking, but it only lasts a moment before she bursts out laughing, "All right, all right, maybe not right away. After this seal business is taken care of and I decide if I'm going to stay, then we'll talk about it. It's a nifty trick to be able to tell if people are trustworthy or not."

My heart gives another lurch at the thought of her not staying, but I ignore it as we step up to the tailor's shop, "Come then, let's get you fitted for the gowns."

She grins and goes inside.

Lilith

My jaw drops open as we enter the store. There's a sea of fabrics in a rainbow of colors laid out before me. In addition to the beautiful fabrics, there are amazing dresses on display here and there as well. I release Graves' arm and flit around the room, running my hands across the soft fabrics and inspecting some of the dresses. I'm in the midst of the sea of colors when an amused voice says, "Well, this is new. I can't say I've ever seen Lord Graves bring a woman here."

I turn and find an older gentleman with graying hair and a sweet smile looking at me. I flush and let my hands drop from the fabric, "I'm sorry?"

"No need for that," he waves my concerns away, "What can I do for you, dear?"

Graves walks up, leaning a hip against the edge of the desk and crossing his arms, "We're attending a ball in a fortnight, she needs a dress that can be put together quickly for that. She'll also need a customized ensemble for the Solstice Ball."

The elderly man raises a brow, "What kind of customization are we talking about? Tailored to her specifications, or Aegis custom?"

"Aegis," Graves says his voice becoming all business, "She has an idea of what she'll need, but your touch as a master will be needed to ensure that it works as intended."

"Very well, let us start with the simpler task. I have a few pre-made pieces that should suffice for the first event." He looks me over, "Dark colors?" he asks.

I consider the options and scan the room, "Probably for the best, I look better in darkness."

He laughs, "I feel you'd look lovely in whatever you'd like, but that's beside the point. I think for a ball darker, richer colors are better. If it were a daytime outing that'd be one thing." He holds out his hand, "Come, I've got a red piece that I think will work well."

I smile and follow him, Graves tails behind us. The tailor gestures at a counter, "Wait here," he says as he disappears into the back of the shop. I fidget as we wait, I can feel Graves's gaze on me and it's making me antsy, but I'm also pleased for some reason. The tailor returns a moment later with a long gown.

I stare as he lays it out on the counter, it's a wine red with silver beads on the bodice that glint in the light. "That's," I say reverently, "beautiful."

"Thank you, would you like to try it on?"

My face lights up and I meet his gaze hopefully, "Can I?"

He chuckles, "Of course, let me get my granddaughter, she can help you change."

It feels like a heartbeat later I find myself changing in a whirlwind of cloth and colors. I stare at myself in the mirror; the dress sits loosely on my form and is too long for me, but the color compliments my pale skin and dark hair. The bodice is meant to fit snuggly, creating a delicate curve, and then flairs out just above the hips. The tailor's granddaughter Victoria smiles at me in the mirror. "It looks lovely."

"Are you sure?" I ask, "I... I've never worn something so nice, and it doesn't look as if it fits" I pick at the fabric and pull it toward me in an attempt to make it fit properly.

She pats my arm, "It looks wonderful, and we're going to alter it so it fits you properly. Would you like confirmation from grandfather," she pauses and a secretive smile spreads across her face, "Or perhaps Lord Graves?"

I spin to face her, a flush spreading across my cheeks as my hands flutter in front of me, "I don't know if that's necessary."

"Too bad," she says with a grin bright enough to blind someone. She grabs my arm and pulls me out of the changing room. We step out of the space and a conversation stops, the whole shop falling eerily silent. I look at my toes and wring my hands, shifting my weight back and forth, waiting for their judgment but too afraid to ask for it.

"Well," the older man says, "You look lovely, Miss Callam."

I flush and roll my shoulders forward, "Are you certain?"

Footsteps approach and a finger hooks under my chin, raising my head to look at Lord Graves. He's looking at me with such intensity it makes my heart clench, "You look lovely Lilith," he says my name softly, "this will be perfect for the Hurts' ball. Now, let Geoff and Victoria get it pinned so they can make the necessary changes."

I nod, unable to look away from him, "Okay,"

"Wonderful," Victoria says, grabbing my arm and dragging me across the store.

As I'm standing on a small pedestal being pinned into the dress by Victoria, Geoff sits nearby with a pad of paper. "All right, Miss Callam," the older man says, "I understand you'll be undertaking some daring deeds during the Solstice Ball and need something custom-made for your escapades."

"Yes sir,"

"Very well, what all do you need?"

"It'll need to be lightweight, I'll have equipment with me. I'll also need the bodice to be flexible and breeches of some sort underneath a detachable skirt."

Both tailors raise their brows at me, Victoria looks surprised but Geoff seems impressed, "That's quite an interesting ensemble. I assume you'll need pockets?"

"On the breeches," I look at Graves, "Can we send someone over with my toolkit so the pockets are suitable for my needs?"

Graves nods, "Absolutely, when we get back you can get everything together and I'll have one of the footmen bring it over."

We go over a few more details, also settling on a deep green fabric for the solstice dress. Once we're done, I've been properly fitted into one dress and we have a sketch of the new one.

"We'll have the red dress delivered as soon as the alterations are done," Geoff says, "And I'll keep you updated on the custom design, as well as let you know when it's ready for fitting."

"Wonderful," Graves says, paying the man before we head out.

We walk a way away from the shop and I mutter, "Did you truly think the dress looked good?"

He looks over at me, not a trace of judgment in his gaze, and a surprising amount of warmth, "I think you look beautiful in it,"

I flush and look away, "Thank you,"

He chuckles and pats my hand, "You'll feel better about it once it's fitted. Trust me."

I smile weakly, "If you say so."

Fifteen

In Which Truths are Revealed

Lilith

I carefully balance the books on my head, keeping my body steady to keep the stack from falling off. Coral is droning on about something she's told me at least twice before, but I'm focused more on the books than her words. The door to the library is propped open and I can see the sunlight streaming in the window in the hall. I watch the movement of the plants, wondering at Lord Graves' strange behavior over the last few days. He seemed flustered when I met him in the hall and was chatty during our walk yesterday. I try not to grin as Coral continues to drone on.

Coral spins to face me and scowls when she sees me looking out the window, "Are you listening?"

"No, Ma'am. I've heard this lecture before and fail to see how hearing it again will help me in any way."

Her scowl deepens, her magic crackling in the air and making the hairs on my arm stand on end, "If you're so certain of yourself, tell me what the point of the lecture is."

I sigh, a vague movement of my shoulders that doesn't disturb the books, "The point of the lecture is to understand how one is supposed to address nobility as well as ways to tell what rank a noble is by sight."

She sighs and turns away again, "Very well, try to create an illusion."

"I'll need a moment to focus,"

She nods and waves me away as she turns to face the window again, "Very well,"

I wonder what I can try to create when I notice movement at the door. Lord Graves is standing there, staring at me again like he did yesterday. I think of an idea and grin, "I think I shall try to create an illusion of a person, " I say, raising my voice so I can be heard clearly.

Graves raises an eyebrow at me and I raise one back, Coral is still facing the window and has not noticed his presence, "You were struggling with plants a few days ago," Coral says, her voice cruel, "and you expect me to believe you can manage a person today?"

I roll my eyes and look at Graves again, trying to ask my silent question again, "I've been practicing at night, it's easier when there are more shadows. I think I can do it."

He smirks and then nods once, I grin in response, pleased that he's going along with my prank. I reach out with my shadows, they slide across the floor and wrap Lord Graves in magic, giving him a shadowy cast that looks identical to my illusions. "I think I can manage an image of Lord Graves," I say, winking at him and then flicking my eyes toward Coral.

I muffle his footsteps as he enters the room and stands in front of me, facing Coral with a neutral expression on his face. I'm smiling like an idiot, as Coral turns around and gasps, covering her mouth with one hand. "My word!" she cries, "This is, amazing!" she walks around him, inspecting him from every angle, "You've covered pretty much every detail," she stands in front of him and looks over his clothes, "This is exquisite. Is it solid?"

I hesitate for a second, but I notice the barest movement of Graves's head and I smile, "Yes! It's a little shaky, but if I focus hard I can," I squint my eyes and bunch up my nose to prove that's what I'm doing.

She touches his chest, "You've improved a great deal, I'm impressed." She raises her hand and pats his cheek, which seems to irritate him a bit.

"Are you quite done?" he says in a dry tone.

Coral yelps and leaps away from him, "What?" she asks, looking horrified and embarrassed.

The look on her face is too much for me and it breaks my concentration. I double over laughing as the shadowy shroud disappears from Graves. I hear Graves chuckle and Coral screams again, "You little Bitch," my attention snaps up and I see that she's got magic gathering in her hands. She raises one and stalks toward me.

I'm ready to bolt when Graves steps between the two of us and grabs Coral's wrist. "It was just a harmless prank, there is no need to attack her for it," He says and I notice there's a layer of what looks like frost forming on her sleeve.

"It was cruel!" she shouts, "She's a brat and isn't fit for this sort of work, you should get rid of her immediately!"

I wince at the accusations, and I can feel myself shutting down. I take a small step back and lower my head.

Graves makes a noise I've never heard before, like a cross between a growl and a hiss, "Need I remind you that Lilith is a contracted member of Aegis, and you are simply here for her benefit? If anyone in this room should be dismissed for their behavior it is you."

I feel my mouth drop open at his adamant defense of me. Coral steps away and glares at me, "Then perhaps we should discuss the terms of my employment,"

"Perhaps," Graves turns to me, "Go get lunch then get to combat training,"

"But it's not-"

"Please don't make me repeat myself, Miss Callam," Graves says, his tone leaving no room for argument.

"As you say, sir," I turn on my heel and rush from the room, not sure I want to know what's going to happen next.

I race downstairs and find the twins in the kitchen, they both look up when they see me, Philip looks concerned and Damien looks surprised. Phil looks at the clock and then back to me, "Your lessons aren't done yet,"

"Ah... something came up and Lord Graves sent me away..." my brow creases, worried they'll think it's my fault.

Their eyes darken, "Is he okay?"

"I think so. Coral was mad at me and I think he might be about to fire her."

A few shocked gasps echo from the other people in the room but the twins look even more worried and hurry past me.

Graves

Coral and I enter the ballroom, "Coral, you're forgetting your place."

"She's a brat! And a thief! And... and..." she crosses her arms and looks away with a pout on her face, "This is outrageous, Samuel, she's nothing, but you seem hell-bent on making her something."

"She's more than she seems, and I have on good authority that she's crucial to Aegis. That being said, your treatment of her needs to change. First the thing with the food, the constant insults, and now this. The prank was harmless. I don't understand why you felt the need to attack her over such a thing."

Coral turns away, a petulant look on her face, "She's a brat." As if that's an explanation for treating another person as she has.

I rub a hand over my face and take a deep breath. I understand why the twins and Marie were so worried about Coral being Lilith's teacher now, "Her being a brat is no reason to condemn her. If you can't give me your word that you'll start treating her better then I'm going to have to let you go." As I speak the doors open and the twins barge in, worry oozing off both of them. I wonder why they're so concerned, it's not like I can't handle myself.

Coral scowls at the twins, her ire quickly transforming into a rage, "I refuse to treat that brat as anything more than the whore she is. I don't know what she's done to wrap you all around her finger, but I can't imagine it was anything decent."

Damien growls as the two of them stalk closer, his hands shifting to stony gray and growing claws.

My anger spikes and frost spreads from my feet as I lose the restraints on my magic, "Lilith is the most powerful shadow mage and one of the most powerful psychometrics in the history of Aegis. As such she is the greater asset by far. You are dismissed. I'll find another teacher if I feel Lilith still needs one."

She spins to face me with wide eyes, "You can't do this!" her voice becomes shrill as her magic starts exploding outward, knocking all three of us backward as she screeches at the top of her lungs.

I slide across the ground as the twins quickly regain their footing. I stagger to my feet as one of the ballroom doors opens, Lilith and Marie are standing in the doorway. Lilith looks horrified as Coral's magic spreads outward. "No!" Lilith cries as Coral flings magic at Damien, her eyes wide as she moves toward him.

As the bolt is flying toward him Damien shifts the rest of the way into his gargoyle form and bellows a challenge. Coral's magic bounces off his stone hide and he launches toward Coral. She throws more magic around the room, aiming for Damien and Philip, but avoiding Lilith and Marie, thankfully.

"Coral, enough of this!" I shout, trying to get her to stop and doing my best to keep my magic contained.

She just screeches again and throws magic in my direction this time. Philip intercepts the attack, his magical blade cutting through the magic and dispersing it.

Then the far door of the ballroom opens. Roland, Helga, and a few of the other servants barge in and skid to a halt, their eyes wide with shock. Coral screeches, her voice echoing through the room, and throws magic at them.

I stare in horror as the magic flies across the room. The people at the door don't have the resistance to magic, or the ability to block it. There's no way I can get to them in time, there's no way the twins can either. My mind whirls with possibilities, all of them coming up useless as I watch my family being attacked.

"No!" Lilith's voice cries out again, and I turn, she's sprinting across the room at full tilt. I feel something shift in the air and darkness spreads out from Lilith's feet, casting a gloom across the entire room. Lilith's eyes begin to glow an eerie green before she disappears and reappears in front of Roland and the others. The shadow she cast gathers around her in a rush, rising like a tidal wave of darkness that surrounds her. She crouches low and raises her arms, the shadow leaping up and creating a large wall between them and the hostile magic.

Coral's bolt slams into the darkness, creating ripples of color within the wall. Coral screams again and shoots more magic at Lilith. Each bolt hits the wall with a ripple effect and is absorbed into the mass, creating a kaleidoscope of colors.

Lilith has a look of concentration on her face as the second and third bolts hit. Lilith lets out a war cry and the wall collapses, becoming a wave that rushes Coral so quickly I can't keep up with it. It crashes into the elven woman with enough force to knock her onto her back, proving she's no match for Lilith, especially when her magic is turned against her.

Phil darts forward before Coral can recover and starts tying her hands together, so I turn my attention back to Lilith. The young woman is kneeling on the floor, her torso curled over her legs as she breaths in heavy gasps. All the servants are staring at her too; none of us have seen her use that much magic, and it was a spectacular display.

Lilith coughs heavily a couple of times, covering her mouth with one hand and it comes away with a bit of blood. She winces and the blood breaks me out of my shock enough that I start moving to her side.

"Lilith," Marie says, taking a tentative step toward her.

Lilith looks up, her eyes scan the room, and the color drains from her face. I pick up my pace as her emotions scream with fear and pain. I only manage a couple more steps before she gets to her feet and bolts out the door.

Damien looks up from where he's helping Phil, "Fuck," he looks at his brother, who nods before he can ask whatever question was on his tongue. Damien darts into the air and dives toward the door Lilith ran out of, "Hellion! Come back here!" he disappears through the door as well and I can hear him stomping after her.

Behind me, Phil shouts, "Go after them!" I don't bother asking questions and run after them as directed. My mind swirls with possibilities as I rush up the stairs. How badly is she hurt? Did she over-exert herself? Why is she scared? We owe her.

I get to the hall outside Lilith's room and Damien is standing outside banging on the door with a fist, "Do not make me come in there, Hellion. I'm being nice and not walking through these stones right now."

"Go Away!" Comes the muffled reply.

"Damnit, Lilith, it's not what you think! Come out here and talk to me for fuck's sake." Damien demands, slamming his fist into the door with enough force to shake the whole wall.

"What's going on?" I glare as he beats on the door again.

Damien looks at me and sighs, shifting down to his human form he gives me a wary look, "Lilith hasn't had the best experiences with people finding out the depth of her magic... what we just saw wasn't even everything she has access too."

"I see," I walk up to the door and he steps aside.

I knock, only to hear a soft sob followed by another, "Go away,"

"Miss Callam," I say, keeping my voice low and gentle, "Please open the door."

"I'll leave, I promise, I just need a little while to..."

"Lilith," I cut her off, "Please."

There's a brief pause that's pregnant with tension, then the lock turns and the door opens. On the other side, Lilith is looking at her feet, her hair creating a drape over her face and hiding most of her features. I can still see the tear tracks on her cheeks and the puffiness of her eyes. "Look at me," I say, holding a hand out to her.

She winces and curls her shoulders forward.

I step closer and hook my finger under her chin, lifting her face so she's looking at me. Her emerald eyes shine with tears, the fear and pain she's feeling becoming almost too much to bear now that we're touching. With my other hand, I brush her hair from her face so I can see both eyes, "Thank you, If you had not stepped in the others would have been hurt or killed."

Her eyes widen at that, and her lips part, "You... you're not upset?" she asks in the smallest voice I've ever heard.

"I am not upset with you in the slightest." I pause and turn my head to the side, "Though, I am concerned that you ran off as soon as you were able. Will you tell me why?"

She winces and tries to look away but I grab her chin, and her lip curls out in a pout, "They always leave," she whispers, "Everyone who sees... who feels what I can do... they leave or make me leave."

"We're not going anywhere," I say unable to keep the frustration out of my tone, "And neither are you."

I'm swamped with a hit of vulnerability, and beside me, Damien's putting out sadness as well. Lilith swallows hard and more tears spill, "You promise?"

"I promise," I nod. She sobs again and darts forward, wrapping her arms around my middle and burying her face in my chest. I'm too startled to react for a second, but then I put my arms around her and hold her.

Damien smiles warily and runs a hand through his hair, "I'll go tell the others she's all right, and see that lunch is ready."

He turns to walk away but Lilith extracts herself from my grasp and wipes her eyes, "No, I'll go down too."

Damien looks at me and I nod, "All right," he agrees.

I put a hand on Lilith's back and guide her to the stairs, "Come on, the others are worried."

Philip

I finish tying Coral to a chair in the kitchen with an enchanted cloth over her mouth to keep her from casting. I stand a pace or two away from her and rub a hand over my face, "That could've gone far worse."

Marie comes up beside me, "What the hell happened? Why did Coral lose her shit? Why did Lilith run away? What is going on?"

I look at her and sigh, "I'm not entirely sure what caused Coral's meltdown. Nor am I sure what caused Lilith to bolt, but if I had to guess..." I trail off as the far door opens to Damien, all eyes turn to him with concern.

He steps in a bit and turns to reveal the doorway, Lilith is standing in the entrance looking warily at the rest of the room. Sam is at her back and when she hesitates he puts a hand on her side and nods, "I already told you what would happen," he whispers, "You do recall that my word is final here, yes?"

She looks up at him with apprehension, but nods and steps into the room. Graves looks at the room, his eyes holding the threat of violence as Lilith moves. She walks toward the table in silence, all eyes on her while her own are on the floor.

Marie approaches her slowly, as one would a frightened deer, "Are you all right?"

"I'm not hurt," Lilith says, keeping her shoulders forward and her head bowed.

And like that Marie, Helga, and Roland descend on Lilith like a flock of hens to their only chick.

"What were you thinking!?" Marie shouts.

Roland practically elbows Marie out of the way to grab Lilith by the shoulders, "Coral's a master mage with almost a hundred years of experience and could've easily killed you!"

Helga does shove Roland aside and picks Lilith up, only to plop the girl in a chair at the table, "Ask questions later, for now, she needs food," The massive woman glares at both of the others so they back off for a moment.

Lilith looks shell-shocked as Helga produces food and slaps it onto the table in front of her. She stares at the food and then looks up at the others, "You're not mad?" she asks in a small voice.

Roland scoffs, "The only thing I'm remotely mad about is how reckless you were! What possessed you to throw yourself in front of us like that?"

Lilith slaps her hands on the table and shouts, "Nobody hurts my friends when it's within my power to stop it! How many times do I have to say this to you people?"

Everyone stills and turns to look at Lilith. Her eyes widen as she realizes what she's said and a flush races up her cheeks, "I... I mean," she looks down at her food and picks up a fork to poke at it with, muttering under her breath as she does.

The others look at me as if expecting me to have something to say. I sigh and walk over to Lilith, wrapping an arm around her shoulders I rub her arm, "Don't you all go gaping at her, you should feel honored. Lilith Callam has deemed you all friends. And that's no easy feat," I ruffle her hair, "Ain't that right Lil?"

She bares her teeth at me as if to yell then sighs and rolls her eyes, "You say that like it's so dramatic that I like you people," she nudges some of the food around on her plate and props her head up on her hand, "It'd be hard not to like a bunch of people who treat you well and look out for you, despite you being a bit of a brat."

"A bit?" Damien asks.

She sticks her tongue out at him, "At least I'm not an ass, like some people."

"You're a pain in one,"

To my surprise, it's Roland who snaps, "Leave the girl alone, Damien, she saved all of us today, even if she was reckless both with her life and with her magic." The older man turns on Lilith with a serious expression, "No more grand displays of magic until you've been practicing with that magic young lady," He puts his hands on her shoulders again and stares right into her eyes, "Do you understand me?"

Lilith's mouth opens and closes a couple of times, then she nods, "All right, I'll be more careful."

He smiles and hugs her to him, "Thank you, lass, for protecting us."

She smiles up at him, and Sam clears his throat, "Just to be clear, after her display, Lilith is officially a member of Aegis. She has all the rights, protections, and aids of that position." He pauses and looks at Lilith, "That does give you the freedom to leave when you wish, but

I would ask that you at least inform us if you choose to go anywhere. I think at least half the house would lose their minds if you went missing."

She grins at him, "I won't go running off Sir," she makes a bit of a face, "Wouldn't want you and Damien chasing me down again."

"Oi," Damien snaps, "I was nice enough not to walk through your walls Hellion, the least you can do is thank me for that."

She rolls her eyes and glares at him, "I'm just lucky the door held, sounded like you were gonna bash it down."

He just growls and turns toward me and Coral, "What're we going to do with her?" he says looking to Sam.

Lord Graves turns to look at Coral, he stays silent as he studies her. I begin to grow uneasy, shifting my weight slightly to be ready for anything. Samael steps closer and his eyes are still locked on Coral as if he's trying to divine secrets by staring at her.

Graves is standing over Coral with that intense look in his eyes, then he turns and looks at Lilith. She's still sitting at the table, a fork in her hands as she watches Graves. Her eyes are still red from crying, and there's a paleness to her skin that wasn't there earlier.

Samael turns back to the elf and I inhale sharply. The look in his eyes is dark and dangerous, a look I haven't seen in over a thousand years. I take a step back, giving him space to do whatever he's decided. Then, quick as a snake, he strikes out.

The blade he always carries with him slides across Coral's throat and makes her eyes widen in shock. The knife is so sharp it takes a heartbeat for the blood to start flowing, but when it does it gushes from the wound. One of the maids screams and flees the room, everyone else is shocked into silence. Cook grimaces and looks at the blood on the floor in annoyance.

My fangs itch at the sight of all the blood rushing down Coral's throat and chest, but I don't make a move. It takes only a few seconds for her to bleed out and she doesn't even have a chance to struggle before her eyes glaze over.

Nobody moves for a while, I think most of the staff is just startled by Graves' actions. At length Graves steps away from the corpse and turns back toward the group.

"Marie," his voice is calm, but there's an undercurrent of violence in it that has everyone at attention, "Would be so kind as to use your magic to clean up the blood? Don't want to stain the floor."

Marie nods and steps forward, "Sure, what should we do with the body?"

Graves looks at Helga, "Does your brother still own those pigs?"

"Aye," Helga nods, "I can take it to them. Won't be anything to find when they're done."

"Excellent," Graves nods back and moves to leave the room. He pauses near the door and looks back, "Lilith, no more training today. You've over-exerted yourself."

"Only magically," she argues.

"Don't make me repeat myself," he says, his voice mostly a growl.

She sticks her lip out in an exaggerated pout but doesn't argue further. Then Graves storms from the room as if his ass is on fire.

Graves

I barely keep myself from slamming my office shut as I flee from the kitchen. Planting my hands on my desk I make a concentrated effort to slow my breathing and get a hold of myself. I can scarcely believe that I let myself act so recklessly. There's no regret, the bitch deserved to die, but I should have thought it through, I should have been more careful. I shouldn't have done it in the fucking kitchen, and I sure as shit shouldn't have done it with most of the staff around. Now we're going to have to keep an eye on the entire household for a while. Ice spreads across my desk as my panic rises, I need to get a hold of myself.

A knock on the door nearly has me jumping out of my skin. I turn to look at the wood, baffled that anyone would try to bother me right now. I think that they've moved on when I hear Lilith's voice cut through, "Oh for fucks' sake."

The door opens a moment later with an annoyed Lilith gesturing into the room with Roland and Marie standing awkwardly in the hall. They all look over at me, then they march into the room in a row. Marie is holding a tray of food and Lilith has one too. Roland has a table in his hands and plops it in the middle of the office before starting to rearrange the seating.

"What are you doing?" I manage as Lilith sets her tray down and plops into one of the chairs.

"You told me to relax," she says, she's changed into sparing clothes and throws one leg over the arm of the chair, "So I'm relaxing. Being all proper and shit ain't as relaxing as this."

I stare with my mouth open as she lays her head against the back of the chair while Marie and Roland finish setting out what looks like lunch. "I meant what are you all doing in here?"

"You didn't really think we were going to let you be alone after that, did you?" Roland asks, giving me a narrow look, "You're in no condition to be on your own."

I can't form an answer to his declaration. Are they that concerned about my reaction? Did I react too rashly? Shit, did I upset all the people I trust? I can feel myself begin to shake, frustration racing through me faster than I can tame it.

I hear someone talking, their voice is distant and it's hard to make out what they're saying. Suddenly something grabs my face and pulls my head downward, "Graves," that voice cuts through some of the swirling thoughts, but I'm still unable to ground myself.

I bring my own hands to my face and pin the hands that are there against my cheeks, the voice softens further and I feel someone step closer, "Samael, it's okay,"

Hearing my name snaps me out of whatever hole I'd dropped into and I find myself staring into Lilith's vibrant green eyes. "There you are," she says softly, her tone heavy with relief and her expression sympathetic.

A glance tells me that the others have left, though I'm not sure why they'd leave me with Lilith unless they're too afraid to be in here with me.

Before I have the chance to ask anything Lilith says, "What are you upset about?"

I frown and release her hands, taking a step away from her, "I killed someone."

"Do you regret that you did?" she asks quietly.

I scowl, "No, she tried to kill members of the household! The unarmed ones!"

"Right," She says with a nod as if that makes perfect sense, "so are you upset that it was you who did it? You could've asked one of the twins, I'm sure they would've done it for you."

"What? No, I wouldn't ask them to do that. I'm the idiot that refused to send her away when she caused problems before."

She crosses her arms and looks up at me, "Then what are you upset about?"

I run my hands into my hair and grip the strands, staring down at the floor and away from her. But I don't answer her, I can barely bring myself to look at her and explain that I lost control of myself. That I could've put everyone in as much danger as Coral did.

"Then it's cause you let your temper get the best of you," she says brightly.

I snap my attention to her, she's watching me closely with a soft look in her eyes, "What?" I ask, my voice mostly a croak.

She shakes her head, "You know what I mean."

I scowl at her, and she just raises an eyebrow at me. We stand there staring at each other for a few moments before I shout, "FINE! Yes, it's because I lost my temper and didn't think about what I was doing before I did it. Are you happy now?"

Lilith snorts, "No, not happy. Largely because you haven't taken one major thing into account."

"And what's that?" I snap, getting riled up all over again.

"You have thought about it," she states.

"What?"

"You're always thinking, always calculating, and always planning. You take the time to think even when you're being asked questions directly. You're always thoughtful and careful with your responses and your actions. Because of that, I'm certain that you have thought about what you'd do if the people who rely on you were threatened. I'm also sure that you came to the same conclusion then that you did today. So, Samael, stop over-thinking it and trust yourself."

I stare at her, not able to articulate what I'm thinking now. She just waits patiently while I think, because she knows I need the moment to make a decision. I open my mouth and then close it, "How?" I finally ask, wanting to know how in the world this thief we picked up off the streets a couple of months ago seems to know me so well.

She grins up at me and pops a grape I didn't see her grab into her mouth, "You're not the only one who pays attention."

I chuckle at that and sit down, "We're not going to be able to eat all this ourselves," I gesture at the table of food.

"Oh! Right," she skips over to the door and I watch as a layer of shadow dissipates from around it. She pops the door open and says, "Come on back!"

"Is everything okay?" Marie asks, looking between the two of us.

"Yep!" Lilith says before plopping back into her seat, "Graves just needed a moment to get himself collected."

The two of them give me a questioning look, but I just grab some food and sit down, the company calming me.

Sixteen

In Which There is Fear

Lilith

I do my stretches in the middle of the training room. Phil is a few yards away stretching as well, "I'm going to up my speed a bit today," he says to me.

"What does that mean?" I ask, leaning to one side.

"It means I'm going to move closer to my normal skill level," he holds up a hand, "And before you get mad at me for holding back at all. I'm a vampire, even at your fastest, you're not going to be able to keep up with me at my maximum speed. So just accept that I think you've gotten good enough to be able to push you a bit harder."

"Am I that predictable?" I smirk at him and raise my eyebrows.

"Yes, and I'd like to point out that the reason I am giving you this information is because we were ninety percent sure you and Damien would butt heads until he lost his temper."

I shrug, holding my hands out in a 'what can you do' gesture, "Not my fault he's so grumpy,"

Phil rolls his eyes and gives me a look, "True, but it is your fault that you always push him so far."

"Well, I'm not going to argue this time, let's get on with it." I wave at him and take up my ready stance.

He smiles at me, the expression shows a hint of fangs and I know with certainty one or both of us is going to regret this. We stand there staring at each other for a long while, both of us bouncing on our toes as we watch the other. I briefly wonder if I can outlast him, patience-wise, but I'm already getting antsy and need to start moving.

I take a deep breath, then with a slight twist of my shoulders, I disappear into the thin shadows around us. "Shit," Phil says softly, scanning the area for me, "Lil, you're supposed to be fighting me, not hiding from me." He turns slowly, trying to pick me out of the shadows.

But I'm not staying still, bouncing rapidly between the shadows in as chaotic a pattern as I can manage. He turns so his back is to me, and I leap at the chance. I reappear directly behind him and drop a kick on the back of his knee.

His leg buckles for a moment but he recovers quickly. He drops low and spins, grabbing my foot before I'm able to regain my balance. He shoves my entire leg backward and I tumble to the ground. He's moving toward me so fast that I scarcely have time to think before the shadows envelop me. Philip makes a noise in his throat that sounds akin to a growl, "Come on, Lil, we're supposed to be fighting."

I keep moving through the shadows as I speak, "I am fighting. You said you were going to hold back less, so I'm holding back less. You're faster and stronger than me. I know with certainty I can't beat you head-to-head. But even you can't see me in the shadows."

With my constant movement, he's unable to pinpoint my location, his head swiveling around rapidly. He makes that growling noise again and says, "If we're including magic then..." he trails off and then pulls a small stone out of his pocket.

He flips it in his hand a few times then grins almost maniacally and throws it at the ground. The stone hits the mats and bright light flashes from the point of impact, briefly lighting the space up so brightly that all the shadows disappear and I'm thrown from my hiding place. My feet falter as I move forward, stumbling into the mats. The light begins to fade and I'm vaguely aware of him moving toward me.

I shift to a kneeling position and roll away just before he would've tackled me. I blink rapidly, trying to regain my vision. As I roll to my feet and turn toward where Phil is, I hear movement behind me.

I turn as the newcomer approaches, not quite able to make them out. A low voice whispers, "Poor Lily, always being beaten up and taken advantage of."

The name rips through my mind like a gunshot, drawing up memories that seem like nightmares, or perhaps nightmares that feel like memories. I scramble away from the voice tripping over something else in my haste. "NO!"

My vision begins to clear from the light, but the memories crowd in too fast. I scream in terror and curl in on myself, a bubble of magic forming around me as I'm dragged into the depths of my fears.

Damien

I hear a scream and turn. Lilith and Phil are in at the sparring mats with the mutt nearby too; Lilith has curled in on herself like she's being dragged to the ground. I sprint across the room as Lilith's magic forms a bubble around her, throwing Philip and Gavin back. Phil manages to keep himself from falling over, but Gavin is launched into a wall and tries to get up but falls back down.

I'm not too concerned with Phil's well-being, he can handle himself, but the magic is rushing from Lilith in a massive explosion. If it isn't stopped it'll hurt someone. I throw myself against the wall of the magic, hitting it as hard as I can.

"Damien!" Phil shouts, "Don't be stupid!"

I ignore him and slam myself against the wall again, which seems to halt the progress of the magic. "Hellion!" I shout, punching against the barrier and sending a shock of pain up my arm. Behind me, I hear other voices, but their words are indistinct as I try again to get through the barrier. "Lilith!" I shout again, but nothing changes.

I hear someone walk up behind me as I shift and slam my fist against the barrier, "HELLION!"

"What is going on?" Sam demands as he comes up beside me, the wind snapping around me telling me his magic is coming out too.

I growl and claw at the darkness, "Something triggered her, I'd be willing to bet you're getting a fuck ton of panic from her. And her magic is reacting to protect her,"

"Panic is an understatement," he snaps, his voice sharp and his expression tight.

The aura flares and we're pushed back a step as a thin wail sounds from inside the bubble. "Fuck," I growl, slamming my fist into the wall, "We need to get to her."

"It seems pretty clear she wants to be alone," Sam says, but he steps beside me and puts his hands on the wall as well. I watch, startled as ice spreads from his hands creating a sheet over the wall, "If she gets mad at us for this I'm blaming you."

I grunt, "She can hate me for eternity if it means this bubble doesn't get bigger. I think it might take out the house if we're not careful." I shove against the barrier again, "Lilith!" I shout again, clawing at the magic.

Sam steps closer, more ice spreading from his hands as the earth below us rises to wrap around his feet, "Miss Callam," he says, his voice strained.

Phil stumbles up behind us and puts a hand on my shoulder, "The mutt," he says his breathing labored, "He called her Lily and this happened," he squeezes my shoulder, a knowing look in his eyes.

I close my eyes and take a steadying breath, trying to keep my own maelstrom of emotions in check. I don't think we've ever seen a flashback that transcended lifetimes but of course it'd be one like that. "Fuck," I mutter then claw at the magic again, "Lilith! Hellion, you're all right. We're here!"

To our right I hear a dry laugh, I turn and Gavin is sitting up, eying us with a satisfied but grim look on his face, "What?" I snap.

He smiles with blood on his lips, "She can't hear you, and it won't work. She'll only calm down once something dies."

"What did you do?" Phil demands, making his way toward him.

Gavin shrugs, "Not entirely sure, I just know that whenever someone calls her Lily or even mentions the flower, she freaks out," He smirks then coughs and shifts his weight again.

"Bastard," Sam says from beside me, slamming a fist against the magic and spreading more ice, "Miss Callam!" he hesitates then actually puts his forehead against the field, "Lilith," his voice drops to a near whisper, "We're here, let us help," the way he speaks reminding me who he truly is; no one else utters her name quite like that.

A scream tears out from the center of the bubble, then it collapses in on itself and both Sam and I stumble as it stops supporting our weight. I don't give myself time to question the situation as I sprint to Lilith's side. She's curled over herself and rocking back and forth sobbing. We get to her and Sam tries to put a hand on her, she yelps and scrambles away from him, her eyes wide and staring, but obviously not seeing us.

"Wait," I say, holding an arm out to keep him back, "She's overwhelmed and her magic is hyperactive, if you touch her now her psychometry is going to kick in," I sit down in front of her, keeping a good distance but also staying in her line of sight, "Lilith, you've let us in, now let us help,"

Sam takes up residence at my side, sitting as well. Lilith is still rocking back and forth in front of us, tears dripping down her face. "Lilith," Sam says softly, holding a hand out to her, "let us help,"

She shakes her head and for a moment I think we need to back up, but then she blinks twice and her eyes focus on his hand, "S-s-s," she stammers, then shifts her weight so she's leaning toward us. She holds her hand out too, reaching toward him but in a way that makes it seem as if she's being held back.

"That's it," Sam says, shifting forward as well.

Their fingertips touch and she yanks her hand back as if struck, "Ow, ow," she scrambles back as Sam recoils too.

"What happened?" I ask, steadying him.

"I'm not sure, her magic... it brought up something..." he presses a hand to his temple and shakes his head, "I'm not sure."

I look back at Lilith and she's curled around her knees, "Hellion, come here."

She looks at me warily and I hold my hand out, "I have a story," I offer gently, "It may help."

She looks up at my face, her eyes watering still. She doesn't speak so I continue, "Do you remember the queen I told you about?" still silent and staring, "Well, she used... she used to have something like this happen at times too. Many people coveted her power and her freedom and that led to her getting hurt very badly on multiple occasions. If you'll come here I'll show you something I used to do to help her calm down. Would you like that?"

She eyes me more then flicks her eyes to Sam, who is also watching her with concern, she nods slowly and crawls toward me, the action reminding me of a wounded animal. She hesitantly reaches to take my hand, before she touches me I steel myself and remember my Queen.

This time no memories are brought to the forefront for me, but I can see Lilith is seeing something. So, for the benefit of others around, I say, "She used to feel panicked and needed to feel safe. So, the King and I would wrap our wings around her while Phil would stand guard nearby."

Lilith looks up into my eyes now and nods, "Okay,"

I spread my wings and wrap them around the three of us, creating a dome. "I can leave," Sam says, starting to stand up.

"No," I say, "She needs to feel safe,"

He frowns but sits down, I hear Phil talking and I assume he's keeping everyone else away. Lilith sits before us, wrapping her arms around her knees once more, and closes her eyes. I can see her breathing deeply and muttering to herself, and I'm certain she'll be okay.

Graves

I'm not sure how long we sit there, under the canopy of Damien's wings, and I'm even less sure what the rest of the household is doing while we sit. But I don't dare leave; when I'd gone to stand up Lilith had begun to panic, and Damien's emotions spiked with fear too. I'm aware of Phil nearby, but it seems everyone else has been sent away. Lilith's breathing has returned to normal and her eyes are still closed as she rests her head on her knees. She seems more relaxed now, but she's still seeping fear.

I wonder what else we can do when she raises her head and looks at Damien, "What happened to your Queen?"

He frowns and sadness seeps from him, he's silent for so long I wonder if he's going to answer her at all, finally, he says, "She died. She and the King were killed and their souls were sent to gods know where. We're not sure how their opponents managed, they were some of the best warriors of the time, their power rivaling most gods, and we thought they were unstoppable when they were together. But, despite all that one day Phil and I went looking for them and found them dead. Their assailant was long gone..."

Lilith nods solemnly then says in a dark, cutting tone, "Did you find out who did it? Did you avenge them?"

Damien's eyes widen and he folds his wings, "We did find out who did it, however, we were unable to avenge them as their assailant proved stronger than us."

Lilith looks frustrated for a moment, then nods again, "Well, once we've done this whole, save the world thing," She waves her hand about as if it's nothing, "Then we'll go avenge them,"

Phil snorts, "Lil, it's not that easy."

She unfolds herself and stands up, turning to look at him and turning her head to one side with an eerie level of calm, "Then we'll make it that easy."

She turns to me and smiles tightly, "I'm sorry for the trouble, I'll..." she trails off for a moment then shrugs, "I'll go talk with Marie about what I need to be ready for the ball tomorrow."

"What?" I stand up quickly, "There's no need to go to the ball, you've just had a meltdown! We're not going."

She gives me a look that cuts me and causes me to take a step back, "I always keep my word," she snaps, "I promised I would do what it took to be able to steal that artifact and I'm going to fucking do it. To do that I need to go to this ball so I'm not a gawking idiot at the solstice. Which means I am going to go find Marie and get ready."

Phil and Damien are staring with their mouths open as I meet her gaze. I see the determination there and realize there's no winning this argument, so I sigh and relax my shoulders, "Very well, I believe the gown is ready to be picked up so I shall send someone to retrieve it. When it arrives Marie can verify the fit."

Lilith nods and turns toward the house, leaving the three of us staring after her.

Once she rounds the corner of the house Phil lets out a low whistle, "Was it just me, or did she look like she was going to rip your head off if you tried to argue with her?"

Damien laughs, "Yeah, it did."

I shake my head, "Yes, I think she may have tried." I look at Damien, "Keep an eye on her for the rest of the day." I look at Phil, "And you keep Gavin away from her. I'm not sure why he did it but we can't afford for him to trigger her like that again."

Phil nods, "Can do,"

"Why do I get babysitting duty?" Damien asks.

I raise an eyebrow at him, "Cause you're the one who helped her calm down."

He sighs and scrubs a hand over his face, "I suppose you're right."

Phil laughs and claps his brother on the shoulder, "Don't complain, you don't have to deal with the mutt."

Damien snorts, "Probably for the best, I'd tear the little fucker to pieces."

"Exactly," Phil says and leads his brother away.

I stand in the room for a long while and look around. There's a small circular burn on the ground where Lilith had been crouched. I walk over and stare, at the center of the circle is a symbol. It looks as if it was drawn by digging her nails into the mat and there's a faint trace of magic wafting out from it. I crouch down and hover my hand over it, the magic seeps up from the surface and brushes against my hand. I jerk my hand back when I realize that there seems to be a memory now embedded in the symbol, and the brief glimpse I got was of a dark cell, tortured screams, and pain so overwhelming I lost myself for a moment.

I back away from it not wanting to think about who or what could've done that to our almost fearless Lilith.

Seventeen

In Which the Thief is a Lady

Graves

I pace the front room of the house, unreasonably anxious about to-night. I can't shake the feeling that something bad is going to happen, but I'm not sure how much of that is my nerves and how much of it is precognition. I pace back toward the stairs just as the front door opens and Sarah enters. She smiles and pats my arm, "It'll be fine," she says reassuringly, "She'll do great and you'll both be fine."

I sigh and give her an exasperated look, "Are you sure it's wise to be telling me that?"

She chuckles, "You assume that everything I tell you is a prophecy. This time it's simply reassurance, trust in her, and yourself."

I sigh again and rub a hand through my hair, "This is ridiculous."

She chuckles and straightens my hair for me, "Perhaps, but you'll see." She turns me toward the stairs just as Marie turns the corner. Marie smiles and holds a hand out behind her. Lilith's glove-clad hand appears and takes Marie's, then Lilith steps down the stairs and I inhale sharply.

I knew the dress she'd picked would look good on her, but seeing it fitted to her is something else entirely. In the last few months, she's put on a good bit of weight and gained a healthier complexion. Her eyes shine in the lights from the chandelier as she wrings her hands slightly, "Does it look okay?" she asks, her voice shaking.

I'm about to answer when the side door opens and the twins come through. Damien is muttering something to Phil who seems to be ignoring him. Phil stops short, staring up at Lilith, and lets out a long whistle, "Damn, Lil, You look stunning."

She gives him a wary look as if she doesn't trust his words. Then her eyes flick back to me, that uncertainty and fear shining in her eyes. I smile and hold my hand out toward her, "You look beautiful in it, just like I thought you would."

A blush races up her cheeks and Damien chuckles as she descends to take my hand. "You almost look like a lady, Hellion." She gives him a dark look and he grins, "Almost."

She rolls her eyes and Sarah comes up behind me, "Ignore him, he's just mad he doesn't get to go with." She takes Lilith's hands and looks into her eyes, "You be careful, yes?"

Lilith nods to the oracle, "Of course, I'm not going to do anything reckless."

Sarah snorts, "We'll see about that, won't we?"

Lilith scowls at her and I sigh, "We don't have time for an argument,"

Lilith frowns up at me and I give her my signature look, which has her sighing and shaking her head, "Fucking eyebrow," she mutters as she comes to my side, looping her arm through mine, "Let's go then."

We make our way out to the carriage, Phil on our heels, when Lilith settles on the bench I see her begin to wring her hands, but can't find anything comforting to say so I keep it to myself.

We roll up to the large manor and I make an effort to keep my face impassive. I step out and hold a hand back to Lilith, her eyes are wide as she stares up at the building. "Come along, Miss Callam," I say firmly, she looks down at me and the wash of her anxiety hits me like a wave. I hold steady, not wanting to show my nerves when she clearly needs stability.

She swallows nervously but takes my hand and steps down to my side. I squeeze her hand and help her from the carriage. The cool air flicks her hair around for a moment before settling as I draw her to me, tucking her hand in my arm.

Phil hops down after Lilith and stands at our back. We make our way to the door and I quickly notice that Lilith is practically clinging to my arm, her breathing quick. I put my other hand over hers and squeeze it, "Deep breaths," I say as she looks up at me, "They're just people. They're no better than anyone else, no matter what they think."

She nods and takes that deep breath, just as we step up to Hurst at the door. The man looks worn and defeated as he stands there, kindly greeting his guests. I briefly wonder if Clarissa is the reason this ball is happening.

I shake the question off as we approach. Hurts' eyes narrow on me and his aura reeks of contempt. "Graves," his voice is sharp, "I'm surprised you decided to show your face here."

I don't bother to react to the ire in his tone, "I received an invitation, I figured I was welcome."

He huffs out a breath, "You know some invitations are just formalities."

I shrug, "Perhaps, but it was sent and you have no right to refuse me now. Besides, I am no threat to you, Duke Hurst."

Hurst sighs, looking frustrated as he casts his gaze around the steps. His eyes catch on Lilith and widen, "Who is this?"

"This is Miss Callam, her father is an associate of mine and has asked me to introduce her to higher society. I do hope that's no trouble."

Hurst relaxes substantially, his smile returning and all the tension bleeding from his aura, "Not at all," he says giving Lilith a beaming smile.

"Excellent," I say, gently pulling Lilith along and making my way into the building.

We're moving through the entryway when Lilith whispers, "What was that about? He seemed upset at first, then calmed down when he noticed me."

I glance over at her and fight back a grimace, "It's a long story I'd rather not get into, especially not here."

She nods, "Ok-" she freezes when her eyes land on our surroundings.

I look up and take in the massive ballroom, trying to picture it from her perspective. It's a huge space, marble floors sprawl out from the doorway. Leading to gilded walls with thick tapestries. The whole place is decked out in gold, greens, and burgundy. I know it to be the Hursts' family colors, but I doubt Lilith is aware of the meaning.

I look back at her and realize she's locked up, her breathing has become shallow and her eyes staring. "Oh no," I mutter then usher her to one side of the room.

She pulls her gaze away from the massive room but doesn't seem to come back from the anxiety. I squeeze her hand, "Miss Callam?"

She looks at my face, the fear still present. I glance around, "Can you shroud us? Make us seem less noticeable?"

Without a word shadows descend around us concealing us from the ballroom and hiding us away in the safety of the alcove. Her breathing steadies as the sounds from around us settle.

"There, deep breaths," I encourage.

"I don't know if I can..." she mutters, her eyes shining with tears.

Her panic spikes and is colored with doubt and fear. I want to reassure her but I'm not sure how to. Her tears spill over and I cup her face in both my hands, making her gasp. "None of that," I say firmly, "You can do this. It's just another persona, another act to get what you want."

Her eyes widen and she raises her hands to grip my wrists, "But I've never- what if I'm not-"

I wipe a tear from her cheek, careful not to smudge the makeup there, "You'll do brilliantly, as you always do. Just embrace the expectation of being a lady, but..." I trail off, unsure if this piece of advice will actually help.

"But?" she squeezes my wrists, drawing my attention back to her.

I smile now, "But don't let Lilith get lost in Miss Callam. Here you're just another version of yourself, no need to pretend too hard."

A smile plays across her lips, "Are you giving me permission to be a smart mouth, sir?"

I chuckle, "Within reason, I'll let you know if you're overstepping."

She grins now and drops her hands from my wrists, excitement mixing with the previous apprehension, "I'll be careful to listen,"

"Mmmhmmm," I hum noncommittally, I know without a doubt she's going to overstep, "Come, let's get to the festivities."

She loops her arm with mine and beams up at me, "Can't let all Marie's work go to waste."

Lilith

I drop the shadows from around Graves and me, I look around, "Where's Phil?" I ask, feeling bad for missing that he disappeared.

"He's considered a servant, so he's in another room keeping an ear out for anything useful."

I grip his hand and look up, "Do I need to listen out for things too?"

He shakes his head, "No, I can handle that just fine. If you hear something file it away, but don't stress over it."

I nod and steel myself before looking back out at the massive ballroom. This time I take account of the space instead of letting it overwhelm me. The large room spans the length of the building, stone floors shine as if they're rarely walked over. Crystal chandeliers are hanging over our heads, each stone glittering and dancing. There are a few doors along the left wall, but the right wall is all windows. The snow outside shines in the night and reflects the warmth of the fire inside. Heavy curtains are draped around the windows and are embroidered with gold on a green background.

I look out over the dance floor and take in the crowd that covers the floor. Women in brightly colored gowns dance in circles with men in suits. The skirts flare out around them like the wings of butterflies as they flit and float. They all move with such ease that I'm a bit envious of their comfort. Graves leans close, "Ready?"

I nod, "I think so,"

He squeezes my hand and nods at a group of people, "Those are some of Aegis' affiliates, they'll be welcoming, though for now let's keep your membership quiet."

"Fair," I straighten my shoulders and we make our way over to the group. There are four of them, three men and a woman. One of the men has his back to us, but the other three are at an angle that allows them to see us. They all look like nobles based on their bearing. Two of the men are wearing well-fitted suits in colors that complement their features. The one with his back to us doesn't seem to be holding onto the formality of things and is speaking in a loud voice.

The woman is practically radiant, her bright golden eyes and large smile feeling contagious. She's wearing a gown with a fitted bodice and a wide skirt that flares out from her hips. The red-gold color compliments her dark hair and warm complexion.

They nod politely as we approach, and the woman smiles brightly at me and says, "Charles, look who's here."

The third man spins and a grin splits his face. He's big enough to match Damien in size, tall, wide shoulders, and a large smile. His suit is of high quality and looks like it's fitted, but he's already unbuttoned the front and loosened his tie.

He throws his arms out to the sides, almost like he's going to hug Graves. "Lord Graves! You came! It's been far too long since you graced one of these events with your presence."

"Earl Evans, you know my work with Aegis keeps me busy," Graves replies, though his tone is amused not chastising.

"Aye aye," the big man waves a dismissive hand, "keeping us all safe from dangerous magic. We appreciate all your work, but I for one appreciate your presence too."

Graves sighs, "Yes, well, you know how much these things bore me."

Evans rolls his eyes and finally notices me, his eyes widen and his mouth drops open for a moment, "Hello, who is this lovely creature? Is she what brought you out today? Wouldn't blame you if she were."

"After a sort," Graves' tone shifts slightly, sounding more rehearsed, "This is Lilith Callam, she's the daughter of one of my associates. They asked that I introduce her to higher society, as a favor."

Evans grins, bows to me, and holds out his hand.

I step away from Graves, smile and return a curtsy, then take his hand.

He drops a kiss on the back of my hand, that grin returning in a heartbeat, "It's a pleasure to meet you, Miss Callam. I'm Charles Evans,"

"Earl, Earl Charles Evans," the woman adds brightly, "He always leaves that bit off."

Charles rolls his eyes and shoots the woman a dark look, "You're always quick to remind me, Leah, and tell everyone." He looks back at me, "It's a relatively new title, forgive me."

I grin, "It's quite all right. But you must introduce me to your friend."

Leah laughs and pushes Evans aside, "Leah Mortimer, I'm Charles' sister, though sometimes I wonder if he wishes to claim me."

"I know how it is, I'm certain there are times when Graves wishes I were not his responsibility." I sneak a glance over my shoulder and Graves is giving me his signature expression.

Leah loops an arm around my shoulders, "You are quite the delight. Here, meet my boys." She gestures to the two other men in the small circle.

I look at them and they're both smiling at me, the one on the left steps forward and bows, "Dante Mortimer, Leah's husband."

"Andre Mortimer," the other man says with a bow, "Dante's brother."

I smile, and curtsy, "It's wonderful to meet all of you. I'm glad we spotted you, I was afraid my first introductions would be to... less than welcoming folks."

Leah sighs, "Oh that would have been horrible," she turns to Graves, "You'd best keep a good eye on her, don't let any of these fussy types give her a hard time."

"Hence why I brought her to you," Graves replies, his voice matching his name.

Leah shakes her head, "Oh forget it, I'll just have Charles do it."

Graves makes a noise somewhere between a grunt and a growl, then says, "You'll be pleased to hear that Lilith is perfectly capable of taking care of herself."

That gets surprised expressions from all of us, he rarely uses first names in public. Besides the fact that the statement was sparked by some level of protectiveness. He meets my gaze, something strange lurking in their depths. I realize that there's a stunned, awkwardness to the whole group. Even Graves seems unsure of how to proceed and I suspect he didn't quite think his reaction through.

So I break into a fit of giggles, "Now you've gone and startled everyone, m'lord. They aren't aware of the fact that you only call me by my name when I've irked you." The lie rolls easily from my lips and he narrows his eyes at me.

"Indeed," Graves says slowly, "Perhaps we should introduce you to a few others. While these four are excellent company, there are others I think would make good contacts for you."

I sigh dramatically but walk back toward him, "After you introduce me to some others, can we come back to them?"

"Of course, while I am to keep an eye on you, I've long since realized that none can prevent you from getting what you want."

Graves

Lilith stays by my side, her demeanor much calmer than it was before. Her energy is brighter now, drawing attention to the two of us as we make our way through the ball. We pass a group of people, I recognize a few of them but don't think they'd be good to introduce Lilith too, so I keep moving.

Unfortunately, one of them spots us and calls out, "Who's that Lord Graves? Some poor pauper you took pity on?"

Lilith stops short, her eyes shuttering for a moment before a smile spreads across her face and she spins to face the speaker. "Miss Callam, Lilith Callam," she holds her hand out to the woman as if for a handshake.

The young lady eyes Lilith's hand as if it's a snake, then says, "That doesn't answer the question, your manners are deplorable." She waves her fan at Lilith's hand.

"Forgive me, my father is a merchant. Lord Graves has been so kind as to introduce me to some higher social circles. I haven't gotten used to all the different expectations yet," Lilith holds her hands out to her sides, shrugging as if to say 'what can you do?'

The lady snorts, her friends tittering as well, "I hate to break it to you, but you've gotten a horrible deal. There are quite a few who don't take kindly to Lord Graves and Aegis. You'd be better off asking his guards to teach you to fight than you are getting connections."

Lilith opens her mouth to reply, but before she can another woman is speaking, "Though, perhaps Lord Graves is the one getting the short stick here, given he has to deal with such an uncouth woman at his side."

Lilith laughs at that, but it's neither a happy nor amused sound. "You're making an awful lot of assumptions," Lilith declares.

The ringleader's eyes widen and raises her chin, "And you suppose to correct me?"

"It would be my pleasure," Lilith says with a condescending smile, "First and foremost you're assuming that you and your friends are the type of acquaintances I wish to make. And you've assumed that I am not taking advantage of the skills of Lord Graves' household."

"Do you even know who I am?" the woman says taking a few steps toward Lilith as if to intimidate her.

Lilith steps closer to the other woman, her eyes flashing emerald, "I'm perfectly aware of who you are, Laurel Ribald. The second child of Count Dean Ribald, Lord Mayor of Moreland. Your family is well known for its long time as the overseers of Moreland. However, since the dire illness of your elder brother, your family's ability to lead has been brought into question."

Laurel's mouth opens and closes in surprise, "Why I've never had anyone speak to me like this!" she presses a hand to her chest.

"I would get used to it," Lilith says, that shining smile returning, "Reputation is everything after all and it seems yours is hanging by a thread."

I cover my mouth with one hand and cough to hide my grin,

"Miss Callam, I think that's quite enough. No need to torment the poor woman."

Lilith looks up at me and pouts, "But Sir, I was just getting started."

The expression is equal parts innocent and mischievous and I don't bother to hide my smile this time, "I am aware, but as I said, no need to torment her. She's got enough problems without us bringing them to light, and we have other people to meet as well."

Miss Ribald seems to recover at that then turns to glare at me, "Do you believe that this," she waves an accusatory hand at Lilith, "is the kind of person you should bring into polite company?"

I regard the woman with a calculating stare for a moment, she's insulted and trying to find footing or some way to get back at us. I can't have that, so I put a hand on Lilith's shoulder.

I offer Miss Ribald a raised brow, "I think Lilith is the kind of company I prefer to keep, and if that means upsetting pretentious folks such as yourself then I'll be sure to bring her to every event."

Miss Ribald gapes as I lead Lilith away from the whole group. We get a bit away and Lilith begins to snicker, one hand covering her mouth. Once we're out of sight of the group she grins up at me "Do you think that'll get us in trouble?"

"I doubt it," I shake my head, "Trevor Ribald's illness is a magical curse, Aegis has been helping their family fight the affliction and Count Ribald wouldn't dare say anything ill against us."

She giggles now then gives me a mock-serious look, "Though there will be rumors you know, Lord Graves with a woman at his side is one thing. But Lord Graves openly declaring that he is going to bring her to every event. The gossip mills will have a field day."

I shrug, "Let them think what they will, the more uncertainty the easier it'll be to hide you in plain sight. Come on, let's head back to Evans and company."

She hooks her arm through mine and grins, "Of course, must set off a few more rumors, yes?"

I snort, "Perhaps, but we'll see, won't we?"

Her grin widens and she practically skips by my side as we head back across the room.

Eighteen

In Which There is No More Patience

Lilith

We make our way back to where we left Leah and her family. Only Charles is still there, "You came back!" Charles says with a grin.

"Of course, like I said, you all seem nice. I may have gotten us into some trouble with Laurel Ribald though." I look down at my feet to play up the contrite young lady.

"Miss Ribald is always looking for someone to put down," Charles says with a snort, "if you put her in her place it's better for all of us."

"Miss Callam has a talent for cutting to the center of things," Graves says with a fond smile in my direction, "it's one of her many skills that can be both endearing and infuriating."

I can't help but preen a touch at the praise, "Just like my stubbornness?" I challenge.

"Yes," Graves states, then shakes his head.

Charles laughs, "It's nice to see that someone can get him to react to things. For a while there I thought…" he trails off and shakes his head when Graves gives him a dark look.

"Where have Leah and the others gone?" I ask, breaking the sudden tension.

"Dancing, I uh," Charles blushes slightly and rubs the back of his neck.

I turn my head to the side and smile at him, "Did you want to dance?"

His eyes widen, "I- Yes. That is," he takes a moment to collect himself then bows, "Miss Callam would you honor me with a dance?"

I grin and look up at Lord Graves, "I promise not to piss anyone else off,"

"I'll believe it when I see it," Graves replies dryly but he releases my arm so I can take Charles' hand.

"I would love to dance," I tell the earl with a huge smile.

He grins and sweeps me off toward the dance floor, nodding to Graves as we go. Evans easily leads me into the dance, effortlessly integrating us with the dancers that are already there.

"Tell me the truth," he says suddenly, "What did you do to get Graves to come out here?"

I blink at him, "It was his idea, well mostly his idea."

"Truly? He hates these things, and this household in particular has always been one he disdains."

I frown, "I did notice that Duke Hurst seemed unsettled by Graves' presence. But yes, this was Graves' idea. He felt that I needed more experience with being actually around nobles and the like. Instead of just the people at the manor."

"Ah, yeah," Evans nods, "That makes sense. Regardless of the reason I'm quite glad you're here. It's nice to see Graves out and about doing something not work related."

My smile falters a bit at that, "Yeah, he is always working away, isn't he?"

"As long as I've known him." Evans shakes his head, "But enough talk of Graves. Tell me more about you, what connections does your father have to put him in contact with Graves? Is it related to Aegis?"

I hesitate at that then smile, "Well, my father was in the war, and he did some work for Aegis, but a bomb damaged his legs and he wasn't able to do that anymore. Aegis took good care of him afterward and let him go back to his family business of mercantile. Unfortunately, my mother passed in childbirth and... well it's just me and my father. He's always wanted better for me so he reached out to Graves."

Evans nods, "That sounds exactly like Graves," the song is winding down and we step out of the middle of things, "Will you be at the Solstice Ball?"

I nod, "Yes, Graves was quite adamant about that one. Apparently it'll be the best place to make some high-standing acquaintances. Not to say that you and your family are low ones," I frown and flush, "Sorry."

Charles laughs and lifts my chin, "No harm done, but if you'd like to make amends..."

"Yes!" I say hurriedly.

He chuckles again, "Save me a dance at the solstice?"

I giggle, "Absolutely, your company has been refreshing."

He glances behind me and frowns, "As delightful as this is, you may wish to go rescue Lord Graves. It seems Duchess Hurst has found him."

I turn around and there's a large, buxom woman invading Graves' space. Her mouth is moving as if she's speaking but he's staring straight ahead with his jaw clenched. "Oh no," I mutter, I look back at Charles, "I'll have to go. Thank you again."

"Of course, I'll find Leah and we'll come to be back up. Clarissa is..." he shakes his head, "Just hurry."

I almost sprint across the room to Graves' side. As I approach I take a better stock of the woman standing next to him. She's tall with a tiny waist and large breasts. She looks elegant in her golden dress with her curls piled high on the top of her head and a fan in one hand. I suspect she's a shifter, given the way she carries herself and the almost predatory way she's watching Graves.

"Oh Samuel, I was so hurt when I heard you were here but didn't come to see me. We could have been spending time catching up!" she fans herself dramatically and bats her eyes.

Graves is sternly ignoring her, looking off into the distance and keeping his fists clenched at his side. "Lord Graves," I say brightly as I step up to them, "Who's your friend?" I look at the Duchess.

She looks down her nose at me as Graves shakes himself and looks at me his expression relaxing, "Lilith, there you are," he glances at her, "This is Duchess Hurst, our hostess for the ball."

"Oh," I curtsy to the woman and smile broadly, "Thank you for letting us into your home, it's lovely."

She glares down her nose at me and fans herself, "Of course it is, we have one of the best houses in the city. Though, I'm afraid I haven't been informed of who you are."

"I'm Lilith Callam," I say with a smile, "Lord Graves is doing my father a favor and introducing me to high society. And so far I'm quite enjoying your party,"

She snorts, "It's a ball, not a party like the riff-raff throw." She looks away from me and looks at Graves, "Honestly Samuel, if you're going to bring some commoner to a ball at least have the decency to bring an educated one."

I look away from her and act coy, but use the distraction to take a hesitant step toward Graves. "I'm sorry ma'am, I am still learning."

Her scowl deepens as Graves ignores her and asks, "How was your dance?"

"It was lovely, Charles is very sweet. He asked me to dance again at the Solstice."

"Ahem," the duchess says loudly, "I don't know who you think you are, Miss, but Samuel and I were talking before you barged in."

I tilt my head to one side, "Were you? I'm sorry, I must've gotten too excited. What were you talking about?"

Hurst glares harder, "Nothing that you need be privy too," she tries to wave me off.

Graves tenses and comes closer to me, "I'd rather Lilith not be alone, these balls can be quite overwhelming if you're not used to them."

I smile sweetly at Clarissa, "Then it seems I'll be part of the conversation regardless." I shift my weight as someone passes by, they bump into me and I exaggerate the force.

I stumble forward and grip the duchess's arm as I fall. I focus on Graves as my hand makes contact, using my magic to find out what the hell this woman has done to fluster him.

I get a flash of her speaking to Graves, a devastated look on his face as she fans herself and kisses the Duke. I straighten up and look at Graves, who is frowning at me now. "I'm sorry, ma'am, I lost my balance."

Clarissa is staring at me as Graves puts a hand out to steady me, "Are you all right?"

"I'll be fine," I say tightly, my eyes flicking to Clarissa, "Just..." I pause for a moment and take a steadying breath, "May I... make a decision, which may or may not be in alignment with your idea of what constitutes 'out of bounds'?"

He frowns, then glances at Clarissa and smiles slightly, "If you've reached the point of no return I'll let you know, and I'm sure you can think of a way to get Phil in here if you need him."

I feel my grin widen and step closer, "Oh good, I think I've hit my limit of behaving for the night."

Graves

I look down into Lilith's face, pleased that she's asking permission before causing a scene, but a little worried at what might happen. I'm unable to look away from Lilith, her warm smile drawing me in and comforting the anxiety the Duchess's presence brings. Despite Clarissa fuming next to us, her hands clenched at her sides and her face turning red.

I wonder if I should stop Lilith and prevent this from getting out of hand as is my job. But then again, I never allowed myself or anyone else to get back at Clarissa for the pain she caused. And if anyone is going to exact revenge, it'd best be the one who's helped heal the pain.

I smile down at her and her grin widens, "My one stipulation is that no one is harmed, can you do that?" I tuck a strand of hair behind her ear and let my fingers trail along her cheek as she nods.

"What is going on?" Clarissa snaps, shoving me away from Lilith and glaring at me, "Is that any way to behave, Samuel? Ignoring a long-time friend because of some, some... trollop?"

I clench my teeth, but before I can reply Lilith steps in, "Look, Duchess, Graves may have the patience of a saint but I sure don't."

"How dare you speak to me that way," Clarissa snarls, taking a step toward Lilith and balling up her fists as her eyes shift to gold, signaling that her animal is near the surface.

"I'll speak to you however I please," Lilith retaliates, there's not a single hint that she's losing her temper other than her tone as she steps into Clarissa's space. "You seem to think that your previous affiliation with Lord Graves somehow entitles you to his attention. However, your very presence is irritating to the point that, despite this being your home, almost everyone is staying away from you." Lilith gestures to the room with one hand, and sure enough, there's a decent gap between us and the rest of the crowd.

Clarissa takes this in and her face starts to turn red, "It is only because you're causing a scene!" Clarissa declares.

"I'm causing a scene?" Lilith asks, her voice mocking, "I, Ma'am, am trying to rescue my friend from a situation he wants nothing to do with. I feel that, if you are unable to read a room well enough to see that people are distressed, then you should not then host events where people are meant to feel welcome."

"I can-" Clarissa starts, but Lilith isn't done.

Lilith raises her index finger and her brow, silencing the shifter, "If you can read a room well enough to see people's distress, then I must conclude that you don't care enough to consider their feelings. Now, don't get me wrong, I would never suggest that you entirely dampen who you are for the comfort of those who are judgmental. However there is a certain level of decorum to these things that requires one to, at the very least, consider how their presentation of themselves might affect those around them."

Clarissa stands there, her mouth opening and closing in shock. Evans comes up with his family in tow as the shifter gets her bearings and cries, "How dare you speak to me like this in my own home! I will not stand for it," she takes a step toward Lilith.

I think I'm the only one who sees the tendril of shadow that lashes out and trips Clarissa, causing her to fumble forward.

Lilith lithely steps to the side as Clarissa crashes to the floor. Looking down at our host, Lilith, in a wry tone says, "I didn't think you meant literally."

The whole crowd is staring at us now and Duke Hurst comes hurrying up and waving his hands about as Clarissa starts to wail on the floor like a child. I hear the murmurs spreading through the room, then Hurst turns on me and snaps, "Why would you bring such a tramp here? I thought with the girl you wouldn't torment my wife, but now this?" he gestures at Clarissa.

"Actually," Evans says, stepping up behind Lilith and putting a hand on her shoulder, "Duchess Hurst started all this. She was antagonizing Lord Graves and when Miss Callam stepped in to help rescue him from the situation the Duchess wouldn't back down. It may be that Lilith has over stepped her bounds here a bit, given that she doesn't have the standing to truly call out a duchess like this, but my family and I vouch for the situation. Lilith is not in the wrong." Leah and her companions nod along behind him.

Duke Hurst looks between Lilith and Clarissa and Charles and myself a few times before he sighs and pinches the bridge of his nose. "Regardless of who is to blame, neither of you is welcome here any longer. Leave."

Lilith shrugs and gives me a look that says 'what can you do?' then turns to Earl Evans and curtsies, "I'm sorry we didn't have more time to get acquainted, but it seems standing up for Lord Graves has cost us our invitation. We'll see you again at the Solstice."

"Of course," Charles says with a grin, "You do owe me a dance."

Lilith giggles and turns to me, "Shall we fetch Philip?"

I chuckle and hold my arm out to her, "I think that'd be wise,"

Philip

I lean against the wall of the servants' room. It's filled to the brim with footmen and a few women littered among them. Most of the people here are as air-headed as their masters, but a few of the women are gossiping and allowing me to pick up a little information. Not enough of it is pertinent to anything we deal with for me to put much thought into it.

A high-pitched wail from the other room has me turning to stare at the door that leads back to the main ballroom. I take a few steps in that direction but pause when no further sound other than some-one sobbing can be heard. A few of the other footmen are muttering amongst themselves, all of us wondering what the hells is going on out there.

A few minutes pass and then the door opens. A murmur spreads across the room as Graves and Lilith saunter through the door, arm in arm. Both of them are smiling and Lilith's grin has that curve to it that lets me know she was up to mischief. I walk up to the two of them with my hands in my pockets and my brows raised.

"Phil!" Lilith beams up at me, "We have been ordered to leave."

My eyes widen and flick to Sam, "What?"

The lord shrugs as if it's no big deal, "Clarissa wouldn't leave me alone."

I scowl, wondering how the fuck that lead to us being kicked out.

Lilith pulls Graves up to my side and hooks her arm through mine as well, "Come, we'll explain more in the carriage. Best not to entice further chaos, we might get banned from another event."

We let ourselves be pulled out into the carriage and get in. Lilith plops down on the far seat, a grin still plastered on her face as Sam and I settle against the other side. "What the hell?" I snap, "I thought we were supposed to be getting Lilith exposed to society a bit."

Lilith giggles, "We did! I had a blast. It was a little iffy there at the beginning, it was overwhelming. But! I made some friends."

"And enemies," Graves says dryly, "Though one is a bit more problematic than the other."

"How did you make enemies? Why did you make enemies?"

Lilith rolls her eyes and fluffs her hair over her shoulder, "Miss Ribald had it coming, she didn't know a thing about me and was trying to put me down!"

"Is that who screamed?" I ask.

Graves chuckles and Lilith laughs, "No," Graves says with a shake of his head, "That was our illustrious hostess."

My mouth drops open as they regale me with the rest of the tale, Lilith taking great pride in how she managed to trip the Duchess.

I cover my face with my hand when they're done, "And here we were worried about Damien coming along, I didn't think you two would be just as bad."

Lilith grins, "I'm a bad influence,"

"I'm not sure you should be proud of that," Graves says, but he's smiling too, "You'll have to tell Damien how it all went, he's been wanting me to get back at Clarissa for a long time."

Nineteen

In Which There are Strong Emotions

Lilith

I frown, "Oh? What did she do?"

Graves' expression falls and I can practically feel him retreating into his controlled mask. I expect a measured explanation but it's Phil who answers, "The short version is that she's a cunt. The long version is Graves' story to tell."

I turn to look at the man in question and he just shakes his head. I sigh, "So I need to tell Demon?"

Phil laughs, "Yeah, he might be pleased enough to hug you. Like Boss said, he's been wanting to get back at the duchess for years now."

I laugh at that and shake my head, "I get on his nerves too much for a hug."

Graves snorts, "You don't get on his nerves half as much as he wants you to think."

"He calls me a hellion."

"While the moniker may have started as an insult or a threat," Graves states flatly, "it's certainly not anymore. I'd be willing to bet you're the only person in this world who has an actual nickname from the man."

"You've got a nickname," Phil interjects.

I grin at Graves, "Damien gave you a nickname?"

"It's merely a shortening of my given name," Graves says with a shake of his head, "Hardly a nickname,"

My eyes widen and I laugh, "He calls you Sam?"

I get a dark look and Graves replies, "It's a holdover from when I was younger, and I believe we've discussed not using my name often."

I roll my eyes and grin, "Then I take it you'd rather I didn't call you Sam?"

He drops his hand and flat-out scowls at me now, "Correct, I would rather you didn't."

Phil chuckles, "Aw, come on Boss, a nickname never hurt anyone. Right, Lil?" he looks at me as if asking for my permission to give Graves a nickname.

I chuckle, "I've never had much trouble with them, but..." I glance at Graves who is now giving Phil a death glare, "Lord Graves isn't fond of them, so we'd best be nice and do as he asks," Graves looks over at me with a raised brow, "Though, I do wonder what the parameters for using your given name are?"

Phil chuckles, "He's not fond of that either,"

Graves gives me more of his attention now, "I'm fairly certain we discussed that as well," there's a brief pause where he searches my face then says softly, and I could swear almost affectionately, "Lilith."

The warmth in his tone has me flushing but I don't bother to hide it and smile, "I do recall that we did." He's used my first name multiple times tonight and I find I quite like it.

Philip is looking between the two of us with a very confused expression on his face, finally, he says, "I've missed something."

I can't stop the giggle that bubbles up, "You have, and I'm not in the mood to explain," I smirk at him and wink at Graves.

Lord Graves shakes his head as we roll up to the estate, "We're home," he says as he opens the door and holds his hand out to me.

I grin and take his hand, hopping out after him. I hear Phil chuckle and go up to talk to the driver, "I'll meet you two inside."

Graves doesn't seem to pay him any mind as he helps me down and leads me toward the door, "Thank you," he says, keeping my arm intertwined with his and placing his hand over mine.

"For?" I lean into him and look up at his face.

"For respecting my wishes in regards to my name,"

"I think you're making it a bigger deal than it is,"

"Perhaps," he's silent for a moment, but it's in that way of his that tells me he's got more to say, so I just wait. As we're nearing my room he stops and turns to me, "I may be making it a big deal, but you're one of the few people to readily accept my request. So for that, at least, Thank you. And..."

I wait again for him to get his thoughts in order. Eventually, he says, "I think that's the most fun I've had at one of these events in a long time. It was refreshing to see the people who look down on everyone be faced with someone who doesn't simper for them. So, thank you for that too."

I smile up at him, "Why, Lord Graves if I didn't know any better I'd say I've grown on you. Wasn't too long ago you didn't even like me."

He raises a brow at me and leans close, his eyes searching for something in mine, "I don't recall saying I didn't like you. Didn't trust you, perhaps, given that I didn't know you; but I've never disliked you," his expression warms as he smiles at me, "And now I wonder why I ever doubted you."

I feel the heat rise to my cheeks and I have half a mind to look away, to hide from the sudden onslaught of warmth swirling between us. Instead of looking away I meet his gaze and smile back, carefully choosing my next words, "In that case, I'm glad we seem to have learned how to trust each other. I hope we can continue to grow closer." I stand on my toes and kiss his cheek.

"Goodnight, Samael," I say as I slip through the door, not giving either of us any time to react.

I lean with my back against the door, my heart racing in my chest as I truly think about what I've just done. My face gets even warmer and I cover it with my hands, "That was foolish," I mutter, but even that knowledge can't keep the stupid grin off my face.

Graves

I stand staring at Lilith's door, too shocked to think, let alone walk away. I raise my hand to my cheek, the warmth of her touch seems to still linger, though I know the notion is ridiculous. I stare at her door for a few more moments then make my way to my office where I know the twins are waiting.

I think about the events of the night. While Lilith was dancing with Evans it took all I had not to stare at her. I'd told myself it was because I wanted to make sure she was all right. In truth, I was wishing that I had asked her to dance myself.

When Clarissa arrived I was hesitant to leave for fear of Lilith not being able to find me. And then, Lilith came to my rescue. She saw that Clarissa was bothering me and stepped in to stop my discomfort. Not only that, she was ready to pick a fight with a Duchess simply to protect me. It was incredibly foolish, but I wouldn't have expected anything less from her.

I realized something tonight; Lilith belongs here, with Aegis, at the estate, with Marie and Helga and Roland and Philip and Damien, and… me. Ever since she arrived she's done everything to belong, even when she's played pranks or caused trouble she's never done any permanent harm. That's not even to mention how scarcely a week ago she put her life in danger to protect the people of the house, even those that don't care for her.

My thoughts drift to Gavin, another person Lilith would give her life for. I almost panic as I realize that there's a legitimate possibility that when the contract is over she'll choose to leave. That when all is said and done her loyalty to us will come second to him. The mere thought makes my chest ache and I raise my hand to my cheek again, remembering the brief show of affection and the sweet smile that followed it.

I get to the office door, close my eyes and take a deep breath. I need to get Lilith to stay, and I have a sneaking suspicion that the two immortals on the other side of the door know of a way to do it. I open the doors and go straight to the sidebar. Phil has beaten me here and Damien is slouched in one of the chairs with a bottle next to him and a half-full glass in his hand. I pour myself a glass and turn to look at them.

They're both watching me with serious expressions. I take a sip of my drink and Phil sighs, "So, how bad was the altercation with Clarissa? Did anybody get hurt?"

"No," I shake my head, "Duke Hurst got there before Clarissa could lose her cool anymore. Besides, I think most of the crowd was on Lilith's side in the matter and would've come to her defense. Earl Evans and his family did openly take her side, I think Charles was quite charmed by her." I stare into my drink instead of letting them see my frown.

"I knew you shouldn't have gone," Damien growls, "What if things had gotten out of hand? Huh? Or if Clarissa decided to be a bitch? She could have hurt one or both of you."

I chuckle which earns me two raised brows, "Somehow I doubt

that any harm would've befallen either of us. Clarissa is all bluster. Had she tried to cause any harm Lilith would have taken matters into her own hands, more so than she already did. She did trip Clarissa when she tried to come at her," I swirl my drink as I stare into it, thoughts still swirling on what to do, "I do need your help with something though."

"Oh?" Phil says, "Did you hear something interesting?"

I don't reply for a moment, then Damien growls, "What is it?"

"I need to find a way to make sure she stays," I whisper into my glass.

"What?"

"When the contract is up. When she has the choice to leave, I need your help to give her every reason to stay."

"What makes you think she'll leave at all?" Phil says with a frown, "She seems pretty intent on being here."

I don't look up from my glass, "I..." I pause to collect my thoughts, not sure what I should tell them, or whether I'm just being paranoid, "I'm worried that her loyalty to Gavin will outweigh her regard for us; I find myself quite frightened by that potential."

They exchange a look and everything falls silent for a moment, "You..." Phil says slowly, "Are afraid she'll leave?"

"Yes, I realized tonight that my regard for her has surpassed what I'd expected," I find myself smiling into my glass, "It seems Lilith cannot help but beat my expectations."

I shake myself and look up at them finally, "And I want your help to see that she stays. I know you both care for her deeply as well,"

"I do..." Damien begins but I hold a hand up.

"Please don't try to lie to me about this," I give him a long look, "Your emotions are not as locked down as you'd like to believe. Now, you two know more than you let on. Is there anything we can do to help her want to stay?"

Philip scrubs a hand over his face and sighs, "Honestly there's not much you can do that hasn't already been done. You've given her a place to call home, people who care about her, and the freedom to do and be what she wants. Not to mention the skills needed to succeed in this world, no matter what she chooses to do."

"So, there is nothing more to do?" I ask, seeking verification.

"Not really," Damien says with a pensive look on his face.

"What?" I ask, "You're thinking hard about something."

He sighs and looks up at me, "There's nothing more you can do, but there is something you can make an effort not to do. Don't take away what she values, and if you don't know what that is then you should think about it."

I consider it for a moment then look up at him, "Do me a favor," he raises an eyebrow at me, "Don't let me do anything to jeopardize what she values. I'd never forgive myself if I did. And in the end, I'd rather watch her walk away than do anything to harm her."

He scrubs a hand over his face and nods, "All right, we won't let you fuck it up."

Phil chuckles, "I think it's safe to say that we should all keep each other from fucking it up,"

Damien chuckles as well, then holds up his cup, "To not fucking things up."

Damien

I sit on the ledge of the roof, staring down at the gardens as I sip from my glass. The last few months have been hectic, and it seems they're not going to settle down just yet. I smile to myself, I would've paid good money to have seen the look on Clarissa's face when Lilith took her down a peg. I can't wait to see what the two of us can do the next chance we get to fuck with the two-timing bitch.

I shake my head and set my glass down, I'm getting ahead of myself. As Sam said, there's no guarantee that she'll stay right now.

Until she agrees that she wants to remain with Aegis, the likelihood of more vengeance is low. She has implied that she's sticking around until the issue with the seals is dealt with, but has not said for certain. Regardless, there are more important things to be worrying about right now.

I hear a door open behind me and sigh, not wanting to talk to Phil and his smug face. "Go away, asshole," I grumble.

The door clicks closed and I'm about to turn and snap at him when a hand slaps the back of my head, "Rude,"

I spin and Lilith is standing behind me, she's bundled up in a thick gown, what looks like a coat, and a blanket, "What in the hells are you doing?" I ask.

"I was going to look for cookies in the kitchen, but I noticed the door open and came to see what was going on." She says sharply, "Only to be called an asshole just for opening the door! Did you know it was me?"

I sigh and rub my neck, "No, I didn't know it was you."

She glares at me for a long minute, as if trying to uncover secrets just by staring, finally, she sighs and sits next to me, "All right, then the one slap will have to do."

"Who said you could sit?" I ask glaring over at her.

"Who said I couldn't?" she argues, raising an eyebrow at me in a gesture that looks eerily similar to Sam's.

"Gods you're going to be the death of me," I mutter, scrubbing a hand over my face, "Fine, you can sit, but don't be reckless. The rest of the house will have my head if something happens to you."

She snorts but doesn't comment.

We sit in silence for a while and I wonder why she bothered to come out here, why she even thought she needed to. Finally, she says, "You're worrying about something,"

I look over at her and she's staring down at the yard, "Says who?"

She rolls her eyes and looks up at me now, giving me one of her signature sassy looks, "I've been here for almost three months. In all that time you've never been out here."

"So?"

She sighs and dramatically gestures around, "There's boxes, a chair, some bottles, and a few glasses stashed about, which means you do come out here often enough to need those things. But, given that in three months you haven't been it means it's a refuge when you're feeling a certain way."

"Okay…" I say slowly, watching as she continues to scrutinize the space, "How do you know I haven't been out here in the whole time you've been here?"

She snorts and tucks the blankets around her more, "You're perfectly aware that I've been getting cookies from the kitchen every day. I know your routes when you're patrolling. You've never been out here."

"Fine, fine," I shake my head, "Yeah, I'm worrying about stuff."

"Want to talk about it?" she asks gently, her tone coaxing.

I turn to look at her, she's watching me with wide, understanding eyes. I take a swig of my drink and look away from her probing expression, "No,"

I expect her to pry, push, or something, but instead, she just sits there quietly, watching the yard with me. My glass is empty and I scowl down at it, Lilith glances at me but doesn't say anything. I sigh and grab a bottle and another glass. I pour myself a new drink and hold the other cup out to her.

She smiles and takes the cup. I pour her a splash of booze and set the bottle aside, "You could go back to getting your snack," I say.

"I could," she agrees as she takes a sip of the drink and makes a face before glaring at the glass.

"Why aren't you?"

"I'm not sure," she admits, turning her head up to the stars she smiles serenely, "I was just going to see what you were doing then leave, but when you told me to leave..." she trails off and looks at me, "Something else said I should stay,"

"You're not psychic," I state flatly.

She laughs, "I certainly hope not," she takes another sip then grins, "Though, I am fairly good at reading people. And I do know that something is bothering you, whether you want to talk about it or not. I just..." she trails off and toys with the edge of her glass, "I'm worried about stuff too."

"I'm not the best for airing worries," I reply, downing the rest of my current drink and pouring more.

"I know, but sometimes when you're worried it's nice to not be alone,"

I look over at her and stare, the moonlight is shining off her hair and her expression is closed and pensive as she stares into her glass. Her hair has fallen to create a bit of a curtain between the two of us and I can't resist pushing it behind her ear, "Yeah, that's true,"

She gives me a pleased smile, "So I guess, thanks for keeping me company while I worry."

I frown, then I realize she's shaking and her lips have taken on a blue cast, "What did I say about being reckless?" I snap, trying to escape the surge of affection I'm feeling for the little hellion. I can't let myself fall for her, not when we're so close to getting this right, not after what happened last time.

"What?" she says, looking about her in confusion.

I growl and shift into my gargoyle shape, using one of my wings to drape across her shoulders and pull her toward me, "Are you wearing anything warm enough to be outside in this weather?"

She goes to protest but stills when I throw my arm around her as well, "I hadn't planned on sitting out here," she argues, but settles closer to me and rests her head against my chest.

"Yeah, yeah," I mutter, rubbing her arm to try and restore warmth to it. Only a moment or two passes before I realize it won't be enough, so I growl softly and she starts to pull away.

"Nope," I snap, picking her up and knocking both our glasses onto the roof, "Time to go inside Hellion, enough worrying on the roof."

She yelps and clings to me, her eyes wide as I march her inside and toward the kitchen. I plop her on one of the chairs and she opens her mouth and I glare at her, so she closes it.

I go to the pantry and get her cookies, "Here," I say, pushing them across the table to her.

She stares at them, then looks up at me, "Want one?"

I can't help but smirk, "No, I'm not big on sweets."

She shrugs and takes a cookie, "Your loss," she takes a big bite.

I chuckle and sit down across from her.

"So," she says slowly, "How are you so freaking warm?"

I laugh at that, "Perks of being immortal,"

She grunts, "Unfair," she takes another cookie then pauses, "So, you..." She looks away and sighs.

"What?" I ask, leaning toward her.

She looks back at me and sighs, "Do you still hate me?"

I recoil as if she'd struck me, shocked at the statement as much as the sorrow in her eyes, "What?" she opens her mouth to answer and I shake my head, "No, Lilith, I don't hate you, and I never did. Fuck."

I scrub a hand over my face and look away, "Was I that much of an ass?" I demand, looking back at her.

Her mouth is hanging open, "I... um..."

I shake my head and hold up a hand, "Don't answer that. But the answer is no, Lilith, I do not hate you." I laugh humorlessly, "But I'm starting to hate myself,"

She reaches across the table and puts her hand on mine, "Thanks," she says.

I look at our hands then at her, "For What?"

"For telling me," she smiles, "I'm glad you don't hate me." She gets thoughtful, "I like it here, and I don't want to have to go away," and with that, she stands and leaves me staring after her.

Twenty

In Which Limits are Broken

Graves

Another set of reports sits on my desk. The twins had thought that they'd dispatched the demon who'd been causing problems, but with the new information, it seems they were wrong. Either that or there are far more demons on our side of the veil than we thought.

I rub my forehead and sigh, "This isn't good. We can't move up the plans to take the seal. It all hinges on the ball. And even then we'll only be one step closer, there are two other seals to find." I close my eyes and pinch the bridge of my nose, trying desperately to think of some sort of plan.

Suddenly my office door slams open, making me jump and glare at the intruder. Phil is standing there with Lilith on his heels, she looks annoyed and he looks frustrated. "What?" I ask, surprised that the two of them seem to be upset with each other, for once.

"Phil is being a prick," Lilith snaps, walking around the large man and plopping herself in one of the seats across from my desk.

Philip glares at her, "I'm not being a prick, I'm trying to keep your dumb ass safe. You can't possibly handle Damien or me at our full strength. You're still a mortal, and a small one at that!"

Lilith scowls back at him, "So you're not even willing to push me a little harder? You said you wanna see how I'd do in a fair fight!"

He bares his teeth at her and hisses slightly, "That's what I mean, it wouldn't be a fair fucking fight!"

"Why does this need to be happening in my office?" I ask, needing to focus on the mess of cases in front of me, more than their arguing.

Phil turns to me and rubs a hand across his face, "Lilith needs to have a more even match..." he stares at me for a long second.

Lilith raises her eyebrows at him, then looks at me, "You can fight?"

I scowl over at her, annoyed that she seems to think me incapable, "Of course I can, everyone in Aegis is capable of physically defending themselves. And most of the staff here are at least trained well enough to get to a safe room."

She looks impressed for a moment, then says, "You'd use your magic?"

I frown, "What?" I hadn't realized she even knew about my magic, let alone enough to realize I didn't use it often.

Lilith crosses her arms and gives me a penetrating look, it seems to sink into me as she takes me in, "You always keep a tight leash on your magic, even though it seeps out when you're frustrated. I'm not even sure I've ever seen you openly use it, you always push it back."

"My magic can be..." I pause, wondering how much I should admit to her, then shrug, "Volatile. I keep a tight reign on it to avoid hurting people. The elements are rarely kind on their own, let alone when wielded by a person."

She leans forward in her seat, her eyes dancing with excitement, "Elements? Your magic is elemental?"

"Yes, But that's not important at the moment." I look over at Phil, "Are you sure that she's ready for a proper match?"

Phil nods, "I'm pretty sure the two of you would be evenly matched at this point." He looks at Lilith, concern flitting across his expression for a moment before he sighs and looks back at me, "If you both use magic, and you fight as you usually do, then you're matched."

I sigh and rub my forehead, "Okay, I take it you'd like to do this sometime soon?"

"That'd be preferable, but if you're busy," Phil's eyes fall on the stacks of paper on my desk and he winces, "It can wait."

Lilith looks at the papers too, her eyes scanning across a few pages before her expression turns grim. She meets my gaze and we both stare, her expression shifts ever so slightly, a small smirk curling at the corners of her mouth, "You look like you could use a break from," she waves at the papers, "All that. I don't know about you, but I always feel a bit better after beating the shit out of something. So maybe it'll help you clear your head and get a better idea of what to do about it."

I frown down at her, her bright eyes flashing with mischief. I take a deep breath, debating if I want to risk fighting her; I'm somewhat worried about hurting her. Then I look into her eyes and see a fire in them, I wonder if she's that intent on fighting me. When she shifts her weight in the chair and meets my gaze more directly, I see that it's not about the fight.

She doesn't want to fight, she wants to prove herself; I know she's been worried about belonging since she got here. The look in her eyes is determined and dangerous, and I know that if I turn this down she's going to find a way to aggravate Damien into a fight. So, I make up my mind, if a fight will help her feel like she can stay, then that's what she'll get.

I sigh and stand up, "Very well, give me a bit to get changed and I'll meet you in the workout room."

Her face lights up and she's on her feet in a flash, darting for the door before Phil or I can react to her sudden movement. I stare at the open door and look over at Phil, "Are you sure this is a good idea?"

He smiles, though the expression isn't friendly, "I'm sure it'll be interesting," he hesitates for a moment, "Word of advice? Don't hold back on her, she'll be able to tell."

I can't help the answering smile that curls my lips, "Don't worry, I'm not so stupid as to hold back against that woman. If I did I'm fairly certain I'd end up with my head handed to me."

He laughs, "Sounds like it'll be fun, I'll go tell the rest of the staff." And with that, he walks off.

Lilith

I bounce on my toes at the edge of the training ring, unable to keep my energy in check. I hope that if I can beat Graves I'll feel like I deserve to be here. I know they've said that I can stay, but I still question if I've earned that trust, especially with the secrets I'm keeping. I do a few stretches and hear someone come up behind me, I spin, ready to fight whoever is there. I stop when I see it's Gavin. I smile brightly at my friend, "Hi!" I say with a grin.

"What're you so excited about?" he asks, his eyes scanning the room, "Where are your babysitters?"

I frown and glance at the space as well, "They're not my babysitters. And I'm going to fight Graves. Phil says I'm ready for a full fight." I grin brightly, "Isn't that great?"

He frowns, "Why does it matter? I thought you weren't going to need to fight for this job?"

I hesitate and shift my weight, "Well, they're probably going to give me a permanent job. And Aegis agents must be able to defend themselves."

He scowls, looking away and crossing his arms, "I don't see why you want to stay here, it's stifling."

Before I have a chance to reply, Phil strides into the room with half the household on his heels. My eyes widen in surprise as Phil gets to my side with a wide grin, "What's going on?" I ask.

Marie skips up to me, wrapping her arms around my shoulders, "Phil said you and Lord Graves were going to spar. We haven't seen Graves fight anyone in quite some time; we're looking forward to it!"

I look at Phil with wide eyes, "What?"

Roland circles me with his hands folded behind him, "Lord Graves is a skilled fighter, but he doesn't fight if he can avoid it. It'll be quite the treat to see you two face off." The older man smiles, the expression warm and full of pride, "I'm looking forward to watching both of you."

"Oh," a flush spreads across my face, "I didn't expect to have an audience."

"Well it seems we have one," Graves says as he walks up, the crowd parting for him.

My mouth drops open despite myself. He's changed into a set of workout gear similar to what the twins wear. Snug pants and a light sleeveless shirt with tall leather boots. He's in the process of wrapping his hands and wrists with cloth, just like mine. The whole ensemble is dynamically different than his usual suits that I end up staring at him.

He raises an eyebrow at me, "Is the audience going to be an issue?"

I shake my head to clear my surprise, "No, just unexpected," I shift my weight, "Uh, weapons?"

Roland's eyes widen, "I don't know if that's wise,"

Graves turns his head to the side, his expression growing distant for a moment, telling me that he's thinking deeply about my question. At length, he says, "Are training weapons acceptable? I don't think actual blades would be wise."

I turn my head to look at him as well, then nod, "Yeah, I can agree with that."

He smiles at me, "Excellent, we are aiming to make this as realistic as possible, yes?"

I shift my weight back and forth then grin at him, "I believe that was the plan, Sir."

His expression morphs, the cool smile spreading into something far more dangerous, "Philip, you know my preferences. What weapon would you like, Lilith?"

I grin wider, "Phil knows what I prefer too."

"You're not going to tell each other?" Gavin says, sounding concerned as his gaze flicks between the two of us.

Graves turns to regard the shifter with something akin to contempt, "The likely hood of knowing your opponent's preference of weapon beforehand is very low. I think it would be best for the intention of this match if we kept it a secret for now. Agreed?"

"Agreed." I step into the ring and stretch, I offer Graves a cocky grin, "Are you sure you want to go through with this, sir? Nobody would blame you if you backed out."

He snorts and shakes his head, "You forget that I don't share Damien's temper; you won't so easily rile me up."

I shrug, "Worth a shot."

Philip returns from the shed with his hands behind his back, "All right children," he says, "either side of the ring, facing away from each other."

I roll my eyes and turn.

A few moments later Phil walks around me and looks down at me, "Don't go thinking this will be easy, Lil. Graves has trained with us for longer than you have."

I grin up at him, "I'm not an idiot,"

He sighs and hands me the training daggers, "Don't say I didn't warn you."

I roll my eyes as he walks away and stands outside the ring. "All right," he says, his voice carrying through the room and all those assembled, "Begin on the count of three,"

I close my eyes and take a deep breath, steadying myself and relaxing my hold on my magic, just a little. I don't let the tendrils of shadow spread from me just yet, but I'm prepared to use their reach to my advantage. I'm distantly aware of Phil counting as I tune out all sound but him. I take one more deep breath and hold it for a second.

"THREE!" Phil's voice cracks across the yard.

I spin on my heel and Graves is already moving, veering to my left with a modified longsword in his hand. He's rushing toward me, but I hold my ground, still keeping my shadows close to me. He gets close, his expression shifting to one of concern. On the sidelines, I hear someone shout, "Lilith!"

Graves brings his sword down and I slip into the shadows, leaping out from behind him and finally letting my shadows loose. They spread out like ink from my feet, creating a sort of puddle around me and spreading under his feet too. I take one of my daggers and slam the hilt into his side, not hard enough to do too much damage, but enough to make him stagger even more than my sudden disappearance did.

He recovers his footing quickly and turns to look at me, a pleased gleam in his eyes, "Nicely done," he says, "I haven't seen how your skills have expanded lately."

I just grin, "Good, all the more realistic."

His smile becomes even more sinister, which has me frowning, and then a sharp gust of wind hits the side of my head blowing my hair from its binding. It doesn't completely come undone, but enough strands are knocked loose that it impairs my vision. Graves shifts toward me and thrusts his sword at my stomach. I barely manage to dance away, using the shadows to help me slide across the spongy mats.

I narrow my gaze on Graves, I've only ever seen him use ice. And though he had just told me the nature of his magic, it hadn't occurred to me that other elements might be at his disposal. I can't help the wicked grin that spreads across my face as I use shadows to pull my hair back, pinning all the loose strands down. "Seems I'm not the only one with some extra tricks."

Graves nods, "I've worked long and hard to ensure that my magic remains concealed. I suspect there's quite a bit you're not aware of."

"Excellent," I say then shift my weight and launch toward him for a more direct attack. His eyes widen as he brings his blade up to block my dagger. I bring the other dagger around to hit him in the ribs but a layer of ice appears, locking the blade in place before it can make contact.

I hiss and drop into the shadows, dragging the daggers with me as I jump through the darkness to get a better vantage point. I reappear behind him and he spins, his sword meeting my daggers moments before it would've met me. I scowl at him, unsure how he managed to pinpoint my location in the darkness. "How'd you do that?" I ask, "Even the twins can't accurately trace me anymore."

His eyes light up, "If you can beat me I'll tell you,"

I grunt and shove him away, dancing back and shifting my weight to look for weaknesses. We stand a few yards apart, both eying the other. "This is getting boring," someone in the crowd calls.

I roll my eyes and Graves shakes his head, but neither of us bothers to verbalize a response to the heckling. I take a deep breath and let shadows crawl up my arm and onto one of my daggers. The shadow curls across the wood and spreads out, making it into a sword similar in length to Graves's.

"Changing tactics?" Graves asks, shifting his weight as he eyes the modified blade.

I nod, "You've got me beat on reach, and my usual tricks weren't working. So new tactics." Before he has a chance to respond I jump into action again.

Damien

I march into the workout room and pull up short. The entire house is standing in the room staring at the center ring where we usually spar. I hear the dull clash of wooden weapons as I weave through the crowd and come to a stop next to Phil.

My jaw drops when I see that it's Lilith and Sam in the ring, they're currently circling each other. But I can tell that they've been fighting for a little while. There's a bruise on Lilith's cheek, as well as one on Sam's arm, both of their training gear is out of place and I'm pretty sure I see a tear in Lilith's shirt.

"What's going on?" I ask Phil, watching the two of them closely.

"Lil wanted to test her strength, since they're both human she and Graves are equally matched," He says softly, but I wonder if he sees how little humanity remains in them as they fight.

As I watch I see some of Lilith's shadows snap out and try to trip Graves up. In response ice slicks under her feet causing her to slide haphazardly before she manages to regain her footing. Lilith hisses at Graves, her eyes flashing, "Really, ice under my feet?"

"Like you didn't try to trip me with shadows," he replies, a grin on his face.

She bares her teeth, then takes off at a sprint, right toward him. A sharp gust of wind buffets us in the face and I realize Graves is using more of his magic than usual.

Lilith easily manages to keep her footing, and I notice that she's using the shadows to wrap around her feet. Her eyes glow, magic seeping from her strong enough to make the air smell of apples.

Graves goes to back up and get a better stance but his movement is halted. He looks down and there are shadows wrapped around his legs up to his knees, keeping him firmly in place.

Lilith's eyes flash, and a short wall of shadows appears, which she then scales as if they're steps.

Graves throws his free hand out, ice forming in the air where the stairs should be, only to fall to the ground and shatter on the floor.

Graves's eyes widen in surprise as Lilith suddenly has the height advantage; he brings his sword up in an attempt to block her incoming attack, but she deftly leaps over him.

Lilith lands lithely behind Graves and swings her wooden dagger at him, the wooden blade stills at the point where his shoulder and neck meet. If this were a real fight he'd be dead, and as it stands he's immobilized and breathing heavily.

The crowd around me is holding their breath. I find myself taking a half step forward, ready to intervene if this goes further even though they're using training blades. Lilith and Graves stand still save for their breathing. All is silent for a long moment, then Graves starts to shake slightly.

I frown, then he lets out a laugh, the sound deep and pleased. "I concede," he says, dropping his sword to the ground. The crowd around me starts clapping and cheering, all of them having enjoyed the show.

Lilith grins, the shadows fading from his legs as she pulls her blade away. Graves spins on her, grinning widely. To everyone's surprise, he scoops her up in a hug and spins her once, drawing a startled laugh from her, "That was amazing, Lilith."

He sets her on her feet and she laughs, "I thought you were gonna be mad," a slight blush colors her cheeks.

"What for?" he asks with a frown, "Using every advantage you have? I'm pretty sure that's exactly what I told you to do. So it'd be rather hypocritical of me if I got mad at you for it now." He ruffles her hair, uncharacteristically affectionate.

Lilith laughs and bats his hand away. Phil and I walk up and the two of them look at us, both smiling, "Impressive, Hellion," I say, my voice gruff as usual.

"You didn't even see the whole fight, Demon," she sticks her tongue out at me.

"I did see that excellent takedown," I counter, "But regardless you've improved a lot since you got here."

She beams up at me as Phil slings an arm over her shoulders, "So, how should we celebrate?"

"No time," I say, getting me a collective dirty look. I roll my eyes, "Got a lead on our demon infestation."

Phil and Graves both scowl, "Shit," Phil says, "Where?"

"Narrowed it down to a few block radius near the docks," I explain, "There's one problem though,"

"What is it?" Lilith asks, looking equally concerned.

"Based on their patterns I doubt Phil and I are going to be able to draw them out. We're going to need help from another agent."

"Who do you think can help with a demon?" Graves asks, his expression shifting to all business.

"I can," Lilith says, drawing all our attention.

"No," Phil says firmly, sounding a lot like me.

She shrugs out from under his arm and crosses her arms, "Give me one reason why not."

Phil hesitates, "Uh,"

"Exactly," she snaps, "You have none," she turns to Graves and me, "I can help, I can hold my own against the twins and I just took down Graves. I can do it."

I look at her and can't help but smile, the look she's giving me is a familiar one. She looks like my queen with fire in her eyes and a grim determination in the set of her mouth as she stares me down. I know without a doubt that she's going to help, whether we like it or not.

I chuckle and shake my head, "All right, all right. You can help, it might work out for the best. I trust your ability to defend yourself better than other agents since I'm the one that taught you. Let's go to the office and you two can rest while we hatch a plan."

Phil makes a frustrated noise, "Are you sure about this?"

Lilith turns on him, her eyes flashing. I put a hand on her head, silencing her before she can yell at him. "Yes, I'm certain," I say, "Lilith is more than competent enough, and she can hide her magic so well the demon won't be able to tell she's not vulnerable."

Lilith grins up at me but doesn't comment as I pull her toward the office. Phil and Graves follow us and we go hatch a plan.

Twenty-One

In Which the Thief Fights a Demon

Lilith

I walk down the dimly lit street, flanked by the twins. Phil seems to be nervous as we walk down the quiet path. Damien, on the other hand, is relaxed and looks casual as we walk along. My eyes flick across the alleys and people that we pass as we go. I don't see anything or anyone that seems blatantly out of place, except us.

I'd insisted we wear plain clothes, but even the simplest things I own now seem out of place here by the docks. I run a hand across my hair and tug at the end of my braid, "Are you sure this is going to work?" I ask quietly, not turning toward them as I speak.

"I'm not," Damien admits, "But it's the best chance we have."

He stops at the edge of an alley, "Phil, this alley is in the center of its territory, set your trap." He turns to me as his brother walks away.

He looks me over, his eyes filled with something I can't quite name, "Mask your magic a bit more," he says, "I can still detect some of it, and for our best bet you need to seem helpless." He grits his teeth as he says it, clearly not appreciating that little detail of our plan.

I nod and close my eyes, centering myself further and pressing my magic even further down. When I open my eyes Damien looks even more concerned than he did before, "That's... eerie." He finally says.

"I take it that I did a good job?"

"Yeah if I didn't know better I'd say you're a typical human. I hope that's enough to bait out this demon."

"You don't think having you and Phil's residual energies will be a problem?"

He shakes his head, "We went over this, for whatever reason you don't retain traces of other people's auras unless you want to. And I presume you don't want to at the moment?"

"Yeah, I want this to work."

"Good," he nods and stretches, "I'm going to trail behind you, do you know these streets well enough to get back to this alley?"

"Yeah, it'll be easy," I hesitate and look away, "What're we going to do to it? You were vague on that point at the manor."

He sighs and runs a hand across his face, "We're going to question it, then attempt to banish it. If banishing doesn't work then we'll have to kill it."

I bite my lip and nod, "That... doesn't sound pleasant."

"It won't be," he shakes his head, "Trot along Hellion; it's getting dark and I want to get this done as soon as possible."

"All right, see you later, boss." I give him a mock salute that has him scowling at me angrily, before I walk off, forcing a spring into my step.

I keep myself moving for a while, taking in my surroundings and trying to stay aware but not openly alert. The task is proving harder than I anticipated, given that this situation is far more dangerous than any other time I've tried this. I see a flash of movement to my right, but it's just a small dog.

I turn my head to the side, listening for footsteps other than the near-silent padding of Damien a few blocks back. I don't hear anything obvious, so I keep going.

I turn a corner and stop short. Standing in front of me is a man, or at least what looks like a man. His skin is grayish purple and strangely clings to his bones. There's a dark residue on his chin, neck, and chest that, as I look at it, seems to be dried blood. Its ears are pointed weirdly, and its hands end in claws. It turns its head to the side and regards me, its mouth opens and I see sharp teeth.

"Well aren't you a tasty little morsel," it says in a raspy voice.

I swallow and take a half step back, not needing to feign fear of this creature.

It cackles and takes a few steps closer, "Come now sweet one, if you don't run I'll make it quick."

I take another step and shake my head, "I-I don't want any trouble," I say, acting as if it's just some other person.

The demon cackles again and stalks closer, "You've found trouble regardless, little girl."

I shudder, goosebumps rising along my spine. I turn on my heel and sprint away, knowing that it's probably not the smartest idea, but not caring as long as I get back to Phil and the trap. The beast lets out a noise that's a cross between a roar and a screech. I turn quickly around the corner, knowing that I can't use too much of my magic too soon or it's going to stop coming after me.

I race through the streets, keeping my magic under wraps as I leap and slide around the hazards that fill the darkened streets. The beast screeches again and I feel a disturbance in the air around me as it makes a swipe at me. I hiss and pick up speed, my legs burning and all my instincts screaming at me to use the shadows to get away.

I bite my lip as I turn the final corner, the demon still hot at my heels as I barrel past a startled Philip.

Philip

A loud screech has me looking up at the corner of the alley. I can't see anything at the moment but I recognize the sound of a demon when I hear it. Lilith turns the corner and sprints past, her feet slapping against the cobblestones with uncharacteristic volume. She slips on something and stumbles to a stop halfway down the alley, not close enough to the trap.

I watch in horror as a mostly humanoid demon charges straight at Lilith. Its claws extend as its cackling laugh resonates through the alleyway, it gets to Lilith's side and slashes at her; the tell-tale rip of fabric makes my heart skip. If she's hurt, if this demon kills her. An image of Lilith, our Lilith, dying and bleeding out rips through my mind, terrifying me in a way I haven't felt in centuries. I rush forward, needing to get to her side before the monster tears into her further.

My awareness of the scene before me returns just in time to see Lilith bare her teeth at the demon, her eyes beginning to glow green in the dim alley. "Big mistake, asshole," she hisses, her voice sounding so dangerous even the demon hesitates.

She disappears from in front of it, reappearing at its back with her blades at the ready. She brings one down on its left shoulder, towards where a human heart would be, and the other goes into its back, near the spine. The crunch of bone and a short gasp emit from the demon as Lilith rips the blades from its back.

The monster falls to the ground with a thump, then starts trying to scramble away. But Lilith is too quick and slams her booted foot down on its back, "Ah ah ah," she says, waving a bloody blade as if wagging her finger, "We're not done here," she says, her voice still holding that dangerous edge.

The demon is staring up at her, terror in its gaze, "I, I," it stammers, but no more sound escapes as Lilith applies pressure to its chest.

"You, are going to answer some questions about how you got here, then you're going to go back to where you came from," she crouches down, her foot still planted on its back, "and if you're very lucky, we might not make you suffer first."

As if on some demented cue, Damien rounds the corner and takes in the scene, his eyes widening at the fact that I'm standing there, gaping at Lilith. While she's got a demon, who's larger than her and seemingly more powerful, pinned to the ground and bleeding, about ten paces before the trap I'd set. "What the hell?" Damien says softly, glancing between me and her.

She looks over her shoulder and grins, "There you are, I thought you were faster than that." She jumps to her feet and walks toward us, but the demon remains in place.

"How are you doing that?" he asks, looking and the demon now.

Lilith's smile is both sinister and mischievous as she flips her blades in her hands, "Come now Damien, surely you've realized that I'm adept at using darkness to my advantage," Her eyes flick to me for a moment, hesitation in their depths. She continues, "It's a simple matter to solidify them enough to use them as restraints, obstacles, and so forth."

"Didn't you struggle with that while working with Coral?" I blurt, confused and wondering how her skills have advanced that far in a couple of weeks.

A flush spreads across her cheeks and she shifts her weight back and forth on her heels, "Ah, well,"

Damien crosses his arms and gives her a look so disappointed I almost feel guilty myself. She sighs dramatically and fluffs her hair over one shoulder, "I was faking it."

Her flat statement has my mouth dropping open, "What? You faked it? Why?"

She shrugs, "I have my reasons."

"Hellion," Damien says slowly, his scowl dark enough to scare a lesser being to death.

She scowls back at him, "You said it was my choice."

"Really?" he asks, "You're going to keep it under your hat now?"

Lilith's gaze flicks to me and I feel like I'm being judged in that moment. Before Damien can press her further I put my hands up in surrender, "If she doesn't want to tell me I'm not going to press it," and I can't keep the hurt out of my next words, "If she's not ready to trust me with that secret I understand."

Her expression softens and she sighs, "I'm sorry, Phil, I'm just so used to hiding it." She relaxes her pose and closes her eyes, her magical signature slowly grows in strength, filling the alley with power until she opens her eyes and it snaps back to her. "I'm a lot stronger than I let on," she wrings her hands, "Usually it scares people off, so I keep it hidden." She glares over at Damien, "I slipped up once and Asshole here won't let me hide it."

A gurgling noise draws our attention back to the demon, who I can now see is being held to the ground with ropes of shadow. We all look at each other and Damien sighs, "We need to get answers before the damn thing dies,"

I nod and we make our way over to the struggling form. We look down at it and Lilith crouches next to it, passing her hand over its wounds shadows fill the spaces and it seems to stabilize enough to regain its speech. "Bitch!" it spits, glaring at her.

She arches a brow at it, "Really? I'm keeping your sorry ass alive and you're gonna call me names?" she shakes her head in disappointment, then looks up at Damien and me, "I'm not sure what questions to ask. I can keep him stable long enough for you to talk to him, but it won't last forever."

Damien crouches down too and looks the creature over, "How did you pass through the gates?"

The demon spits at him, "None of your business."

I roll my eyes and look down at it, "I'd answer his questions, we're not all we seem either," I nod over at Lilith and she grins down at it, I see the ropes tighten just enough to make it gasp.

It hesitates, "I didn't,"

"Didn't what?" Damien prods.

"Come through the gates," it replies then seems to decide on something and it starts to cackle madly, "The veil is thinning, without the King and Queen to regulate things the worlds are starting to merge." It grins wickedly, "Soon the denizens of hell will be able to walk into this world without resistance. Soon, Discord will reign."

I wince and Lilith frowns, clearly concerned but also not understanding, "What's that mean?" she asks, looking at us instead of the demon.

"It means that we need to find the Seals of the Lost," Damien says slowly, his eyes sad as he looks at her.

"The Lost," her eyes widen as understanding dawns, "The King and Queen, the ones you served, they're the Lost?"

I nod, "Yeah, we... we've been looking for them for a long time."

We look back at the demon and it's grinning evilly, "You'll never find them, never fix what was broken, you're going to fail. Again."

I wince, knowing that it's drawing on the deep fears I harbor.

"Is that all you have to say?" Lilith asks sharply, her eyes starting to glow and her hand beginning to shake.

The demon laughs, "Yes, that's all I have to say to you pathetic beings. You're go-" it cuts off as Lilith slams her blade into its skull, right between the eyes.

My eyes widen in shock and Damien looks equally startled as a greenish light flashes from the blade and the demon starts to sizzle and crumble.

"What did you do?" I ask, not having seen something like that in so long that I'd honestly forgotten it was something that could be done.

She shrugs and stands up, "Nobody hurts my friends when I can intervene," she tosses me a look over her shoulder and says, in a tone that reminds me she holds the soul of my Queen, despite how intensely I'm aware of her current mortality, "You haven't and aren't going to fail, Philip. We're going to find them and fix this. I promise." With that, she tucks her hands in her pockets and starts to walk away.

Damien and I both stare after her, and I wonder if he's feeling the same level of awe as I am. It's then that I notice the tear in her shirt, remembering that the demon had gotten a shot in before she tapped into more power. I stare at the hole, noting that her skin isn't even red, though I'm fairly certain the attack made contact. I frown and look at the remains of the demon, "Should we be afraid?" I whisper to my brother.

He stands next to me, also watching the way Lilith went. "No, I don't think we should be afraid, but I do think we need to be ready because it seems we've forgotten how ruthless our Queen can be." He looks down at the crumbling remains of the demon, "If she'll destroy something like that simply for it preying on your fears, I pity the creature that harms one of us."

I snort and Lilith reappears at the end of the alley, "You idiots coming or what? I wanna get back in time for dinner to still be hot."

Damien

We make it back to the manor, Phil is unusually quiet, and Lilith doesn't seem too chatty either. I'm not sure who was more shocked by what happened with the demon. Lilith for the deadly rage she felt, or Phil for the stark reminder of how fragile she is. We near the manor and I clap my hands, making them both jump, "If you two go in there looking like you've lost everyone is going to be worried."

Lilith scowls at me, "We don't look like we lost,"

I shake my head, "Yes you do. You look like you're scared of something, and he looks like he's seen a ghost."

"Or a demon," Phil mutters.

I snort, "You've seen plenty of demons and not reacted like this. I understand that the encounter with the demon was weird, but you two are going to freak everyone out if you go back like this."

Lilith and Phil exchange a wary look and Phil crosses his arms over his chest, "What do you want us to do, then?"

Lilith turns her head to the side and eyes me for a long time, "Yeah, do you want me to mask that the demon scared the shit out of me?"

I look over at her, "Well…" I trail off, not sure how to react to that question.

Lilith sighs and looks away, "I guess I can mask how badly it scared me," she rubs her arm and whispers, "And I scared myself." I don't think she meant for either of us to hear that, but the way Phil turns to look at her proves that both of us did.

Phil sighs and rubs his neck, "All right, fine. I was mostly worried cause I thought it got Lil," he gestures at the tear in her shirt.

She frowns and rubs the side of her shirt, "Well, it didn't, not even a scratch." She shows him the skin under the tear, "I'm fine."

"But it was close," he argues, "What if you hadn't gotten out of the way fast enough?"

I scowl, "But she did," I argue, "And she will every time," I look back at Lilith, "Won't you?"

"Of course," she says, straightening her shoulders and meeting my gaze defiantly.

Phil frowns, "You can't guarantee that!"

Hellion spins on him with a scowl, "And you can't be sure that I won't! I will always do everything I can to survive whatever the fuck gets thrown my way. I will fight you if I fucking have to. And I will not let you try to put me on the sidelines because you are afraid!" Her magic flares around us and the look in her eyes is one I'm familiar with, one that our Queen used on us every time we tried to keep her out of a fight.

Phil takes a step away from her, his eyes filled with conflicting emotions. He doesn't reply to her ire and just turns to march away angrily. Lilith stands there breathing heavily, then turns to me with a challenge in her eyes.

I hold my hands up in surrender, "I may have been concerned about your capability at the beginning, but you've more than proven yourself. Honestly, I think it'd be more dangerous to keep you out of things."

She snorts, then laughs, "Damn straight."

I grin and ruffle her hair, "Come on, let's go find him before he scares one of the maids." Lilith smirks and we make our way into the house.

Lilith

Damien and I make our way into the kitchen and all eyes turn to us. Marie and Roland come to my side looking me over, turning me back and forth to check for damage. "Phil came through here looking like someone had died! Are you two okay?" Marie asks, cupping my face in her hands to inspect me further.

"We're fine," Damien says gruffly, "There was a close call with Lilith and Phil isn't too happy about it."

"He's being dramatic," I say sharply, "the stupid beast didn't even scrape me," I say, picking at the fraying fabric of my shirt. I neatly omit the fact that I briefly became a shadow to avoid its attack. I'm still not sure if I can trust them with the entirety of what I can do. Though once I get the first seal I'm going to show them.

Marie hugs me tightly, her perfume tickling my nose, "Good,

good, I don't know what we'd all do without you. You've become so important around here."

My face flames at the affection in her tone, and the murmurs of agreement that echo around me. I shrug out of her grip and look at the ground. The far door of the kitchen opens and Graves's voice fills the room, "Did you guys manage to stop it? Did you get answers?" he comes toward Damien and me.

"Let them eat!" Roland says, grabbing my arm and pulling me toward the table.

"We did catch it, and got some answers." Damien says, "We managed to trap it and found out that it's worse than we thought." He glances at the other people in the room, "We should probably keep this between us."

Some of the servants in the room look worried as Graves frowns, "Okay," he glances at me, "I'd prefer to get a run-down of what happened now, rather than later. Are you all right waiting to eat?"

"Can I eat in your office?"

"Lord Graves doesn't let people eat in his office," Riley snaps her hands on her hips.

Graves ignores her and replies, "Sure you can eat up there,"

Riley's mouth drops open as Barry hands me a plate of food, "Go on," the big man says gesturing at the door.

I follow Damien and Graves up to the office and plop in one of the chairs. Phil is already in the office sitting in a chair with a glass of alcohol. He raises his eyebrow at me when he sees me with my food. "How big did the puppy eyes have to get?"

"Didn't even bring them out," I quip, taking a bite of the mashed potatoes on my plate.

Phil shakes his head as Damien and Graves take their seats. "So, what happened?" Graves says, "What did it say?"

Damien explains what happened, then pauses when he mentions the way the demon was taken down. He glances at me and doesn't even have to make a face for me to see the question. I bite the corner of my lip and he sighs, "We managed to trap it, and then asked it some questions,"

"What answers did we get?" Graves asks quietly, apparently sensing the severity of the situation.

Phil rubs his face, "It's way worse than we thought. The thing didn't come through the gates; the veil is so thin that it was able to cross over without going through them."

The color drains from Graves's face, his eyes widening, "Oh no," he whispers.

I shudder and close my eyes, remembering the look on the beast's face as it cackled about the twins' failures. I clench my fist around the fork in my hands, "We need to hurry," I say softly, "We've got to get this seal and stop this."

"We can't rush the theft," Graves says, "I've looked at it from every angle and I can't find a good opportunity other than the Solstice Ball."

"Is there more information on the other seals? Can we go find the second one in the meantime?"

"No," Phil says with a shake of his head, "The other seals are hidden, thoroughly. You have to have the first one to find the other ones."

I scowl, "How do you know that?"

Damien coughs, "We helped hide them,"

"Then you know where they are!" I cry, standing up and almost knocking my plate to the floor, only for Damien to grab it before it hits the ground.

"No, we don't," Damien says, "We helped hide them, we didn't do it. Besides, the people it was given to for safekeeping are nomadic, they won't be in the same place we left them."

I scowl and sit down, crossing my arms over my chest, "Fuck,"

"Indeed," Graves says absently, "For now, we'll stick to the current plan. I'll reach out to Sarah and see if there's anything else she can tell us."

"What if it's already too late?" I whisper.

Phil makes a stressed noise and looks away, "Then we're all fucking screwed, and the world as we know it will end in chaos and death."

I run a hand down my face then clench my fists again and sit up, "I'm not going to fucking let that happen," I stand up and glare at the three of them, all of them looking hopeless, "What the hell has gotten into you three?"

"What do you mean?" Graves's brows furrow and he looks like I've grown an extra head.

"The three of you are the most confident, powerful men I've ever heard of. You've done everything you can to fight back against the bad things of the world since the moment I met you. Why do you all look like you're going to give up? Because it's more difficult than you expected? You've all gone on and on about how Aegis must protect people, about how the point of all of this is to make the world safer. And now you're going to sit here and act like all is lost?"

The twins exchange a loaded look, but Graves is the one that speaks, "Your confidence in us seems to outshine our own."

"Then fucking trust the people that depend on you. Roland, Sarah, Marie, Helga, all the others who live and work here, they all trust you to do this," I snap, shadows snapping around me dramatically as I slam my hand against my chest, "Trust me when I say that if anyone can stop this from going to shit, it's you. It's us," I emphasize the last word, "And I'll be damned before I let the world be destroyed, it's the only one I've ever known! Now, I'm gonna let you three get your heads out of your asses and think of what we need to do once the first seal is retrieved." I take my plate from Damien and leave the room, dedicated to my words, but also terrified I overstepped my bounds.

Twenty-Two

In Which an Artifact is Stolen

Graves

Lilith shifts in the seat across from me, clearly worried. Beside her, Philip is trying to remain calm, but I can tell he's worried too. The only one in the car who seems unaffected by the situation is Damien, who is next to me looking us all over with an amused expression. "Hellion, stop fidgeting, it'll make you stand out in the crowd."

She looks over at him with a glare, "I'm sorry, Demon, not all of us are unfeeling assholes who can be calm all the fucking time. So get the fuck out of my face."

He smiles and leans forward, looking her right in the eyes, "Make me," he challenges.

I half expect her to haul off and punch him. Instead, a coil of shadow wraps around his throat and yanks him back onto the bench, his back slamming against the seat and shaking the carriage. Lilith bares her teeth at Damien the shadow still wrapped around his neck, "Don't make me repeat myself."

Phil's eyes widen in surprise, looking at his brother with shock written plainly on his face. Phil looks almost scared, but Damien grins with a satisfied gleam in his eyes, "There's my Hellion. Now stop your fretting, you can handle this."

She glares at him, then the shadow dissipates and she sits back on her side, "Asshole," she mutters as she looks out the window.

I chuckle and shake my head, "You two are going to cause a scene."

Phil snorts, still looking shocked, "I'm just amazed there wasn't more violence as it is"

Lilith rolls her eyes and props her chin on her hand, "I'm not about to damage or dirty my dress just to kick Damien's ass," she smooths out the fabric, "no matter how much he might deserve it." She looks up at Damien and smiles with saccharine sweetness.

Damien just smiles back, showing off his fangs, "The point was to help you feel better."

"Odd way of doing it," Phil grumbles, "Though, I do suppose that's how you usually help people feel better, making them wanna fight you."

"You weren't gonna do it. You're just as nervous as she is."

"I think we're all a bit nervous," I comment, "This is important and we have to tread carefully."

"Yeah," Lilith whispers to the window of the carriage, "We've got to be careful, so much hangs in the balance. I think I'll be fine with the stealing portion, it's everything else that I'm concerned about." She wrings her hands and then sighs.

"We'll figure it out," Phil says, patting her leg.

She looks up at me, our eyes meet and I can see the wariness and determination shining in their depths. "Sir," she says quietly, "Do you think this is the right decision?"

The twins both frown and I lean forward and take both of her hands in mine, "I've told you once before, I think you're right where you should be. I am completely certain that you can do this."

Her smile widens, the tension in her shoulders eases, and the twins look even more confused, "Thank you,"

"Anytime," I release her as the carriage rolls to a stop.

"Show time," Damien says as he hops out, holding his hand out to Lilith.

We all exit the carriage and Lilith comes straight to my side, hooking her arm with mine. "Let's do this," she says, plastering a big smile on her face.

"Remember, you don't have to sacrifice being yourself," I remind her before I squeeze her hand and we make our way inside, the twins flanking us.

The ballroom is grand as always, but instead of her previous gawking Lilith strides through as if she belongs, holding herself in a way that makes her look like a noble. I can feel the pride radiating from the twins, and I'm not afraid to admit I'm proud of her too. We're scarcely on the floor before a young man walks up to Lilith.

"Miss Callam!" the man, I believe his name is James Fisher, says as he rushes to her side, "May I have a dance?"

She smiles and pulls out her dance card, "Of course, though I promised one to Earl Evans at the Hursts' ball, he's got a slot before you."

"So I'll be second?" he asks hopefully, his eyes lighting up at the prospect.

Damien snorts behind us and earns an elbow from Phil. Lilith shakes her head, "Third I'm afraid," she looks over at me, smiling warmly, "Lord Graves has also been promised a dance."

I have to make an effort to school my features to avoid showing both my surprise and my pleasure, but I'm sure I fail when Lilith's smile widens.

The young man visibly deflates, "Very well," he eyes me and I raise a brow at him. He looks away, "I suppose that makes sense, he is your benefactor after all."

Lilith doesn't seem to know how to respond so I squeeze her hand, "Miss Callam, I think we should find something to eat before you dance with anyone. Marie and Helga will have my head if you come home hungry,"

Lilith giggles, "I'd like to see that."

"I'd rather spare myself the experience," I comment dryly, I turn back to the boy and bow slightly to him, "I'll see that she finds you later."

He nods and scurries off.

"You'd think the boy had never asked someone to dance before," Damien says from behind us.

"Lilith is lovelier than the women here," Phil states in a wistful tone.

Lilith snorts, "Don't be absurd. If anything, I'd say he's intimidated by the fact that I've got the three of you looming like bodyguards."

"Regardless, we should find food," Phil says, surveying the room.

"You two get to listening for gossip, we have to make sure Lilith is seen," I say, patting her hand and looking down at her.

Lilith's expression turns grim for a breath as she scans the room, "Keep an eye out for Earl Evans, it'll be better if I'm seen with more than just you three."

Damien grunts and I feel he doesn't agree with that sentiment, but I nod, "You're right, let's go."

Before we walk away from the twins, Lilith shakes her shoulders and relaxes, her expression returning to one that's soft and pleasant. I still marvel that she's able to make that change so quickly, even though it is one of the reasons I hired her for this.

Lilith

I stay close to Graves' side as we weave through the crowd, "I shouldn't eat much," I mutter to him, "At least not until after…" I leave the rest of the sentence hanging.

"Just a few things, it'll work to get you seen."

I take a deep breath and nod, "Right,"

Graves looks over at me and squeezes my hand, but he doesn't say anything, and I realize I know what the silent gesture means. It's his way of letting me know he's there; of ensuring that I know he has my back. I smile, comforted by the fact that it has become so easy to communicate with him.

We get to the food tables and I grab a few small things and put them on a plate, Graves keeping vigil at my back. We wander the room quietly while I eat. The room is grandly decorated, and there are more people here than at the Hursts' ball. This is the biggest social event of the year, so it stands to reason that there are more people here. The press of so many people is making me nervous, despite knowing that I should be safe here. At least until I've claimed the artifact that's waiting for me deeper in the building.

We finish our loop around the room and I hear a booming voice from across the hall, "Miss Callam! Graves!"

I turn and grin as Earl Evans marches through the crowd and to our side, "Evans,"

"Please," he says dramatically, "no need for formality. You can call me Charles."

I laugh, "Very well, you may call me Lilith."

His face lights up, "Wonderful!" he bows with a flourish and holds his hand out to me, his eyes searching my face as he waits, "I believe I was promised a dance," he glances at Graves who tensed up as he approached, "May I steal your companion for a bit?"

Lord Graves nods, "Of course, far be it for me to keep Miss Callam from doing what she wishes."

Charles laughs, "I get the impression that very little can keep Lilith from doing anything she desires."

I snort, "I'm not some wild thing with no control,"

Graves chuckles, "Could've fooled me,"

I gasp and turn on him, "Excuse me?"

He smirks at me, his eyes dancing with amusement "How many pranks have you pulled this week?"

My mouth drops open, "They weren't all me! Phil did plenty of them too!"

"So you admit to some of them?" he raises that questioning eyebrow at me and I roll my eyes.

Evans laughs, a full-bellied sound that booms around us, "Just as I suspected. Lilith Callam does as she likes," he gives me a big smile, "I am more than willing to be subject to your whims, assuming of course they're not going to put me in danger."

I shake my head, "I'm not stupidly reckless," I pause to consider my words then shrug, "most of the time."

Graves shakes his head, "Go dance, I need to check in with the Twins," he nudges me toward Evans and walks off.

I take Evans' hand and he smiles, "Lord Graves seems rather fond of you, I don't think I've ever seen him smile that much."

I can't help the blush that rises to my cheeks, "He is quite the austere person, isn't he?"

"That is an understatement," he says as we step onto the floor and the music starts up.

We get through the first rounds of the song and he says, "I see my suspicions at the Hursts' Ball were correct."

"What?" I ask startled and meeting his gaze. Does he suspect that it's all a farce? That I don't belong here at all?

He smiles, his eyes gentle as he inspects my face, "Lord Graves may have taken you in as a favor to your father, but his fondness of you goes beyond that. As does yours for him,"

I flush deeply, "Ah, I... um..." I'm equal parts relieved and flustered by his assessment, casting my eyes around I try to find something else to talk about.

He laughs and squeezes my hand, "No need to be embarrassed."

"I don't know that his fondness is what you think. I merely amuse him. Which, I suppose, is more than most people can say."

"If you wish to stubbornly remain oblivious so be it." He says with a good-natured smile.

I shake my head, but can't come up with words to refute his claim.

He chuckles at my silence, "I'm glad to see that he's happy, we may not be very close now, but we spent a good bit of time together when we were younger. He's always been serious, but it's gotten worse as he's gotten older." He pauses and smiles, "I just hope we can be friends as well if that's to your liking."

I smile up at him, "Of course! You and your sister are the only people I've met at these balls who seem to truly like me. All the others only wish to garnish favor with Lord Graves."

"Those who seek power will always do whatever it takes to earn it," he says seriously, almost like a warning, "I am content with my lot and as such see no need to press for advantages."

We fall into silence for a while and as the song winds down I hear a clatter and a bang from somewhere nearby. Evans turns to look at what's going on and I spot Damien behind him, gesturing away from the sound and toward the fainting rooms on the far side of the ballroom.

I stumble and sway into Evan's side, gasping as if I'm having trouble breathing.

"Lilith? What's wrong?" Charles asks, putting a hand on my hip.

"I, I'm feeling faint." I say hurriedly, "C-can you take me to one of the fainting rooms," I gesture in the direction Damien had indicated and Charles quickly whisks me away.

We get to a door and Charles goes to come in with me but I put a hand on his chest, "I don't think that's appropriate," I say hurriedly.

He hesitates and then looks at the room behind me, obviously seeing that it's vacant. "Ah," he says, "Yes, I'll go let Lord Graves or one of the twins know. Will you be all right?"

"Yes, I'll just lock the door, thank you."

He smiles, "Good, I'll be back."

I nod and close the door on him before he can come up with something else to say. I grin to myself as I flip the lock, that was a lot easier than I expected.

I chuckle and reach for the ribbons holding my skirts up. I lay the fabric out on one of the chaises that are spread across the room. "Well, it's time to get into some trouble." I grin to myself then use the shadows to easily slip through the doorway.

***

It doesn't take me long to find the inner reaches of the house, I've memorized the layout over the last few weeks and I could probably find my way around with my eyes closed. I turn a corner and back-pedal quickly, a guard is patrolling toward me. I inhale sharply, the air hissing through my teeth as I press against the wall.

There isn't usually anyone patrolling through here, but I'd known it was possible with the ball happening. I cross the hall and tuck myself into the shadows of a corner, using my magic to make the shadows deeper and keep me more hidden.

I wait a few moments, keeping my breathing steady as the guard passes, his eyes passing over the shadows without so much as a flicker in his expression. I grin to myself as he walks off and I dart through more shadows.

I get to the back reaches of the house and find the vault door. My grin widens and I pull my lock picks out of the case at my hip. As I'm reaching for the lock a prickling sensation washes over my fingers. I stop short of touching the metal and turn my head to the side, I focus intently for a while and feel the prickle of magic across my awareness. I bare my teeth at it, muttering under my breath about stupid security measures. I retrieve the charm that Sarah and Marie gave me, it was meant to protect me from the people at the house. But it dulls magic and hopefully, it is strong enough to do what I need it to.

I slip the ward off and wrap it around the handle of my lock pick. I bring the pick near the lock and the tingle of the protective magic is absent, I grin wickedly and slip the pick into the lock. It takes me mere moments to unlock the small lock. It clicks open, revealing a series of buttons, underneath. I take a deep breath and use the back of my hand to touch the button pad.

The pad has a memory of the sequence I need, hundreds of events of the same set of numbers. I press the buttons in the order it shows me and another mechanism clicks inside the massive door. I take a deep breath, this is where the extent of our findings ended, beyond this door, I'm not sure what I will encounter.

The door swings open slowly and I grimace, there's a lot more magic inside the vault, and I can feel that it's going to prevent me from getting across with the shadows.

I shift my weight from foot to foot, drawing my magic to me. I turn my head to the side, listening for more guards, when I don't hear anything I look down at the dampening charm. I stare at it for a long time, contemplating if I can do what I'm thinking. I nod to myself and mutter, "It may burn it out, but it should work."

I pour raw power into the charm increasing the reserves it has to pull from. I can feel the magic around me dulling more and more as the bubble of influence expands. My shadows wink out and the itchy sensation of protective magics eases. I grin and step into the room, nothing happens as I slip across the floor.

The magic stays at bay as I make my way across the room. The vast room is overflowing with treasures of all sorts. There are items strewn across the floors and shelves, it takes some careful maneuvering to get to the small charm nestled on a pedestal at the far end.

The magic in the room is easily held at bay by the small charm I'm holding and I'm suspicious of how simple it is. I look around the pedestal and use the charm to nullify the field around it as well. I pluck the charm off the pedestal with my gloved hands and wrap it in the magic-dampening cloth made specifically for it.

I hear a cracking sound and spin around, two of the statues that were resting against the walls have begun to unfold and stand up. My mouth drops open, they're stone constructs and their glowing eyes are fixed on me. I swallow hard, I need to get out of here, now. I squeeze the charm tighter in my hand, I can't afford to release the dampener, if I do the magical alarms are going to go off. However, it's also created a bubble around me where I can't use my magic either.

I shift my weight, thinking through my options quickly. I swallow hard and do the only thing that I think will work, despite how reckless it is going to be. I take a creeping step away from the construct, their movements no longer constrained by their stony forms. They both move toward me at once, I sprint toward the door and I release my stifling hold on my magic.

In a breath, the whole room is covered in darkness save for the space directly around me. I hear the golems crash into each other, but expand the bubble of my influence to dampen the sound. I feel my magical energy draining rapidly, my breathing becoming ragged. The flooring beneath my feet switches from hard marble to soft carpet and I slide to a stop.

I put the restraints on my magic and turn around to shove the vault door closed. I hear all the locks click back into place and flee the scene without waiting to see if the commotion drew any attention.

Twenty-Three

In Which the Lord takes a Stand

Lilith

I slide back into the fainting room and lean against the door. I close my eyes and let my shadows spread out back through the hallway, nothing amiss. I grin like an idiot as I rush to put my skirts back on. I move over to the mirror along the wall and can't keep the grin off my face as I adjust my hair back into place.

A soft knock at the door has me turning and I hear, "Lilith? Are you all right?"

I make my way to the door and pull it open, Charles is standing there with his entire family, "Oh, hello," I say with a shy smile.

"Charles said you were feeling faint, I was going to come and check on you." Leah says with a sweet smile, "But I see you're doing just fine."

"Yes, I think it was just some nerves," I say with a flush, "I thought I'd be okay after the last ball, but this is so much grander."

Leah nods, "Oh yes, it is. Come, we'll get you some punch and a bit of food. It'll help settle you, then you can go back to enjoying the ball, yeah?"

I nod and let her lead me away with the rest of her family tailing after us. We get to the table with food and Leah hands me a few things while Dante follows behind her and gets a plate as well. I wonder why he's getting food when we get to the end of the table and he hands it to Leah, then grins at me, "She'll feed you all day and forget about herself, I learned some time ago it's best to keep food within arms reach."

I giggle and nod, "I have found that I'm often in the mood for a snack, though my tutor wouldn't be too pleased to hear it."

Leah snorts, "Tutors are a bunch of prissy old biddies as it is, you eat what you want when you want dear. If anybody gives you trouble about such a thing, bring them to me," she takes a bite of something as Charles and Andre join our little circle.

"How do you like the solstice?" Andre asks, giving me a pleasant smile.

"Wonderful so far, I just hope it doesn't end as disastrously as the last ball I attended." I flush again.

Dante chuckles, "We'll stay with you, hopefully, that'll help."

I grin, "That sounds wonderful... though," I scan the room, "I should probably seek out one of the guys before too long too."

Charles shakes his head, "They'll find you when they're ready, I'm sure."

I nod, "You're right, I shouldn't fret."

Leah wraps an arm around my shoulders, "Come now, tell us more about yourself?"

"What would you like to know?"

She leans real close and whispers, the men also crowding a bit closer, "My biggest question is if you're as close with the twins as you are Lord Graves."

I frown, "What? I'm not sure I understand."

She blinks at me, then looks over at Dante who shrugs, "Not everyone makes the logical leaps you do, my love. The idea might not have even occurred to her."

"What idea?" I ask, hating that I'm out of the loop.

Leah grabs me by the shoulders and turns me so we're facing each other, "Lilith, dear one, Samael Graves is entirely enamored with you. My question, is if you've charmed the twins just as thoroughly?"

I just stare at her, unable to quite process what she's telling me. So I end up opening and closing my mouth a few times before replying, "I can hardly speak to their thoughts toward me. And, if it is as you say, it's unlikely that I'd be able to tell anyway."

Leah's head droops and she sighs, "I suppose you're right. I guess I'll just have to observe for myself." She follows that statement up with a grin that has me shooting Charles a concerned look, but he just looks amused.

"Well well," A voice coos from behind me, "If it isn't Miss Callam. Have you already made such a fool of yourself that Lord Graves has chosen to abandon you?"

I tense and turn, Clarissa is standing behind me with a few other women flanking her like a small army. Each one of them is as dressed up elaborately like Clarissa and, honestly, they look like copies of each other. Among their number is Laurel Ribald, who I spurred at the Hursts' ball. I paste on a fake smile, "Ah, Duchess Hurst, I was under the impression that a ball was meant to be for socializing. With that in mind, I sought out company other than who I arrived with. I'm sure if you have questions for Lord Graves you may seek him out; He and Damien were near the food last I checked."

She tenses at the mention of the Gargoyle, her eyes narrowing, "I'm not looking for him,"

One of her cronies giggles, "Is this truly the girl who has enchanted the Lord? His standards have fallen far since the two of you were courting, Clarissa."

I tense, while I'd suspected her previous involvement with Graves, something about having it stated so openly sets me on edge. Before I can reply Clarissa says, "I'm aware, I think she's laid an enchantment on him. The man is so thoughtful and discerning, I find it hard to believe he'd want anything to do with this sort of rabble without magic involved."

"Hey," Charles says, taking a step forward to block me from Clarissa's view, "Leave her alone."

One of the ladies scoffs, "You too?" she looks at me, "Are you truly so low class as to put spells on people to get what you want?"

Leah grabs Charles' arm and whispers something to him before she and Dante hurry away. I'm not sure why they're leaving, but it stings.

"I would never-" I begin, only to be cut off by Laurel Ribald.

"Perhaps it is not as mystical as a spell," She looks me over with a calculating stare, "She's pretty enough I'm sure she could wiggle her way into a man's bed. And I'm sure we're all aware of what sort of tricks harlots will play to get what they want."

Clarissa nods at that, "You're right, Laurel, there's no way anyone would want her around if they weren't getting something from her."

The statement hits hard. I can't help but think they're right, the only reason Graves hired me was because of what I can do. My ability to retrieve the talisman which is currently hidden in my dress, is the whole reason I'm here at all. And Damien only tolerates me because Graves asked him to. I take a half step back, "T-that's not true." I stammer, trying to fight the anxiety that's crowding in.

"Isn't it?" Clarissa coos, "I heard from a little bird that you were hired to help with an assignment from Aegis. That whole story about a merchant's daughter is lies."

Charles and Andre frown, "What? Lilith?" Charles looks at me.

My breathing becomes ragged and I shake my head, "I-I," I try to get a grip on myself but it's a losing battle. This isn't the first time I've only been used for something only to be cast aside. My mother loved my magic until it scared her, until she found a man who would take care of her, as long as I was gone.

I take a step back and shake my head again, "Leave me alone," I manage, my voice coming out as almost a whine.

"Not so brave now, are you? Now that your so-called friends know you're nothing more than a street urchin hired to pretend," Laurel says, a smirk spreading across her face as if she's won.

I have to leave, I have to get away from here, from all of this. I turn and start to walk away, "I'll get out of your way," I say hurriedly, trying to dodge around them.

As I go to get around them Clarissa reaches out and grabs a fistful of my hair, yanking me off my feet and pulling me toward her so we fall in a heap. The harsh pull on my hair draws tears to my eyes and memories to mind, I scream.

Graves

"I haven't heard much, mostly rumors about Lilith." Phil says, rubbing his neck, "Not sure if that's good for us or bad for us. We'll need to be on alert."

I sigh and close my eyes, "She's with Charles and his family at the moment, it should help to dispel some of the rumors but we should probably get back to her."

Damien snorts, "Not sure why you left her with him, he's a good sort but still just human."

"Yes, well he's a noble too and it should help-" I'm cut off by a shrill scream tearing through the ballroom. I'm startled that someone would scream in this situation, but what terrifies me is that I've heard that scream before.

All three of us spin toward the dance floor and see Clarissa and Lilith in a pile. It's clear to see that Clarissa pulled Lilith on top of her, ruining Lilith's hairstyle. And the four women standing near them are crying and sobbing. Clarissa shoves Lilith off of her, yelling about how Miss Callam attacked her.

Lilith's eyes are wide and staring as she tries to scramble away, but her attempts are half-hearted at best. I lose track of all else as I rush to her side, Damien pushes Clarissa away as Phil tries to herd the others away, only for all of the women to start crying and lamenting that they were just talking to her.

Lilith sits on the floor that glazed look in her eyes not fading even though she's freed and separated from Clarissa. I distantly hear the twins talking but I'm focused on the woman before me.

"Lilith," I say gently as I kneel next to her, "Lilith, look at me. I'm right here, I've got you."

She shudders and hiccups out a soft sob but there's no further reaction. I cast around, looking for a way to ground her, to settle her back into this moment. Charles kneels next to me and says, "Is she hurt?"

"No," I murmur, "Not in any way that we can heal. Can you keep the crowd back? The more people gawking at her the more it's going to stress her out."

"On it," he jumps to his feet and I hear him talk to someone before they're ushering the crowd away from us.

Lilith sobs and hugs herself tightly. The action reminds me of when Gavin scared her and a thought occurs. Without further consideration I shed my coat and wrap it around her, I drape it so that her head is partly covered. She inhales deeply and the horror in her eyes clears, she looks up at me and whispers, "Samael?"

I sigh with relief and nod, "Yes, I'm here."

She launches herself at me and I catch her before we both crash to the ground. She clings to my vest and presses her face to my chest, "You're okay, I've got you," I murmur, rubbing her back as she slowly stops shaking.

"Look at that, hanging all over Lord Graves as if this isn't her fault," a sharp voice snaps, drawing my attention away from Lilith, "She attacked Clarissa! She's a menace I tell you!"

Clarissa stares down at us with disdain clear in her expression. A few other ladies flank her, their eyes equally cruel as they survey the scene.

"She's not the one dragging people around by their hair!" Damien snaps, stepping between us and Clarissa.

"Perhaps if she weren't some commoner she'd have better manners. Clarissa was just talking to her and she went wild." One of Clarissa's groupies declares, "Though I suppose talking to you is useless given you're wrapped around her finger. We know she's not a merchant's daughter, just some beggar you picked up off the street. Not even worth the dress she's wearing."

Damien growls and steps toward them his eyes shifting slightly to take on that darker sheen.

Lilith whimpers and presses her face against my shoulder, "I'm sorry, I've fucked all this up."

"No," I reply, "you haven't done anything wrong."

"But they're right, I'm nothing, I'm just here to do a job. Then... Then, you'll send me away." she says softly, her voice heavy with despair even as she tries to pull herself closer.

I won't let these bitches make her think like that, won't let them hurt her by preying on her fears. Not when I would give the world for her. I grunt and lift her face so she's looking up at me.

"W-What?" she stammers as I wipe a tear from her face.

I stand and slowly pull her to her feet and cup her face in my hands, "Please, don't talk about yourself like that. You're far more than what they see. Don't let them tear you down."

"B-but they know the truth. And they've seen... this." She mutters, gesturing at her face which is splotchy from crying.

I wipe a tear away, "They won the round, now it's time for you to take the fight."

She stares at me, confusion in her eyes.

Behind her, Laurel snaps, "This is ridiculous, She acts like some feral thing and is being coddled? She's used some sort of magic."

"She didn't attack anyone." Charles snaps, stepping up next to us as well, "You lot came up and started antagonizing her."

One of Clarissa's lackeys scoffs, "Your word can't be trusted, she's clearly got you wrapped up too!"

Lilith tries to curl in on herself, tears renewed. I lean close and whisper in her ear, "Fake it, put on the persona and make them believe what you want them to believe. Take back the fight, you can do it." I sit back and push her hair behind her ear and raise a brow at her.

She frowns, then Clarissa says, "Is nobody going to get her out of here?" she waves her hand around as if trying to flag down one of the guards.

Lilith tenses then rolls her shoulders and turns to face the ladies, "No need, We'll be leaving now."

Clarissa frowns, her eyes scanning Lilith head to toe. Lilith slides her arms into my coat, putting it on as if it belongs to her. "Damien, Phil, it's time to go. It's clear that this event is no longer welcoming to us."

The twins look over at her with frowns on their faces and she just gives them the same expression I used on her.

Phil sighs and nods, "All right." He makes his way toward the door, most likely to fetch the carriage.

Damien doesn't give in so readily and glares at her, a challenge in his eyes. She holds his gaze until he sighs as well and takes a few steps forward.

One of Clarissa's goons scoffs again, "How do you have them so compliant? It can't have been anything decent. Perhaps she is a harlot as we suspected," she says the last toward the women around her.

Damien spins on his heel, baring his teeth, "At least a harlot would have the decency to charge you after the deed. Unlike you lot,"

"Damien, enough." Lilith snaps, her voice cutting.

Damien doesn't move and Laurel waves her hand at him in a shooing motion, "Go on, follow your little friend."

Lilith steps forward and puts a restraining hand on Damien's arm before he can start swinging. She looks Clarissa in the eyes, "If your accomplices continue to antagonize me in this manner they'll rile Damien into a fight. They may not be aware of the danger that poses, but you are. So I suggest you accept this kindness I'm offering and call off your dogs."

Clarissa blanches, her eyes flicking to Damien as if she hadn't realized how hazardous the situation had become. At this point, the gargoyle's skin has started to look gray. And I can see the tips of his horns peeking out of his hair.

Laurel scoffs, "Are you threatening us? Again?" she asks.

Clarissa shakes her head and grabs Laurel's arm, "No, enough."

The posse looks startled that Clarissa changed her tune. At that Damien grins, a wicked look in his eyes as he turns to Lilith and holds out an arm, "Come on, Phil should have our ride by now," and just like that they leave the room.

I wait until Lilith is out of earshot when I look at Clarissa and her cronies, "I'll only say this once. You will leave Lilith alone. You won't go near her, you won't speak to her, or of her to anyone. If you try to pull something like this again I will make sure that every secret you have is exposed to the world. That goes for all of you."

Clarissa gasps, "You would protect some, some, urchin over a dear friend?"

"We haven't been friends in a long time and she means more to me than you ever did," I don't give her or her cronies time to reply as I turn around and walk out.

Philip

Damien helps Lilith into the carriage and I can't help but fuss over her a bit. I snag a blanket from the floor and drape it on her lap, then button Graves' coat around her. She smiles weakly at me and leans against the side of the carriage, looking worn out.

I'm starting to worry about Graves when he comes out of the hall and to the carriage. "I was about to come get you," I say as he climbs in and settles across from Lilith, his eyes locked on her.

"I just had a few things to clarify with Clarissa." He says, his gaze not wavering.

I get in and sit next to her, Damien sitting across and watching Lilith warily. The carriage begins to move and we're all silent for a while.

Lilith seems to remember something and fishes around in the coat for a moment.

I frown, wondering what she's doing.

Then she pulls out a cloth bag and holds it out to Graves, "Here, it's what we came for."

He looks at it, then looks at her, "You're wearing my coat, which is where I'd normally put it. So just keep it for now."

"You trust me with it?"

Damien growls, "Why the fuck wouldn't we trust you with it?"

Her eyes cut over to him and I see tears begin to gather again, "Why would you? I'm just some beggar and thief you found who happened to be able to do a job. If it weren't for what I can do then you wouldn't have even entertained my presence."

Damien opens his mouth as if to argue but it's Samael who replies in a gentle tone, "So?"

Her attention snaps back to the lord, "What?"

"It is accurate that there's a low chance that you would've been given a position in the house without the need for your skills. However, that does not negate the fact that you're more than that now," Graves explains, "You act as if you're the only one whose original reason for joining the household was money."

She opens and closes her mouth a few times, her brow furrowing, then she whispers, "But, Why? I'm nobody."

He frowns back at her, then leans forward and takes both of her hands in his, looking right into her eyes, "You may not have come from the best of circumstances but you are far from nobody. You are the strongest shadow mage in centuries, with near-perfect psychometric magic as well. You're one of a very short list of people who have ever put Damien Jones in the dirt. You stand your ground when those you care about are in danger no matter the potential threat to yourself. You're an irreplaceable member of Aegis and one of my closest friends. And as such I will never allow someone to hurt you while I have the power to stop it, even you."

Her face flushes bright red and she looks away but makes a soft scoffing sound, "Haven't had that turned on me before," she mutters.

Damien grins wickedly, "Well, get used to it."

"Yeah," I agree, "You're one of us now, we get to protect you as much as you protect us."

She chuckles at that and looks over at me with a small smile, "Thanks," she sighs softly and leans her head against the side of the carriage as she pulls her hands from Graves'.

She tucks the pouch inside the coat, her eyes fluttering closed.

"Are you all right?" I ask, adjusting the blanket in her lap again.

She nods, but doesn't open her eyes, "It took a lot of magic to get into the vault. Then the whole thing with Clarissa drained me further, I'm about magically tapped."

"Oh," I say, trying to find some way to make her more comfortable.

"Go ahead and sleep," Damien says, "We'll wake you when we get home."

She nods and pulls the blanket closer to herself.

Twenty-Four

In Which Everything Changes

Damien

As we roll up to the manor door I hop out and Phil turns to wake Lilith up. She groans softly and waves a hand at him. Phil sighs, "Come on, Lil, you can't sleep in the carriage all night."

She grunts and waves him away again, "Sure can," she mumbles, rolling so her face is tucked against the corner of the carriage even more.

Phil sighs and runs a hand across his face, then looks at me pleadingly as if he thinks she'd listen to me. I open my mouth to tell him to fuck off, but her eyes flutter and open. She level's that emerald gaze on me and, like so many times in my long life, I'm lost.

Samael may have been the one to take me in when my family cast me out, he may have been the one who saved my life. But we all knew she was the one who got me to live again. So, unable to do anything else, I hold a hand out to her, "C'mere, I'll carry you."

Phil's eyes widen and Samael chuckles as Liltih's face lights up.

She tumbles out of the carriage and into my arms with a pleased hum. I easily scoop her up bridal-style and she snuggles against my chest. "You're spoiled rotten, you know that right?" I murmur to her.

"Mhmmm, too tired to care," she says sleepily.

I smile down at her and carry her inside with Sam tailing behind us leaving Phil to deal with the carriage.

Marie is already in Lilith's room when we arrive, a small smile spreads across her face when she sees the three of us, "I take it all went well?" she asks pleasantly.

"Well enough," Graves says, "get her settled."

I deposit Lilith on her bed and go to help her out of Graves' coat. She clings to it and glares at me, "s'mine now."

"Let me get the seal,"

She grunts and fishes about for it herself before handing me the cloth-wrapped bundle and turning away. Marie starts into scolding the thief for trying to sleep in a corset.

Graves and I leave the women to their devices and make our way to his office, where we lock the seal up in the safe. After the artifact is locked away we head to the lounge, Phil is already there pouring three drinks. He hands them out and we all settle into our usual chairs. "So," I say as I swirl the liquor in my glass, "We've got the first Seal. And now Lilith will be able to help us find the next one, using the first."

"Right," Phil says, "Now we just have to figure out how exactly she can do that. So far she has to touch things when she wants to see their past, and even then it's inconsistent."

"I'd rather she didn't touch the artifact," Graves says in a grim voice, "Its power is volatile and we don't know what will happen if she interacts with it."

I scrub a hand across my face, thinking how much I can reveal before I say, "I don't think the Seal can hurt Lilith, nor do I think its power would be corrupting for her. I doubt Sarah would've said she can help us find the next one if doing so posed a threat to her."

Graves doesn't look convinced when he says, "I hope so..."

We all fall into contemplative silence for a while. I soon find myself wondering if things will end up the way they were. I feel like I shouldn't hope they're different, but I keep it to myself, the same way I always have.

"You're thinking hard about something," Phil says, interrupting my thoughts.

I look up and he's watching Graves who, when I look over, is looking very thoughtful. The Lord covers his face with a hand for a few moments, "Officially Lilith's contract is complete. She's under no obligation to stay here or help us with the other seals. She could leave if she wants..."

He trails off as if his thoughts are just too chaotic to voice. Phil and I wait for him to finish, when he finally says, "And if that's what she chooses I'll let her go."

I smile tightly, I knew that would be his choice, it's always been his answer when it comes to Lilith; let her do what she wants.

Phil, the idiot, still looks surprised at the decision, "But the seals?"

"We'll find some other way," Graves replies quickly, meeting Phil's gaze with something like a challenge in them, "From the moment she arrived I tried to control what she did; I put restrictions on her time, her behavior, and her clothing. It wasn't until I stopped trying to reach for that control that her true strength came out. If we want her help, then we have to give her the freedom to choose what she wants to do. Then we have to trust that she'll do what needs to be done for the sake of the world."

Phil just stares blankly at Graves, no doubt confused as hell that he's made that call. I'm surprised that he's so confused, perhaps my brother wasn't as observant as I gave him credit for. Or, worse yet, perhaps he's forgotten what they were like all those lifetimes ago.

So I just grin and say, "Lilith has said more than once that she's going to see this through. She's even talked of helping us find our King and Queen afterward."

Graves chuckles and shakes his head, "That she has, I think that if we ask her if she's going to leave she'll kick our asses for even thinking it."

I bark out a laugh, imagining that fight, "Oh for sure, she might not win but she'll definitely give us a run for our money."

Phil snorts, "We've seen her take down Sam, and she's tricked you more than once."

Graves laughs, "We may as well just, give her the reigns I suppose. She's clearly in charge now."

"How do you figure that?" Phil asks with a frown.

I smirk and shake my head at Phil, "The three of us have led Aegis for years, we've taken on all that responsibility and all that burden. However, Lilith looks at that and sees our strength. She sees who we are and accepts every piece of it, she's not afraid, she's not intimidated, and she trusts us. And if we're completely honest has more faith in us than we do ourselves. With that in mind I, for one, will do anything she asks of me."

"And to think, you were the most against her being here in the beginning," Graves says wryly.

I down the rest of my drink and stand up, "We should sleep, we'll talk to Lilith about the next steps in the morning. Maybe fetch Sarah too and see if she can give us any leads."

Phil shakes his head and pours me another glass, "Sit your ass down, we're celebrating tonight."

I go to argue with him, but Graves laughs and says, "That sounds good," and downs his drink.

Lilith

I wake with a start when my bedroom door bursts open. Marie is standing in the doorway with a tray of food and a huge smile. "So, I understand that last night's event went well?"

"I don't know about well," I mutter, rubbing my eyes, "You startled me."

"Sorry about that, I just want to hear how it all went! You were..." she trails off, "You were pretty out of it when you got back last night like you'd depleted most of your magic."

"I had," I admit, rubbing my neck as she hands me the tray of food.

"What happened? The boys made it seem like everything went okay with the job, but that Clarissa caused some trouble after the fact."

I sigh and pick at the food, "There were more spells than we thought. I had to get creative to get the artifact. Which reminds me," I take my necklace off and hand it to her.

She frowns and takes it, her eyes widening dramatically as she takes in the state of it, "What did you do to it? It's like, like it's..."

"I only changed the strength of the enhancement... Well, and pushed it way past its usual limits. But that's beside the point." I wave a hand dismissively, "It's unstable now and needs to be re-made."

She looks between the charm and me a few times, then says, "How did you know how to do this? What did you do?"

I hesitate and look back at her, I wring my hands then look away, "There's a lot of things I can do that you all aren't aware of."

She frowns slightly then turns her head to the side, "I suppose that makes sense, people always have their secrets, yeah?"

I smile weakly at her, then look outside and see that there's snow falling, "Can I go for a walk? I... I need to get some fresh air."

She nods, "Of course, we'll get your-"

"I'd like some time alone," I interject, twisting my hands nervously,

"Not that I don't appreciate all the care I get but I would like to be able to do things on my own from time to time."

Marie frowns, glancing outside then nods again, "Okay, I'll help you get bundled up."

I sigh with relief and hug her, "Thank you,"

I step outside into the icy morning air, my foot sinking into about four inches of fresh snow. I chuckle as I kick it, throwing the fluffy ice out in an arc. I smile and make my way across the yard and to the gardens, kicking up a mess of snow as I go and enjoying the way the brisk wind clears my head. I weave through the hedges, enjoying the peace of the morning.

Turning my head up to the sky I stare at the clouds overhead, it looks like it may snow more. And I'm glad that I can enjoy it, instead of having to fret over whether or not I'll be able to find somewhere warm enough to stay safe. I turn to look at the house that's come to be my home.

It's still huge and intimidating, making me feel small in comparison, but I'm not afraid as I was when I arrived. I know that when I enter that building I'll be fussed over by Marie for going out in the cold, Helga will sit me down at the table and give me soup, while the twins give me a hard time for going out on my own.

I smile, then a thought crosses my mind that makes me frown. They still haven't seen the full range of my power. They haven't felt all that I can do, and I wonder if they'd still let me stay if they knew. I bite my lip and look back at the building. As I stare at it, that welcoming feeling intensifies, and I know that I want to stay. To do that, and feel completely safe, I have to show them all that I can do.

I roll my shoulders back and nod to myself, I have to go in there and show them everything. If they aren't afraid and are willing to accept me with all that I am on display, then I know I've found where I belong, and I'll fight to the death to protect it.

I turn a corner and stop short, Gavin is standing there with a shoulder bag and a backpack. "Gavin? What are you doing?" I ask frowning as I look him over.

"I was coming to find you,"

"Why? Are you going somewhere?" I peer at his bags.

"Yeah, we are." He says brightly, holding out the backpack, "Now that you've completed the contract we can go. I've got another job we can do, they'll pay better than these assholes," he jerks his head back toward the manor.

I stare at the backpack for a long moment then look up at him with a frown, "I... Gavin I don't want to leave," I say slowly feeling out how he's going to react to that statement, "There are still more seals to find, and... I like it here, I belong here."

His smile falters, then he steps closer, "But, Lil, I..." he keeps stepping closer and I get an ill feeling in my gut. I keep moving away from him until my legs hit a bench. I stumble a bit and Gavin grabs my arm, harshly pressing his lips to mine with enough force that I think his teeth bust my lip.

I grunt in surprise and try to push away, but he grips me tighter and presses closer. I can't break his hold so I use a touch of magic to shove him away from me and stagger as the world spins strangely. "What did you..." I trail off and throw myself forward, knocking into him and sending us both sprawling onto the ground.

His bag is thrown away from us and its contents are strewn about the pathway. My vision swims and I spot a shimmer of red-gold within the pile of clothes and items. I recognize the charm and scramble forward to grab it.

My world spins again and Gavin grips my leg, yanking it back and causing me to fall on my face. I try to reach for my magic and it doesn't respond, still too drained from my stunt last night, and I feel physically sluggish and uncoordinated.

I taste the blood dripping down my face as I groan and roll over to grab the charm. Gavin drags me away from the seal, I try to struggle and use my magic again, but it is still out of reach like something is holding it back. With a bit more squirming I manage to get my foot between Gavin and me and kick him away with all my remaining might.

I rush forward, one of my hands slipping on blood and ice, but I manage to reach the seal. My hand closes around it as Gavin slams his foot into my side. I roll to the side as I grip the seal to my chest, tears spring to my eyes as I stare blearily up at Gavin.

"Why?" I whisper not sure what I expect him to say but needing some answer as to why he'd harm me like this, why he'd try to take me away from what I want. "Why?" I'm vaguely aware of the ribbon of the Seal wrapping around my wrist and warming against my skin, the sensation is reassuring and gives me some clarity.

Gavin scowls down at me and kicks my side again replacing the clarity with pain. "You had to go and take their side," he snarls as my world starts to fade in and out of focus, "You couldn't just do what I wanted and come with me. If you hadn't been so stupid I wouldn't have had to do this," he grabs my wrist and tries to take the charm.

The artifact has woven itself tightly to my wrist and doesn't look like it's going to come off.

Gavin curses under his breath, then draws his fist back, and punches me in the face. I hear a crunch and pain radiates out from my nose, then all goes black.

K.A. Shady grew-up in a very large, blended family. Being the second of 12 kids, most adopted directly from foster care, their life was always very hectic. To occupy their younger siblings and themselves, they would act out elaborate stories revolving around brave heroes exploring fantasy worlds. By the age of 10 they realized they wanted to be a writer, so they started transcribing the adventures they had with their siblings and put together a variety of different short stories.

Kyra spent their adolescence in Georgia, but after living there for over two decades they were ready for a change. They moved to Nebraska with their wife in 2019. When they're not writing, they're traveling to new worlds by way of books, battling monsters with their PC, and organizing the next DnD session with their party.

www.ingramcontent.com/pod-product-compliance
Lightning Source LLC
Chambersburg PA
CBHW071250300726
48975CB00002B/620